KILLING TIME IN GEORGIA

THE SAVANNAH TIME TRAVEL MYSTERIES
BOOK 1

SUSAN KIERNAN-LEWIS

SAN MARCO PRESS

Killing Time in Georgia. Book 1 of the Savannah Time Travel Mysteries.

© 2023 by Susan Kiernan-Lewis

All rights reserved.

Books by Susan Kiernan-Lewis

The Maggie Newberry Mysteries

Murder in the South of France
Murder à la Carte
Murder in Provence
Murder in Paris
Murder in Aix
Murder in Nice
Murder in the Latin Quarter
Murder in the Abbey
Murder in the Bistro
Murder in Cannes
Murder in Grenoble
Murder in the Vineyard
Murder in Arles
Murder in Marseille
Murder in St-Rémy
Murder à la Mode
Murder in Avignon
Murder in the Lavender
Murder in Mont St-Michel
Murder in the Village
Murder in St-Tropez
Murder in Grasse
Murder in Monaco
A Provençal Christmas: A Short Story
A Thanksgiving in Provence
Laurent's Kitchen

The Claire Baskerville Mysteries

Déjà Dead
Death by Cliché

Dying to be French
Ménage à Murder
Killing it in Paris
Murder Flambé
Deadly Faux Pas
Toujours Dead
Murder in the Christmas Market
Deadly Adieu
Murdering Madeleine
Murder Carte Blanche
Death à la Drumstick

The Savannah Time Travel Mysteries
Killing Time in Georgia
Scarlett Must Die

The Stranded in Provence Mysteries
Parlez-Vous Murder?
Crime and Croissants
Accent on Murder
A Bad Éclair Day
Croak, Monsieur!
Death du Jour
Murder Très Gauche
Wined and Died
A French Country Christmas

The Irish End Games
Free Falling
Going Gone
Heading Home
Blind Sided
Rising Tides

Cold Comfort
Never Never
Wit's End
Dead On
White Out
Black Out
End Game

The Mia Kazmaroff Mysteries
Reckless
Shameless
Breathless
Heartless
Clueless
Ruthless

Ella Out of Time
Swept Away
Carried Away
Stolen Away

The French Women's Diet

1

There's something about waiting for trouble that is extremely unsettling.

I'm not sure I should actually be getting paid for it. That just seems wrong on several different levels.

I adjusted my headset and glanced around the office.

The dispatcher's center smelled of bad coffee and sweat, and weirdly, old plastic and paper. I'd already drunk too much of the bad coffee. I watched the buttons light up on my call screen and felt my stomach tighten.

We had the latest in computer technology at the Savannah Police Department. Of course we did. It was 2023. But the office I work in has been in this part of the building since 1948. The air conditioning unit—literally the most vital piece of equipment in the building—heaved and shuddered as if it was on its last legs, often emitting a fine mist rather than cold air.

I reached for my water bottle and took a long sip. I'd been doing the job for over three years now and I knew the drill. Nobody knew it better.

Receive the calls, screen them, determine the nature and

location of the emergency, dispatch law enforcement or emergency responders as necessary.

I was good at it, too. I was fast, competent, and calm with hysterical people, plus I'd incorporated a vast knowledge base of basic first aid that the caller could attempt before help arrived.

Last year I'd delivered a baby over the phone. Up until then, I'd not even seen a YouTube video of a baby being born. But I'd somehow managed to talk the young father through it. There was something distinctly surreal about interacting with people during the worst moments of their lives, and then just going home to watch Jimmy Kimmel as if none of it had ever happened.

The phone buzzed and I reached for the button to connect. I could feel my heart racing as I took the call.

"911. What's your emergency?" I asked.

"My hubs fell offa the ladder," the woman said, her voice whiney and shrill. "He just laying there!"

I checked on the map to see what section of Savannah the call was coming from. Garden City. Not a great area of town.

"I'm sending an ambulance now," I said. "Don't move him."

"Hell, he three hundred pound if he a pound," the woman said. "I ain't touchin' him."

"Is he conscious, ma'am?" I asked.

"No, but his eyes doin' some blinkin'."

I reached for a water bottle. I felt my mind easing into neutral. Sometimes all the calls sounded the same. Bad habit to get into.

I took another long sip, hoping the cold water would jolt me back into the job. I've started having to do that more and more. Usually it worked.

"You still there?" the woman said. "When that ambulance coming?"

"Let me check," I said. I put her on hold while I connected with one of the mobile field medics.

"I have a from a fall from a ladder," I said into my headset. "6 Main Street in Garden City."

"We have someone enroute. ETA ten minutes."

"Ma'am?" I said to the woman on the line. "The ambulance will be there in ten minutes."

"Do I have to be here when it come?"

Nothing surprised me anymore.

"Yes, Ma'am. You need to lead them to the—"

"Well, they can see what happened! He laying there big as life!"

"Ma'am, can you tell me exactly what happened? You said your husband fell off the ladder? Has he regained consciousness?"

But she had hung up. I sat staring at my computer screen, wondering as I did nearly every minute of every day on this job who these people were. Unless I called the hospital later, I never learned how it all turned out.

Would the man live? Was he dead right now? Who was that woman who wouldn't stay with her own husband? What had he done to create that situation? How was the baby I'd helped deliver last year?

"Hey, girl," a voice said from behind me.

I turned to see my friend Jazz standing by my desk holding a pile of file folders.

"Who was that?" Jazz asked, wrinkling her nose.

Jazz felt like the people who called 911 had somehow gotten themselves into these predicaments. She was rarely sympathetic.

"Some guy fell off a ladder," I said

"Ugh. You still up for lunch?" She dropped a folder on my desk.

"Yeah, sure."

I watched her walk down the aisle toward the bull pen to deliver her armful of folders to the various teams and detectives, her long dreadlocks swinging rhythmically behind her as she moved. It always amazed me that even though the office was completely automated in so many ways, we still did so many things the old-fashioned way. Hand-delivering files? And then filing them away in cabinets? I wondered if that's how they did things in Atlanta or Jacksonville. Or was it just Savannah and Pooler that did it like we still lived in the eighteen hundreds?

I stared around the dispatchers room which had been freshly painted. The walls held a faint scent of pine and lemon. All the dispatchers sat like I did in front of large computer screens pinned with notes. A coffee machine sat on a counter next to a stack of stained mugs, which smell of rough morning coffee.

Down the hall, a dozen detectives gathered each morning around a large table in the center of the room. On one wall was a large whiteboard filled with details of the cases—suspects, evidence, alibis, and the like. On the opposite wall hung a giant map of the city with red push pins marking key locations.

My workspace didn't have any windows. I suppose that was so as not to distract us as we dealt with our daily life and death phone calls—as if we might be distracted by seeing a bird fly by or maybe get thrown by the appearance of a rainbow.

I turned back to my desk and glanced at the folder Jazz had left there. I'd read through this particular case file several times already, even committing the details to memory. It wasn't my case, of course. I'm a dispatcher. I don't have cases.

It was a copy of one of Rob Lockwood's cases.

Detective Rob Lockwood worked in another part of the facility. He walked with lazy swagger as if he was constantly bored. His shirt was always crisp, rolled up to his elbows, his shoes always polished. He wore his hair cropped short and his cologne was a mix of musk and sandalwood. I had a fantasy that I might be able to tell Rob something about his case that would impress him. I have a very good eye for detail, a trait extremely useful for a detective which I'd once had high hopes of becoming.

My lack of credentials aside, I knew I had the skills to solve Rob's current case. The way I saw it, it was going to make an awesome story of how we finally got together.

The case involved a conman—one Jimmy White—who had been in the Savannah area for about six months, had a very slick pitch and a long list of victims. White offered shiny new iPhones, the latest models at unbelievable prices to his customers whom he found on the street. His victims—all elderly on fixed incomes—were always giddy to find such a great deal until they took their new phones home and found that none of them worked.

White's MO was to stand outside strip malls, dressed in a natty suit—seersucker usually (and yes, I'm aware of the irony). He would smile at passersby, especially if they came by on walkers or just looked all alone in the world. Promising "the latest, greatest cellphone on the market" he showed them a handful of boxed cellphones, each one identical to the next. Then he offered an unbeatable price, often throwing in a free faux-leather carrying case. The elderly buyers happily bought the phones—happy to have made a new friend on top of getting a new phone—only to find out later that they'd been conned.

I had started my investigation by reading Rob's case notes and comparing the victims' stories against the con artist's version of events, because yes, he had been interviewed under caution. They'd brought White in for questioning but didn't have enough to hold him. It was his word against his victims' word that they'd been sold nonfunctioning phones.

I'd actually driven by White's house once and waited until he came home and then went and looked inside his vehicle. I wasn't too worried about him catching me since I'd seen him go in with a case of Budweiser under his arm. I waited just long enough for him to get started on the beer before I crept over to peek inside his car.

I figured if I found anything then Rob would be able to get a search warrant to nail White. I was looking for any kind evidence but more specifically for a bunch of discarded phones with broken or scratched display screens that White had gotten from repair stores. That was the other problem with the case—there was no evidence of inventory.

When White sold the phones, the boxes that supposedly contained them all looked new to the point of being wrapped in clear plastic. The victims all claimed that White never took the phones out of their boxes. He kept up a steady patter touting the wonders of the product and how it was going to change their lives for a fraction of the retail cost. The victims all assumed the boxes contained brand new working iPhones. Instead, of course, they contained battered cellphones with no battery, no microchip, and no working parts.

I'd overheard Rob talk in the lunchroom the other day about the case and knew he was trying to find where White procured his junk phones. My theory—as yet unexpressed to Rob—was that he bought them unlocked and nonworking on eBay. But I was pretty sure Rob didn't want to hear my theories. Why would he? I wasn't a detective. I just worked the phones here.

Regardless, I felt sure I could solve this case. In fact, I longed for the thrill of unraveling it, of doing the detection work I knew I was capable of. More than that, I longed to see the look on Rob's face—his eyes wide and impressed, as if seeing me for the first time—when I handed over the proof of existence of the junk cellphones that would lead him straight to a conviction of Jimmy White.

I closed the copy of the case file, and turned back to my desk phone, suddenly willing another call to come in and then felt instantly guilty for trying to prompt someone's emergency to distract me. I glanced around the dispatchers center. Cindy, the other dispatcher, was chatting on her personal cellphone. She'd just had a baby and said she looked forward to coming to work to get away from all the noise at home. Becca, like Jazz, was a file clerk like Jazz. She'd moved to Savannah two years ago to follow a man who later dumped her. But the barbecue and the beach were better here, so she stayed.

I wasn't particularly close to the ladies in my office. I knew what they thought of me. I heard the snickers and whispered comments in the lunchroom. They would all be shocked to learn that I'd actually gone to the police academy. My grades were good, my marks high. My instructor referrals, not so much.

I was graded as stolid but timid. And as one instructor so coldly put it:

"This is not who you want showing up on your doorstep at two in the morning with an intruder in your house."

I'd never tell my workmates that I'd gone to the academy because then they'd want to know why I hadn't graduated. They could probably guess the answer.

I hadn't graduated because I'd been too afraid.

Too afraid of the constant barrage of people's problems, of people's anger. Afraid that I couldn't rise up to meet the challenge of helping them. Or of failing them. Afraid of holding a gun. Afraid of facing one pointed at me. Afraid of getting hurt.

Any way you looked at it, I thought as I rubbed a tired hand over my face, while it was true that I'd failed the academy, I'd mostly just failed myself.

2

The magnolia tree stood over the slightly gnarled picnic table giving shade and dropping its dark green leaves in the hot afternoon. To me, it felt like an oasis in the concrete jungle of downtown. Its leaves were dark green and lush. A cool breeze blew through the shade of the tree making the branches sway.

It was a typical muggy, summer day but still nice to be outside. Jazz and I often ate our lunch at the picnic table under the trees on the back side of the police station. It smelled more like gas and garbage than a park landscape—the picnic table was close to the trash bins—but considering what I did for a living, I needed to get out and feel the sun on my face.

Jazz frowned at the contents of her sandwich baggie. She was petite but she had an outsize personality. Her brown eyes were always probing and sparkling.

"I don't know what you're fussing about," she said, as she unwrapped her tuna salad sandwich. " I'd kill to have your job. And you know you could always push yourself if you wanted to do something else."

"Thanks," I said wanly.

"But if you're just trying to get Detective Lockwood's attention, I'm pretty sure there are easier ways to do it than creeping around dodgy neighborhoods after dark to find a phone counterfeiter."

"He's not the only reason I want to solve this case," I said. "My whole life, I always thought I was going to be a detective, you know?"

"Well, you tried, right? You did the police academy thing. And you're a killer with crosswords. Don't think I haven't noticed."

She laughed and I smiled. But it wasn't funny. Not to me.

"Georgia?" a shrill voice pierced the air.

Jazz and I both looked over toward the door leading into the dispatchers center, but we both knew who it was. Sergeant Jennifer Turlington, specialized traffic division and Grade A Bitch.

"Over here," I said, although I knew she knew where I was.

She didn't walk over to me, but stood with her hands on her hips, her feet planted wide, the very picture of obstreperousness. Her hair was pulled back into a severe ponytail and she blinked into the sunlight.

"Dennis wants to know what happened with that last call," she said.

Dennis Gibson was the center's Communications Chief. I frowned. It was true I'd not sent the police to the address, just the ambulance. I hadn't picked up that there was more to the story than just an unfortunate accident. But now I felt a tingle of foreboding. It wasn't Jen's place to track me down to tell me my boss was annoyed with me.

Just her idea of fun.

"The caller disconnected and the ambulance was on its way," I said.

"Protocol says you fill out a report," she said.

"I made a judgement call."

"Okay," Jen said. "I'll just let Dennis know you're writing new interdepartmental protocol now."

She turned and left.

"What a bitch," Jazz said. "Why does she ride you?"

I gathered up my sandwich wrappings.

"I don't think it's personal," I said.

"You're kidding, right?" Jazz scrunched up her face to look in the direction Jen had gone.

I'd like to think that Jen hates me because she's jealous of my perfect attendance record or possibly because she's insecure about how her colleagues interact with me, as if they were willing to see past my dispatcher staff rank. But bottom line, I know it's a lot simpler than that.

Detective Rob Lockwood kissed me at last December's holiday party and Jen saw it. I'm not sure if they ever dated or if he's just on her wish list, but she went from totally ignoring me to actively targeting me.

I stood up and waited while Jazz picked up her own lunch trash. I knew I did a dependable job as dispatcher. I wasn't worried what Dennis would say. It was true he did enjoy chewing people out for his own pleasure, but he wouldn't push me too far.

It wouldn't be easy finding someone willing to do what I did, day in and day out.

3

As I'd predicted, things were just a little too busy that afternoon for Dennis to waste time reaming me for a case that ultimately didn't matter. The guy who'd fallen off the ladder had been picked up by EMS and taken to Candler Hospital on Reynolds Street. His wife either wasn't there or didn't look suspicious since she wasn't questioned. Everyone's life went on as usual. Well, I'm not sure what happened to the husband, honestly.

My afternoon was fairly dull after that. We had a moment of excitement when a woman called to say her daughter was missing only to find the child playing on the other side of the house while I was on the line with her. There were no fires, no heart attacks, no home break-ins, and I was able to spend the rest of my day tracking the location of all on-duty officers in case I needed them, and monitoring traffic in the areas of our jurisdiction, tidying up my desk, and reflecting on my life and how exactly it was I had ended up here.

How that happened was this: After walking out of the police academy, I spent a couple of years doing temp work in Atlanta for various companies before my mother fell and broke her hip, prompting my return to Savannah to take care of her until she mended.

She lived in a small two-bedroom cottage in Pooler, about ten miles from the Savannah historic district, and I used the six weeks I spent with her to sort out what I was going to do next with my life. My mother is a very supportive person which can sometimes slosh over into nagging when the thing she wants to support seems more important to her than whatever you had in mind for yourself.

But since I didn't have anything in mind, I was open to hearing what she said. And she suggested I join the Savannah police force as a dispatcher.

You know how when you're depressed, doing anything, even without much thought is easier than properly analyzing your life? That's how I ended up taking the certification course to be a police dispatcher—or *certified public-safety executive* as we're called before we get our diplomas. After that, we're just police dispatchers, even though most of what I do is dispatch ambulances, not the police.

That was three years ago. Sometimes I wondered if the fact that I was still here meant I'd chosen my path forward well. Or maybe I was just so out of the habit of analyzing my life that I couldn't tell any more.

I left the office at a bit past five o'clock. Once I put my uniform away in my locker, said goodbye to Jazz, and headed out, I started to relax the further I walked away from work. A major part of my job is to sound calm and knowing on the phone.

It's amazing how stressful pretending can be.

I turned left off West Congress Street and headed toward Barnard Street where I live. I have to say that my walk home at the end of a shift is probably the best part of my day. I know that sounds pathetic but at least I'm aware enough that I can appreciate it.

Savannah is beautiful any time of year, day or night. It just is. There's a reason why it's clogged with tourists twenty-four seven. Once I broke free of the worst of the tourist scrum, my walk took a winding path through ancient beautiful neighborhoods decorated with Spanish moss draped on the branches of the rows of Southern live oaks. Shafts of sunlight pierced the tree line and glowed in the dust rising from the streets.

I've only lived here as an adult for three years, but I fell under Savannah's spell when I lived here as a child. With its historic squares and monuments, and its cobblestone alleyways meandering throughout it like a lazy river, it's hard not to be captured by its haunting magic.

Plus, I love a river town. Practically everywhere you walk, the Savannah River makes itself known. It's not just the noise of the horns on the enormous ships and barges that go up and down its length constantly, but the air itself that you breathe on every street in a ten-block distance from the waterway. Air which is thick with humidity and the scent of salt and fish. But also, for me, adventure. A lot of women I know hate what the humidity does to their hair, but I don't care. I wear my hair short, and I like how the moisture in the air clings to it.

As I passed Ellis Square, I began to feel the tight knots in my neck start to unkink even more. Everywhere I looked, there were signs of this city's long and storied past: old brick buildings and churches, each with its own unique story to tell; ornate iron gates, black and rusted with age, standing like silent sentinels against time.

Before I turned down my street, I wanted to visit a shop I'd seen a few times but never had the time to enter. It was called *Antiques and Things*. It looked like the sort of shop where one might find Civil War memorabilia or things from an antebellum estate sale.

I glanced at my watch. My mother had some appointments in Savannah so we were doing dinner at my place this evening. She would do the cooking, so I had time.

The signs hanging from the door of the antique shop creaked in the humid air as I opened the door and went inside.

Inside, there were shelves of dozens of porcelain dolls in delicate lace dresses, dusty books held together with ancient bindings, a few amateurish paintings of lush landscapes, and old photographs of people long gone. An old grandfather clock ticked in one corner of the shop, the sound of the pendulum echoed through the space. There seemed to be something special in every nook and cranny, from rare coins and hat pins to crystal goblets and porcelain figurines.

I looked around and saw a young black woman at the front register. She smiled as I passed but went back to the book she was reading.

I don't know why I am drawn to these artifacts of yesteryear. It's not like I have space for any gee-gaws in my one thousand square foot apartment. Nor am I into dusting said gee-gaws. But I look at them here in this shop and I feel myself drawn to them. I try to imagine who these items belonged to. Were they treasures? Cherished gifts from a beloved? Memories of a happier time?

I have to admit to feeling that life had to be more romantic in the old days. I've probably seen too many old movies. There was something less snarky, more forthright in those days. I don't care what kind of cad Humphrey Bogart played on the silver screen, his character was always genuine at heart. Plus, he didn't fill every available space in conversation with talk about himself.

I know that's probably not true in real life back then. Surely men talked about themselves as much in 1945 as they do now. But it was still an ideal that for whatever reason, I took pleasure in wanting to believe.

Just as I was about to leave, I saw it. It was propped up against the wall, on the floor and unframed. A canvas of an oil portrait—dusty and muted, its colors long faded and dim.

It drew me down the aisle like a strong magnet. My eyes never left it once my feet started moving.

It was a portrait was of a beautiful young woman. She had dark eyes and hair. Her eyes held a hint of sorrow, almost a world weariness, although I didn't think she could be forty yet. Her chin was set firm, and her lips were formed into a determined line. Her suit was cinched at the waist as was fashionable in the 1940s. Around her neck she wore some sort of locket on a gold chain.

The woman in the painting was looking straight into my eyes.

And she was asking: *Remember me?*

4

There was a grayish cast to the sky by the time I made it home through the first few drops of rain. I'd made it back mere minutes before my mother showed up. Although I knew she wouldn't have minded waiting, I hated to make her do it, just because I'd gotten lost down a rabbit hole of would-be dreams.

I swear I thought of that painting and the creepy way it affected me all the way back to my apartment. I couldn't get over the feeling that the woman in the portrait had sat for me and that I'd painted this portrait of her. I wondered if the reason she looked familiar to me was because I'd seen her on some cable TV series.

My mother knocked on the door of my apartment and then used her key to let herself in. She had brought chicken and dumplings which was an absolute boon since I hadn't had time to pick up any groceries. After hugs and shedding her raincoat, we set up our meal on the coffee table in the living room with the beautiful porcelain dishes that she had given me last year. She'd wanted to give them to me on my wedding day but when it began to look like that wasn't going to happen, she just gave them to me.

Amanda "Dixie" Belle has always been the epitome of the true Southern woman to me: beautiful, refined and sharp as a razor. My mother was everything I would never be. She was beautiful, calm, pleasant and always knew the right things to say and do. Her own mother, Pearl, who I'd never met, had been the quintessential southern belle, too, and had raised my mother to be the very picture of genteel womanhood. My mother had mentioned to me on more than one occasion that she was glad her mother never lived to see her divorce my father.

I'm sure she didn't mean she was happy for her mother to have had a shortened life. After all, Pearl never lived long enough to know me either. More than once I thought that was just as well because I couldn't imagine what she would've made of me. Thirty and unmarried with no prospects. Yeah, now that I think of it, I have a very clear idea of what she would think.

"You look tired, darling," my mother said as she spooned up my plate over my usual protests that I could do it myself.

"I'm fine," I said. "I have a stressful job."

I was sorry I said it as soon as the words were out of my mouth. Even though she'd been the one to initially suggest my getting a job as a police dispatcher, my mother eventually decided she didn't love the idea after all. She's never come right out and said it's not ladylike, but I have a strong suspicion that that was Reason Number One with her.

"I wish you would go back to school, darling," she said, scooping up her own meal.

We'd had this discussion many times before. There was no point in my saying anything in response. She could probably imagine my side of the conversation.

"You are such a talented artist," she continued. "And with SCAD right here in town…"

SCAD was short for the Savannah College of Art and Design. It was a famous and well-respected art school in Savannah. I have to admit there had been a time when I'd thought about taking classes at SCAD. But someone in the family had to be practical about where the money was coming from, and it was clear it wasn't going to be my dreamy-eyed mother.

"Jessie in dispatch does sculpture," I said, reaching for the baguette she'd brought.

"Well, there you are!"

Her face lit up as if I'd finally relented and jumped onto her team.

"She pays more to rent the space in the art market where she shows her stuff than she earns in sales," I said.

"Well, maybe she's not very good," she said.

"Her stuff looks really good to me."

This was our same old argument. My mother couldn't imagine that real talent went unrewarded. She couldn't believe that an author who wrote an amazing book wouldn't be nationally recognized and appropriately compensated with money and fame. Or that an artist who created something beautiful would be forced to sell it for peanuts in a strip mall parking lot. On the way to their day job.

I love that about my mother. But this wonderfully romantic notion was not a blueprint for living. Not in today's world anyway. Not with brilliant Julliard pianists playing in subway stations.

"Even if you didn't make a lot of money from your art, think of the satisfaction and joy!" she said.

This was a bit of a detour from Mom's usual argument, and I nearly smiled to hear it.

"I like my job, Mom."

"I can't believe that."

"I'm helping people."

She sighed and leaned back in her chair.

"Daisy and I were thinking of taking a cruise this spring," she said.

Daisy was one of the widows who lived in her neighborhood in Pooler. I think they belonged to the same knitting club or something.

"That sounds nice," I said guardedly. Mom didn't have a lot of money. I would've thought a cruise was financially out of reach.

"She says it's important to keep learning new things, even after one retires."

I think I saw where she was going, and I couldn't help but smile.

"Daisy is right," I said. "That's why I'm constantly updating my accreditations at work."

She snorted.

"It's not all about the arts, Mom," I said. "Some people need their plumbing fixed and their shoes repaired."

"It *is* all about the arts, darling," she said, leaning forward again. "For those with a gift, it definitely is."

"Well, the arts don't offer health benefits," I said. "By the way, these dumplings are delish."

"That's just it, darling! The arts are nothing but health benefits! They feed your soul!"

"Just not your stomach. Mm-mm, so tasty."

She shook her head and smiled, clearly seeing my attempt to reroute her argument.

"You could help people by teaching them," she said. "Daisy has a niece who teaches at Savannah Technical

College. Seems to me that's the best of both worlds. She's in an art community and she's getting paid."

"I'm glad for her. But I like my job."

"Seriously? Darling, you come home, tense and stressed. And no husband at your age? No children?"

"And that's my job's fault?"

"Well, it's not helping."

"There's a woman in my office who does the exact same thing I do, and she just had a baby. And yes, before you ask, she has a husband to go along with it."

"You are so amusing, darling."

She added salad to her plate.

"No wine tonight?" I asked looking around.

"I was running late," she said. "Didn't have time to pick up any."

She glanced around my kitchen and the unspoken but loudly communicated message was: *what about you?* But she already knew the answer to that. After the last major problem with my ten-year-old Toyota, wine had become a luxury I could no longer afford, at least not regularly.

I nearly asked her how she thought giving up a paycheck with benefits to paint landscapes of Spanish moss over the river was going to help me buy wine.

But sometimes, I think it's an act of love to let an argument go and allow the arguer to believe she's won.

Or has at least made me think.

5

The next morning, I felt like I had a better attitude about things. Not to disappoint my mother, but it had nothing to do with her words of wisdom night before. What it had to do with was the fact that there was an office party after work today that I was looking forward to.

After my mother left last night, I'd done a little research on the Internet about the White case. While I don't have access to the National Crime Information Center or any other police database, sometimes just basic curiosity and logic can go a long way to unraveling a mystery. Well, at least that's what my *Idiot's Guide to being a Detective* says.

I found a thriving business of broken cellphones for sale on eBay. While the website made a big loud deal of announcing they did not support the sale of counterfeit phones, the fact was that there was hard to tell what the seller was ultimately doing with the phones if not that. All White had to do was open up multiple eBay accounts in different names and voila, he had his criminal inventory.

I knew it wasn't a huge deal, and possibly Rob had already thought of it, but it was at least a conversation starter with him tonight. I wouldn't be stepping on toes by mentioning my idea to him. I would merely be showing him how interested I was in what he was doing. And if it turned out that my tiny bit of Intel proved useful in closing his case, then I didn't mind at all being the recipient of his gratitude.

Normally I wore slacks and a polo shirt to sit behind a desk all day with a headset strapped to my head. But today I wore a dress. It was summertime in Savannah, and anything more than gauze-thick cotton was always going to be too hot. In the South, nothing is more feminine than a dress, freeing your legs from the entrapment of heavy twill or khaki or, heaven forbid, polyester.

And if the fact that I'd once overheard Rob say how he likes women in dresses comes into play then that's just a win-win.

I put my drivers license and phone into a tiny cross body bag hanging from a hook in the hall and gave my reflection in the hall mirror one last glance before heading out the door. I was traveling light today since I was sure someone else was buying drinks tonight.

I strode down the street toward Bay Street. I'm lucky in a number of ways to live so close to work and shopping—although it costs the earth to live this close to the river. When I need to shop at the Kroger a few miles away, I take my car, but there's a small family run grocery store near me that's just fine for small runs for milk or eggs. Also, because it's in my neighborhood, I've had the chance to get to know the proprietors' at least a bit. They're an elderly very friendly Indian couple.

I've seen a few lemonade stands in the strip mall where their grocery sits and the Girl Scouts own the corner every block or so. Every now and then I see a vagrant, but Mr. and

Mrs. Chakrabarti usually call those sightings in pretty quickly.

This morning as I approached the small strip of stores, I saw a man standing in the shade of a giant live oak tree with two old ladies whom I instantly recognized as living on my street. They were sisters, both widowed. As I neared, I felt the back of my neck begin to tingle ominously. I swear I didn't realize what I was seeing until I was nearly in the parking lot, but some part of me must have, because I instinctively slowed my pace and felt my breathing begin to speed up.

It was him.

Jimmy White.

From the photos I had seen of him in the case file, I knew exactly who it was. He spoke to the two old ladies, his face shifting as he twisted his neck around to survey the area. His hands held out a shiny new box, and I watched as the older sister reached for her purse.

I hurried forward, rummaging in my bag for my phone, my chest tightening with anticipation. Fear pulsed through me, but it was as if the fear itself was driving me forward. I knew White was dangerous. He was a criminal who, when confronted with a potential obstacle, could react violently.

Could I film him without him seeing me?

Just then one of the sisters looked up and saw me. Like a horror movie, I saw her smile and then reach up to wave at me.

Everything slowed down then like it always does when the stupid girl goes down to the basement where the monster is. I watched White turn his head slowly, painfully slowly, until he was looking right at me.

My hand was up, my cellphone positioned in it outstretched. It was clear what I was doing—filming a crime in process. His eyes met mine and that's when the deal got sealed. He pulled the cellphone box out of the hand of the old woman, turned toward me, his eyes now focused on the camera in my hand.

Fear shuddered through me as I looked around desperately. He charged me.

Even then, in the split second of all that was happening, I knew if I dropped my phone, he'd let me go. But right then a light breeze caught the hem of my pretty summer dress, and I was reminded that I was doing this for Rob and that he was going to be so proud of me.

But only if I had the video to show him.

I held my ground, clutching my phone tightly in my hands. My breath hitched in my chest and my legs felt as if they'd been trapped in cement.

I turned to look behind me, ready to run, and then back again where I gasped to see he was not two feet away. Before I could change my mind and run, I watched in frozen horror as a long dark bat materialized in his hand.

It came at me swinging faster than I could imagine anything happening. The explosion in my head immediately sucked all the light out of the world.

My vision went to black, leaving me with a detonation of pain and then, blessed nothingness.

6

It was the smell I noticed first.

Mold and rot with an overlaying stench of antiseptic cleaner—mixed with the scent of blood and decay.

I opened my eyes. A nurse stood next to me, dressed in white, looking at me as if I were a math problem she couldn't figure out. Her frown made her wrinkles deeper, and more severe. Correction. Not a nurse. A nun. In white. Like an angel.

I struggled to sit up and she immediately put a hand to my shoulder to keep me still. I tried to turn my head, but it hurt, and the room began to spin. Something was wrong and only part of it was me.

I was in a hospital but one that smelled like rotting wood and sour breath.

"The doctor said you are to lie still," the nun said.

I tried to remember what religious hospitals there were in Savannah. I knew all the medical facilities according to location and Square. I didn't remember any religious hospital, at least none still in operation. Had I been life-flighted out of Savannah?

My lips were parched. When I licked them, the nun turned to pick up a small paper cup next to the bed. I was so thirsty I didn't hesitate to drink from it, spilling most of it down my front. When she set the cup down again, I remember thinking nonsensically, *no straw*?

"What happened?" I croaked, closing my eyes again, hearing for the first time a muted chorus of moaning noises down the hall.

"You were attacked," the nun said. "The police are looking for him now."

Then I remembered White, the look in his eyes—panicked and desperate—when I'd frozen in his path and waited for the bat in his hand to strike me.

Dear God, why had I done that? I groaned. *Just stood there waiting for it?*

"How badly hurt?" I asked.

"You rest now," the nun said, turning and picking up a large hypodermic needle.

That was the moment I began to wake up. I have never seen needles that large except possibly in horror movies.

From the twenties.

"My mother," I said. "I need to tell her…"

The nun stopped and frowned as she held the needle like a threat over me.

"What is your name?" she asked.

"Georgia Belle," I said. "My mother is Dixie Belle."

She rolled her eyes.

"It's not a joke," I said. "Did you find my cellphone? Her number is there under *Mom*."

Her face was as determinedly unhappy with me now as

if I hadn't spoken. And unfortunately, the needle was even larger the closer it got to me.

∼

The next time I woke up, I was alone and very thirsty. It was dark but I was able to see a little more of my surroundings. There were at least four other people lying in beds in the room with me. I felt a stab of fear at that since I do not know of any hospitals that don't provide private rooms. And certainly none with *four* patients to a room.

I sat up. The room was small, with a single narrow window framed by lace curtains that looked as if they'd been dipped in tea. I was sitting in an old-style hospital bed, with metal railings on each side. Across the room was an armoire, of all things. Its doors were open showing shelves of bandages, gauze, and vials of different colored fluids.

Where am I?

I stretched my neck to look out the window near my bed. A half-sheet of frosted glass stretched down the length of it, letting in only the faintest glimmer of light. My eye traveled to the head of the bed where the figure of a winged cherub —so emaciated it looked like a corpse—hung on the wall staring at me.

The panic started deep inside my chest and began to build like a bird desperate to escape its cage. I didn't know where I was, but I knew there was no reputable clinic anywhere in the country that looked like this. I searched the top of the bedside table, hoping my phone would be there but of course it wasn't.

I glanced down at my night gown which was made of a

rough cotton with irregular stitching on the sleeves and the neck.

"You're awake," a voice said to me.

I was so intent on figuring out what kind of place I'd been taken to, that I hadn't seen him come in. The man who stood there was wearing a complete three-piece checked suit that looked to be made of worsted wool. He had a hat on too.

In Savannah? In summer?

I pulled the sheet up to my chin. He wasn't a doctor or a nurse and he certainly wasn't a visiting relative.

"I need the nurse," I said hoarsely, glancing at the door and wondering what kind of security this place had that any weirdo could just walk in off the street.

"Are you in pain?" he asked, furrowing his brow.

He seemed genuinely concerned but I knew a few things about sociopaths, and they were usually great actors. I looked around frantically for a button to push to call for the nurse.

"Hello!" I called out loudly, clutching the sheets to my chest. "Anyone?"

"Calm down, Miss," the man said. He approached the bed and opened a small leather notebook revealing a badge. "I am Detective Samuel Bohannon of the Savannah Police Department. I've been waiting to talk to you about what happened."

I stared at him.

"What...?" I felt a fluttering in my stomach as I tried to understand what was happening. "I was...where is the police?"

"I am the police," he repeated patiently.

I stared at him and then past him. The nun I'd seen before paused in the doorway of my room.

"Hello, Ma'am!" I called to her. "Sister?"

The man turned to the nun but instead of trying to evade her or make up a story, he folded his wallet and tucked it into his breast jacket pocket.

"She still seems confused," he said to her. "Shouldn't the sedative have worn off by now?"

"Don't talk like I'm not here!" I said. "Where is the doctor?"

"The doctor is busy," the nun said to me.

I didn't forget she could always whip out that monster needle to end any further discussions, so I watched her warily.

"Detective Bohannon needs you to make a statement, Miss," she said firmly. "Do you feel up to doing that?"

I looked from one to the other, my body heat rising.

"I need to make a phone call," I said. "My mother will be worried."

Bohannon pulled out a notebook and a pen from his vest pocket.

"What is your mother's name?" he asked.

I glanced at the nun who crossed her arms as if daring me to give my mother's name again.

"Look," I said. "Yes, it's an odd name. I get that. Her name is Amanda Belle. Her number is 708-342-4533. It's listed in my phone, as I told you...Sister."

Now it was Bohannon's turn to look confused.

"And you are?" he asked gently.

"My name is Georgia," I said.

"Like the state?" he asked, bemused.

"Yes, like the state," I said. "Georgia Belle. I work as a dispatch officer for the Savannah Police Department. Call them. Ask anyone...talk to my supervisor Dennis Gibson."

Bohannon made no move to do anything. He only

frowned and looked again at the nun with a questioning look.

"Her X-rays are fine," she said with a shrug. "No head injury."

"Hey!" I said, feeling the blood rush to my cheeks. "HIPAA much? Don't tell him personal medical information about me!"

She ignored me.

"The doctor believes she might possibly be suffering from trauma-induced amnesia."

"What?" I said, bewildered. "That's not true. I remember everything that happened. He was coming out of the..." I put a hand to my head and tried to remember. "The strip mall. He was talking with the...I was trying to film him, and he saw me and he came running over to me and..."

I stopped speaking as I realized again what I'd done. I hadn't run away. I had just stood there. Had I even tried to block the attack? In any way? I'd been trained in self-defense! I sagged back against the pillow on the bed in disgust. What had I been thinking?

"Can you describe the man?" Bohannon asked.

"His name is James White," I said. "I recognized him from the open case file the department has on him."

I closed my eyes, surprised at how exhausted I was. When I opened them, again, I saw that both the detective and the nun were staring at me. The detective wasn't taking notes. And as weary as I was, I couldn't help but notice that neither were they trying to phone anyone to check out my story.

I felt a feeling of panic begin to well up inside me and I glanced around the room when my eyes fell on a framed photograph on the wall that I hadn't noticed before. It was a black and white photo of an historic hospital built in a distinctive architectural style. The only reason I even recognized it was because I remembered it was featured in a series of Savannah ghost tours that are very popular with tourists.

Built in 1804, the Savannah Hospital had a long and creepy past, which involved caring for Confederate soldiers during the war and Union soldiers after Sherman came through in 1864. It's actually considered one of the most haunted buildings in the entire country.

I shivered at the thought. I've never taken the ghost tour of the hospital—now called the Candler Hospital after the Methodist Church took it over in the late eighteen hundreds—but it's supposed to be so haunted that simply walking past it in broad daylight is enough to witness apparitions and ghostly wails. I read that there was a morgue tunnel that led from it to nearby Forsythe Park.

I realized I was still trembling. The picture of the Savannah Hospital was burning into my brain along with its terrible history—one of the first in the country to introduce shock therapy—until I realized that my brain was trying to formulate an insane notion—one that I desperately did not want to be thinking—and that was that I was sitting in that hospital in the photo this very minute.

My fingers felt frozen, and I was shivering. I sucked in a breath and my lungs felt like they were filled with wet cotton. I gasped for breath, letting the panic attack roll over me like a tidal wave.

The nurse nun came over to me and pushed me down in the bed.

"That's enough, Detective," she said. "I'm afraid we'll need to take it from here."

7

I don't know if I was given some kind of truth pill while I was unconscious—or just knocked out, which is essentially what Sister Ratchet did to me when I had my little panic attack—but somewhere in my brain, I began to think that I was dreaming all of this. I began to believe that I was in some kind of coma and was locked away inside this crazy dream unable to awaken. I imagined my mother sitting by my hospital bed, holding my hand and urging me to come back to her.

When I opened my eyes this time, my mother wasn't there, but the nurse was, and so was a man in a white coat looking at me as if I smelled bad. I assumed he was my doctor.

"How are we feeling today?" he asked as he looked at an old-fashioned clipboard in his hands with no obvious interest in my response.

I sat there, tempted to answer him truthfully. It was at that moment that I knew I was going to have to play a little game with these people—in my dream—if I didn't want to get a one-way ticket to a mental hospital or shake hands with Mister Needle again. It occurred to me that if my dream had concocted this horror show from the remnants of a perfectly innocent hospital, I could only imagine what it would do if I ended up transported to a looney bin.

I've seen enough movies and documentaries to give my imagination plenty to work with. I wasn't going there. In or out of my dream.

Sister Mean-Face had given me the answer to this dilemma when Detective Dreamboat had appeared in my dream. Something told me I needed to grab for that life vest with all the strength and sanity I had in me.

"I can't remember who I am," I said and swallowed hard.

The doctor smiled as if he'd just won a bet and nodded at the nun.

"As I said," he said. "Trauma-induced amnesia."

He reached over and patted my hand and then turned to the nurse.

"Keep her comfortable and let's see if anything starts to come back to her."

"We have a bed shortage, doctor," she said with a frown as she looked at me, clearly thinking that if I wasn't faking it I was at least being extremely inconsiderate.

"Excuse me, doctor," I said. "Am I concussed?"

He looked at me as if the pillow had begun to speak and then handed the clipboard to the nun.

"Find a place for her somewhere," he said. "Maybe in one of charity wards? She's fine physically. She can work for her keep."

Then he walked away. But before he did, he pulled out a packet of cigarettes and lit one up, dropping the match on the floor. It was a good thing I was pretending to have amnesia because I'm sure the look on my face would have convinced anyone that I had just lost my mind.

The nurse came over to me and frowned as if she didn't believe what I'd told the doctor.

"How do you really feel?" she asked suspiciously.

"Hungry," I said.

But honestly, I felt nothing at all. Because in my mind was seared for all eternity the image of that physician in his white coat, smoking as he walked past the other three beds in the room.

The nun turned and left the room. I sat up, my heart pounding in my throat because this dream was getting worse, and I wasn't sure if I was going to survive it. On the wall was a poster I hadn't noticed before that read *Toxoid Diphtheria. Ask your doctor*!

I looked around the ward. The three other beds in the room with me held people too weak or sick to sit up. One of them had a foot sticking out of the bed. It was filthy.

I took in a breath to settle my nerves, and then looked around the room for something resembling a closet where hopefully I might find my clothes. I saw nothing and there was no way I could leave the hospital wearing what I had on unless I wanted to get arrested or committed to an asylum for sure—assuming I wasn't already there.

How could this have happened? I had been attacked by a con artist in the middle of fleecing two elderly sisters in my neighborhood, and I wake up in a hospital in a part of the county I've never been! Did White take me here?

Does that seem likely after hitting me on the head with a bat?

I stood up and walked to the window to get a better sense of what part of the town or county I was in.

The first thing I saw that was not so unusual to see in Savanah was a horse-drawn carriage painted yellow and black. The tourists loved to see the city from this kind of charming vehicle of the past.

It wasn't until that same horse reared up in its harness because a Model T Ford, noisy and spewing black smoke, edged it off the road that I began to breathe really fast. My mouth fell open as I watched the scene as antique cars and horse-pulled buggies trotted beneath my window on a street alive with activity, a virtual river of humanity flowing in both directions. The sights were a blur of movement and color, the smells and sounds a disorienting bombardment of everything I'd ever experienced in a nightmare.

I felt lightheaded as I stared in disbelief at the steady stream of antique vehicles driving by. Since they had no mufflers, the sound in the street was deafening, a clattering roar that rose up and filled the air around me.

And the horse-drawn carriages! Forget the tourist horse carriages! Horse manure was piled everywhere in the street. Women were walking below on the sidewalk in long dresses and wide hats, while men were all dressed in suits with hats. I stared at the scene, transfixed, as if I were watching a movie.

It was unimaginable but in some part of my brain, I recognized that I was looking at Abercorn Street. Only instead of Chipotles and Starbucks on the corner, the road was framed by tall buildings, and quaint shops holding everything from antique clothing and hats, to what looked like farming tools.

How is this possible? Are they shooting a movie?

But the production value of it all was way too detailed. And if it was a movie set, it was for a camera that never took any breaks. No director ever yelled "*Cut!*"

Stunned and trying desperately to see *something* that might explain what I was seeing, I stood there in my bare feet and gawked at the streams of people walking by, their heads down and faces hidden by the brims of their hats.

All of it was unbelievable. But honestly, I could have come up with an answer for what I was seeing—the horses, the strange antique cars, the people all wearing costumes from central casting—even the cobblestone street which I knew was paved with asphalt concrete. I could find a reason to explain all it, except for one thing.

And it was that one thing that clinched the idea of the impossible for me. It was the thing that made me go from *this isn't happening* to *OMG this is happening*. And that was the simple fact that everywhere I looked—on the buildings around me and the very building I was in—*a hospital no less!* —nowhere did I see a single air conditioning unit.

In Savannah?

In summer?

That was the moment I knew I had to at least consider the unimaginable.

8

The hospital ward was old, its walls were peeling in places, its floor a tacky linoleum. The sound of a ticking clock filled the room as the seconds crawled by. The smell of vomit, blood and cleaning products pervaded the room.

After my surreal realization that I was experiencing what looked like Savannah in the eighteen hundreds, I went flying back to my bed and dove under the covers to literally pull the sheet over my head—my body and mind vibrating with confusion and disbelief. That was the moment when a strange little man pushing a tea trolley ambled into my room.

I had in no way even begun to process what I'd seen outside on the street when I found myself watching this creature push his cart up to the side of my bed. He was medium height with blond hair. He wasn't ugly but there was nonetheless something very ugly about him. He wore a name tag that read *Gus Jones*.

On his cart was a large silver teapot, several canisters of

cakes and cookies, a jug of milk and a stack of ceramic teacups and saucers. Not even mugs.

It's the little things that finally make you accept what on the face of it really seem unacceptable. Like being handed a steaming cup of tea in a ceramic cup with a saucer instead of in a Styrofoam cup. And the man himself, who leered at me as if he were trying out for the part of a generic sleazy creep-o in a slash-chop film, someone who could not exist openly in my own time.

Yes, I'd gone there.

There was simply no other explanation for what I was seeing. I should have gotten there sooner. The smoking doctor was a big tell and I'm amazed I didn't realize right then that—unless this is a dream, which I desperately hope it is—I have gone back in time.

Just thinking the words made me want to throw up.

"Sister Beatrice said to bring you a little something for sustenance," the grinning troll said to me, his implication sniveling and predatory all at once. He set a ceramic plate holding a piece of bread slathered with thickly clotted butter and two large wedges of pound cake on my bedside table.

I was afraid to thank him for fear he would take it as the wrong kind of encouragement. I sipped from the teacup, my eyes on him in case he tried something. I could only marvel with horror that he existed at all. This was not a person who would ever have been hired in modern times. Not with the existence of sexual predator databases. To allow him to work around vulnerable people was completely unimaginable.

But then, it seemed that that's what my life was now.

Unimaginable.

In the face of my refusal to engage, the tea man—he was wearing a white coat, but I prayed he wasn't an orderly—finally turned his attention to the woman lying in the bed beside mine. I made a point of clearing my throat every few seconds to remind him that I was watching him. I had to assume that whatever the differences were in this new time, people didn't behave despicable if they thought they might be seen doing it.

After he finally left, I wolfed down the bread and the cake, not at all surprised that they were extraordinarily delicious, and certainly not the product of some impersonal hospital cafeteria or automated food factory.

I noticed the light from outside the window had begun to soften and I was trying to guess what time it must be when Sister Beatrice returned with three young women at her side. Like her, they were dressed all in white, their eyes wide in panic or concern, but clearly there to assist. One was pushing a trolley stacked with trays of food which surprised me since from what I could see I was the only person in the room capable of eating without the help of an IV. I glanced around and saw no IVs.

When the nurse pushing the trolley came to me, she slipped one of the trays out of the rack and settled it on my bed. I saw something that looked like tomato bouillon along with pot roast and string beans. And chocolate cake. Pretty hardy fare for sick folk I would've thought.

"Hello," I said.

She looked at me, startled as if sure I wasn't going to engage her. I wondered if she'd been told I was insane or something.

"Can you tell me the time?" I asked.

She looked over at Sister Beatrice who was busy dealing with a woman in the bed by the door.

"It is half five," she said in a small voice.

Killing Time in Georgia 41

"Thank you," I said. "And the date?"

"The date?" she asked, nervously as she went back to her cart, clearly ready to be finished with our conversation.

"The doctor said I've had a hit on the head," I explained. "I think I've lost track of time."

"Tuesday," she said softly. "May tenth."

"And the year?" I asked, holding my breath.

"You don't know the year?"

"I think I do," I said with a smile. "Is it....?"

She waited until she realized I wasn't going to finish the sentence.

"1923," she said and then hurriedly pushed the trolly past me and toward the door.

It's one thing to figure it out for yourself. But I have to say it's a whole different bucket of fish when you hear it said in words.

Somehow, someway, I was in a hospital bed in Savannah, Georgia.

One hundred years ago.

∽

The rest of the afternoon really unfold for me like a dream. I watched the dying sunlight from the window create moving patterns onto the parquet flooring. I watched the nuns and nurses come and go, tucking in patients, reading notes scrawled onto clipboards and interacting with the one or two visitors who had come to see my unconscious roommates. I didn't see any doctors again after mine this morning and the creepy orderly didn't come around again either.

By the time I was thinking of asking Sister Beatrice for a dose of whatever was in that needle in order to help me sleep, she came in with a stack of clothing in her arms and I realized that my adventure was poised to continue in a different way before I was allowed to sleep.

She laid the clothes at the foot of my bed and frowned at me as if trying to determine if they might fit me.

"Your own clothing was destroyed in the accident," she said.

I couldn't imagine that that was true, but I wasn't going to argue with her. I had been wearing a light-cotton dress with a hem that hit above my knees. If I really was in a different time—and I only say that because it's much more likely that I've had some kind of mental break down—it stood to reason that a nun from 1923 would find the clothes I'd been found in inappropriate.

I picked up the midcalf-length skirt, which was a heavy forest green wool, not something one ever saw anyone wearing in Savannah even in our so-called winter. Most people in Savannah wore as few clothes as possible and certainly never wool.

The suit was comprised of a long jacket with a square collar and cut straight to accentuate a narrow waist. The matching skirt, which was flared, was the same color as the jacket. The silk blouse was cream-colored. That was a lot of clothes given that I was used to just yoga pants and a top for most of the time.

I was surprised to see Sister Beatrice had also laid out a set of women's underwear which included a silk camisole and cotton pantaloons. I didn't wear underwear anywhere near this sexy in 2023.

"Shoes?" I asked.

She handed over a pair of lace-up Oxford shoes. All leather, handmade by the look of them, and polished to a shine.

"I will take you to my sister's," she said as I began to

dress in the clothes, feeling the suit fabric smooth in my hands but somehow stiff and unyielding against my skin.

I knew that flappers came about in the 1920's and they had definitely worn their hemlines elevated but not usually over the knee. This suit skirt, unsurprisingly, was quite modest. I glanced at Sister's own skirt which dusted the floor and decided it could have been worse.

Once dressed, I felt better, more confident and more able to handle whatever was coming next. I slipped on the leather shoes and tied them.

"We will get you hose later," she said with a frown, looking at my legs. "I was not able to find any today."

I wanted to tell her not to worry about it. I hadn't worn pantyhose since moving to Savannah three years ago. They were too hot on my legs. But I could see it was important to her and so I held my tongue.

After that, she led me from the room. I felt my excitement begin to ramp up as I realized I was about to step outside the hospital into this new world which just might cure me of whatever trauma-induced dream I was currently in the grips of.

Or it might ease me more fully into the dementia I was beginning to feel more and more at home with.

9

The late afternoon sun was just beginning to dip behind the rooftops when Sister Beatrice led me down the sidewalk in front of the hospital.

The architecture of the historic neighborhoods that we passed featured all the homes I've become so familiar with over the years—big, impressive structures with gingerbread gables, and elaborate ogee moldings adorning eaves and shuttered windows. Some of the homes we passed were already abandoned, their windows broken, their paint flaking off of what had once been grand structures.

As we passed the hospital gardens, I noticed an elderly black man clipping a hedge of thick cabbage roses along the perimeter. He turned his head to watch us walk by and nodded in acknowledgment.

I had already accepted the outrageous notion that my comatose brain seemed to believe, which was that I had gone back in time, so once outside, I eagerly began to look for the famous oak tree—the "hanging tree"—that anchored the hospital site and that was still standing in 2023. I saw it within minutes of stepping out of the front of the hospital. It was smaller than when I'd seen it last. About a hundred years smaller.

After that, I decided not to spend too much time looking around my surroundings. My thoughts went from wonder to horror at the snap of a finger, the end result being I was shaken and unnerved. Nothing helpful would come from my looking around. If anything, I might be becoming even more unbalanced.

There were at least a handful of times when Sister Beatrice had to stop and walk back to where I periodically had become transfixed in spite of my best intentions on the sidewalk, staring at the cars and the horse-drawn buggies and just the world in general. I knew this street, Abercorn, from my own time. There are no massive magnolia trees lining it in 2023—at least not at this stretch of it—and I tried hard to remember what there was instead but couldn't.

It was so much more beautiful today.

As we passed the Mercer-Williams House—a superior and pristine example of Italianate architecture—I saw that it was a private residence. In 2023 aside from being the setting for a bestselling book, it was a wedding venue and a popular tourist stop. And of course also haunted.

"Hurry up, Miss Belle," Sister said sharply. "My sister is expecting you and it's not right to make her hold dinner."

I wasn't sure how it came to be that I missed out on the charity ward that the good doctor had suggested for me, but since staying at the hospital wasn't an option, I was grateful for a place to stay—especially if it was going to be on this street. In my time, most of these homes are still standing, although they've been significantly renovated to include granite counters and modern bathrooms. And they cost in the million dollar plus range so walking by them was all I could afford to do.

The thought that I might get a peek inside one during its heyday was the first bit of non-horrified excitement I'd had since I opened my eyes in that hospital bed.

As I hurried along behind my companion, I kept my focus on her ramrod straight back. I'd already passed an ancient stable that in my time was a Whole Foods Market; I nearly lost my footing as I realized that. When we crossed a square that I didn't recognize at first, I saw it was fringed on all sides by breathtaking mansions until I realized where I was. In my time, half of these mansions were gone, replaced by towering and seriously ugly condominiums.

After that, I decided that the best way for me to keep my sanity was to roll with what I thought was happening—and to focus as soon as I could on getting back to my own time. I had a few ideas how I might do that—after all, I was pretty sure I was really lying on my back in a hospital bed somewhere in 2023 Savannah in a medically-induced a coma. Getting hysterical about it now would do me no good.

Sister Beatrice began to slow at the intersection of Drayton and East Charlton Street, a block south of Lafayette Square. I didn't remember seeing all the houses on East Charlton Street, but the ones I saw were the epitome of southern elegance and the archetypal antebellum mansion.

In my time there would be a Savannah Coffee Roasters on the corner.

The warm evening breeze carried with it the aroma of fresh baked bread and fresh cut grass. And of course the sea.

"Here we are," Sister Beatrice said as we turned off Drayton Street into a small lane called East Macon Street. She moved to walk up the broad steps of an impressive four-story house painted in cream. Curling green vines trailed up the pillars that stood on either side of a massive mahogany front door with intricate carvings and a gleaming brass door knocker.

It was the height of summer, and the light was still not quite gone, but I guessed that it was about eight in the evening. The lights from within the townhouse were blazing and it looked warm and inviting from where I stood on the threshold.

The door swung open before Sister Beatrice had knocked.

"I saw you from the window," the woman said, smiling at us.

I stared, dumfounded.

Dark hair and eyes, the resolute chin, the sad expression...

"Why didn't Seamus answer the door?" Sister Beatrice said as she stepped past her sister.

But I was still staring at the young woman who stood in the doorway looking at me.

It was the face of the woman I'd seen in the oil painting.

10

"Seamus is not feeling well," Mary said, her glance going to me. She smiled.

I was still reeling from the realization that I had seen her face just the day before in 1923. It was definitely her. The lips, the hair, the clothing. Suddenly, I realized I was staring at her with my mouth open.

"Hello," I said, not sure if shaking hands was appropriate between women during this time.

"You can do all that inside," Sister Beatrice said. "Hurry up now!"

I scurried after her into the foyer catching my slightly too-big leather shoes on the door mat and nearly tripping.

The elegant entryway of the townhouse featured polished hardwood floors made in an intricate checkerboard design. A beautiful chandelier hung overhead and the walls were covered in dark wood paneling with delicate floral and curving designs carved into the panels.

A wide staircase swept up to the second floor, where an ivory banister swept outward and upward. Atop the staircase was a spectacular stained-glass window which was framed by thin, delicate columns on each side. In the foyer itself, a mahogany table held a large bouquet of fresh garden flowers. A beautiful chandelier hung above.

"Have you eaten?" Mary asked as she led the way from the foyer into the living room.

"What's wrong with Seamus?" Sister Beatrice asked.

"I don't know, Sister," Mary said. "He's lying down."

"Oh, for heaven's sake," the nun said, her glance going toward the staircase and presumably where the bedrooms were. "Perhaps he should accompany me back to the hospital."

"I think he just needs some peace and quiet," Mary said.

"You mean he's the worse for drink."

Mary turned to me and took in my attire. I must have put it on wrong because her glance was a little longer than surely was normal.

"Are you weary?" she said.

"No, I'm good," I said and then bit my tongue. Obviously, *I'm good* was a euphemism specific to my century because she frowned when she heard it.

"She has a head injury," the nun said briskly. "She will say all manner of odd things."

I found myself regretting that I'd gone along with the amnesia diagnosis especially since it seemed that the good sister was adding a little more to the diagnosis herself. It was just as well. I wasn't going to get the hang of the dialect in the short time I intended to be here.

"Would you like to see your room, Miss Belle?" Mary asked me pleasantly.

"That would be nice," I said. "Please call me Georgia."

Something passed across her face, almost like a wince, and I realized that in this time, first names were an intimacy I hadn't earned. By asking her to call me by my Christian name, I was forcing her to allow me to call her by hers as well.

"You will call her *Miss Thompson*," Sister Beatrice said to me, eliminating any confusion or consternation my comment may have caused.

She turned to her sister.

"Feed her, give her work. She is not a guest. She is only here until she can regain her memory." She turned to give me an askance look. "I'm sure she has people who are looking for her."

Mary turned to me and smiled. "A husband, perhaps?"

Sister Beatrice snorted rudely as if the very suggestion was absurd. It was true I wasn't wearing a wedding ring.

"You're both spinsters," she said. "Don't let that be a reason to become pals."

And with that, she turned and walked to the front door, letting herself out. Mary Thompson must have been used to her sister's ways because she merely dipped her head as if to signal to me to follow her. Relieved of the burden of making small talk, I followed her up the long, carpeted stairs, marveling at how beautiful and new everything looked.

The bedroom was decorated in soft shades of yellow and white, with a simple country bed in the middle and a wooden rocking chair beside it. The grate in the fireplace was dark and cold. I walked into the room and sat down gingerly on the corner of the bed which was covered in a richly colored handmade quilt.

"If you need anything," Mary said, "please don't hesitate to call me."

"Thank you," I said. I wanted to say more, to express my gratitude but the events of the day had begun to wear on me. I was exhausted.

"The bathroom is down the hall," she said, relieving me of that little worry before I had to ask.

I thanked her again and she left. The window opposite the bed revealed that it was finally dark out. The moon was clearly visible through the trees across the street.

I honestly felt a little shaky and was sorry I hadn't asked for something to eat after all. I hadn't been hungry, but appetite isn't the only reason one needs fuel. I could've used a big glass of Merlot, too.

When I finally got up from the bed, I found that Mary had placed a small stack of clothing on the bed. Clean, pressed undergarments and a long cotton night dress which had also been ironed. I fingered the collar of hand-embroidered rose petals and wondered if something like this would have survived in my time. Nothing this pristine. Even so, the cotton was so soft, it felt like nothing in my hands.

I opened the bedroom door, looking both ways in case the mysterious Seamus was up and about, and then tiptoed down the hall to the bathroom which was amazingly modern for the time I thought. Or perhaps I'd just been fearing the worse.

After I'd used the washcloth and soap to wash my face and neck and also to brush my teeth, I hurried back to my bedroom where I slipped into the nightgown and climbed between the crisp cool sheets of the bed.

Just before I closed my eyes, shutting out the glow of moonlight from my window, I told myself in the form of a sort of prayer that what I was experiencing was real and that I would find my way home.

It was either that or break down and accept the other alternative, that I'd completely lost my marbles.

11

I slept late the next morning.

Even the glare of the midday sun through my window didn't wake me. I know I must have needed the rest—or at least the oblivion. When I finally sat up in bed, I found that I felt much better and that I was quite hungry.

Mary must have come into my room at some point in the morning while I slept because I saw another set of clothes hanging from a quilt rack in the room. I touched the fabric and was relieved to see it didn't have the coarse, stiff texture that Sister Beatrice had procured for me yesterday.

Even so, it was a heavy twill, and I could not imagine sweltering in it in Savannah in late June. After another trip to the bathroom for a much more thorough washing, I put on my new underthings, except for the girdle, that had been included in the neat stack, and then the dress that Mary had set out. It was checkered, the hem hitting my leg midcalf. I stood in front of the room mirror. The collar was Peter Pan style with wide cuffs and piping along the bias in pale linen. I looked ridiculous.

I couldn't remember the last time I'd worn so much clothing. Especially without air conditioning, I felt ready to take another bath before I even left the room. But for now, it would keep me from getting shocked stares from the people in 1923 and allow me to do the research to get home again without causing too much attention to myself.

When I opened the bedroom door, I heard the rumblings of a male voice coming from downstairs. Wondering if it was Mary's servant Seamus, I made my way silently down the long staircase.

The voice belonged to the handsome detective who'd visited me in the hospital, Sam something. As soon as I descended the stairs, he was on his feet. Mary sat opposite him, her ankles crossed primly, wearing a double-breasted silk suit in pale lilac. When I saw her, with her beautiful hair coiled up off her neck, I instantly became self-conscious of my short, cropped hair.

"Good afternoon, Miss Belle," Sam said. "I trust you slept well?"

At first I thought he was being sarcastic, and then I realized he was merely being the epitome of the Southern gentleman—police detective or not. I came into the room and Mary, smiling, indicated the chair across from her.

"Yes, thank you," I said as I sat, my stomach growling.

"Oh, Detective Bohannon," Mary said instantly. "Might we postpone this until after lunch? I know Cook wouldn't mind adding another plate and we would love to have you."

Sam, still standing, nodded at her with a gracious smile.

"That would be delightful," he said.

Mary stood up and I started to, but she gestured for me to remain seated.

"I will have a word with Cook," she said. "I'll be back directly. That dress color suits your coloring, Miss Belle."

She disappeared while the detective sat back down. I really didn't know what to make of his visit. He was clearly here to take my statement on my assault and yet everyone was acting as if it were a social engagement. Was it possible that police interrogations in 1923 were considered some kind of social intercourse?

"I'm surprised to see you again, Detective Bohannon," I said. "Have you found out anything about the man who assaulted me?"

He frowned as if uncomfortable with the word—or at least with it coming out of the mouth of a woman—and pulled out his notebook and a pen from his vest pocket.

"I'm afraid it's a most vexing case," he said. "If you're feeling up to it, do you think you could tell me exactly what happened to you?"

It wasn't until that moment that I realized that what had happened to me in 2023—when Jimmy White attacked me—was not likely to be what had happened to me here in 1923. I knew I could always default to my amnesia cover story but if I did, then I would be making work for the police in an investigation that didn't really exist. As a member of the police force in 2023—not to mention a conscientious citizen—that felt wrong.

"I'll try," I said. "Can you tell me where I was found after the assault?"

He frowned again at my word usage, and I wondered if that word only had a sexual connotation in 1923.

He flipped open his book.

"Witnesses said they saw a man approach you on River Street," he said. "A Miss Lydia Bartram says you stepped into an alley with a man dressed all in black."

That didn't sound at all like something I would do.

"You're wondering if I knew my assailant," I said carefully.

This time his eyebrows shot up.

"Did you?"

Here was the tricky bit. If the interaction was anything like what had gotten me attacked in 2023, I must have known my assailant but not in any way that would make sense to this detective. But if I made up something, as in I said I saw a man acting strangely, or he approached me and asked me a question, and it wasn't the truth, I'd be derailing whatever legitimate investigations he'd already done.

"I didn't, no," I said. "My memory isn't too good, but I think he asked me a question and when I stopped to answer him…well, that's where my memory leaves me."

He nodded as if this all made sense to him.

"Witnesses said you began shouting and when a Mr. Havington approached to see if you needed help, he saw you struggling with a large man."

"So perhaps *he* could identify him?" I asked.

"Regretfully, he only saw him from the back. But he said he was quite tall with blond hair."

"What happened then?"

"By then, you were on the ground, having been…struck by the man and he had fled the scene."

I think both of us were exhausted with this whole exchange, but at least I'd discovered what he thought had happened to me.

"I'm sorry I couldn't be of more help," I said.

"Oh, you have been a very big help," Sam said, his brown eyes intense and probing as he put away his notebook. "The Savannah Killer has never struck this early in the evening before, nor in this area."

I was surprised.

"Oh! So you have an existing investigation?"

I didn't realize my mysterious attacker had done this before.

"We have two other similar incidents we believe are related," Sam said.

"Neither of the other victims were able to identify him?"

Bohannon stood up and I saw that Mary was coming back into the room.

"Lunch is served," she said, smiling and hesitating so that we might follow her into the dining room.

I got to my feet to follow her.

"Detective?" I prompted. "Why haven't the other women identified him? Was he wearing a mask?"

"No, Miss Belle," he said, flushing slightly as if talking about the case now that we were going to lunch was somehow unseemly.

We entered the dining room where the table was artfully set with fragrant flowers and glassware. A golden chandelier reflected sparkles of light off the glasses at each place setting. I had a strong feeling of being in someone's great grandmother's parlor. I'd never had that experience myself but everything—although new—looked dated and old-fashioned.

"Why don't you sit on my left, Miss Belle?" Mary said as she seated herself.

Sam waited until we were both seated and then an older woman came into the room carrying a large tureen. She wore black slacks and a white shirt stained by grease. The crook of her elbow formed a permanent dimple from the weight of pots and pans.

The smell of traditional southern dishes like okra and shrimp gumbo, fried green tomatoes, smoked ham, collard greens and cornbread muffins seemed to infiltrate every corner of the expansive dining room. While she ladled up my plate, I looked up to catch her eye, but she never looked up from her task. Discomfited, I turned again to the detective.

"So why can't the other women identify him?" I asked.

Even if they didn't have facial recognition software back in 1923, I assumed they had police sketch artists.

"We can discuss it after lunch," Mary said as the server filled Sam's bowl full of gumbo.

"Okay," I said. "But it's really a pretty simple question. You have a perpetrator with a modus operandi that you've identified and a series of victims but for some reason you don't have a suspect. All I want to know is—"

Sam cleared his throat as if to stop me from speaking. Mary spoke to the serving woman under her breath at which point, Sam leaned over to me. Instantly I got a whiff of sandalwood and tobacco.

"It is because, Miss, Belle," he said, speaking in a low, terse voice, refusing to give me eye contact, "you are the only victim to have survived."

12

I have to say after that, lunch became a fairly tense affair.

It was clear by Mary's behavior that no real discussion of anything important was going to be allowed during the meal so there was very little conversation. If I hadn't been so hungry, it would've been one of the most uncomfortable hours of my life. Yes, a full hour. After soup came pork chops and then fried chicken along with cornbread and turnip greens and sliced tomatoes and cucumbers. After that, the server returned with a huge coffee pot which she poured for each of us, before cutting wedges of peach pie topped with whipping cream.

It didn't occur to me to look at Mary to see how much of all this food she was eating. But for myself, after the main course, I could barely move I was so stuffed. I could already feel my dress straining at its buttons. I could only imagine my agony if I'd decided to wear the girdle.

But at least the mostly silent and very tense meal allowed me to ruminate over what the detective had told me. As far as he was concerned, I was meant to have been killed in the attack that sent me to the hospital—as the others were.

Of course, if he was having trouble hearing me say words like *assault* and *assailant*, he certainly wasn't going to tell me if any of the women had been raped and I didn't want to end up being committed to an insane asylum for posing the question.

The bottom line was that Detective Bohannon was clearly dealing with a serial killer—before the term had been coined. This was quite a bit worse than selling counterfeit iPhones. I don't know how I fit into the scenario, but I did feel as if somehow I'd had a close call. It helped in a way to explain why this extraordinary experience was happening to me.

Perhaps I'd been killed? And this was the afterlife? Or a kind of reincarnation?

Correction. Forget reincarnation scenarios. I was pretty sure I was in hell.

After lunch, the detective made a fairly quick beeline for the door. I didn't blame him. I followed Mary into the parlor where she sat down with a *Lady's Home Journal* magazine—prompting me to wonder what she could possibly get out of it since she clearly didn't do her own cooking or cleaning. I sat down across from her.

"I wanted to thank you for taking me in," I said, smoothing out the pleats of my dress and wishing I could run upstairs and find a pair of sweatpants to ease the misery in my tight clothing.

"Of course," she said with a perfunctory smile.

"Do you see your sister often?"

She looked at me as if not understanding my words.

"Sister Beatrice," I clarified. "Do you see her often?"

"Rarely," she said. "We're not close."

I nodded having no idea what to say to that. But when Sister Beatrice had rung her up saying she needed Mary to house a crazy person for an indefinite period of time, Mary had presumably acquiesced without hesitation.

"I'm very grateful," I said again, not knowing what else to say.

"You're very welcome."

I looked around the room and saw a newspaper folded on the coffee table. I reached over to take it and saw that she'd glanced at my motion.

"May I?" I asked.

"Of course."

Something about the way she said that made me think that it really *wasn't* okay, but she was too Southern and too genteel to admit it.

Just looking at the date of May 11, 1923, made me catch my breath but I don't think Mary noticed. I opened the newspaper with slightly shaking hands that made the paper rustle. I cleared my throat in an attempt to camouflage the sound.

It was the *Savannah Bugle*, not a paper I'd ever heard of. There was an artist rendering on the front page that looked surprisingly familiar. It wasn't until I began to read the article that I realized the reason was because the picture was supposed to be of me.

A young woman, as yet unidentified, was found in a state of unconsciousness in the early hours of yesterday morning off Whitaker Street. The authorities are already hard at work to bring the assailant to justice. At this reporting there has been no description of the young woman's aggressor. We request that all citizens keep an eye out for suspicious behavior and report it to the authorities at once. Meanwhile, we shall keep our readers apprised of any new information as it becomes available.

I sat back for a moment, astonished to have what I'd experienced reduced to a few lurid lines in what was clearly a very different kind of journalism. In addition to the flowery language, they'd gotten the date and time for the assault wrong. Shaking my head in disbelief, I read further.

This shocking episode marks the third such aggression in the past month. This heinous series of attacks on young women has taken the lives of several unfortunate victims. Just last week, the second victim was added to this monster's devastating list of foul misdeeds. It is expected that these recent acts of violence will continue to foster both fear and outrage amongst our citizenry. An investigation is underway by Savannah's Police Department to identify and apprehend the perpetrator, but authorities continue to urge our city's flowers of Southern womanhood not to venture out in public unless with a husband or other male relative.

"This is incredible," I said.

Mary looked up. "Excuse me?"

I indicated the paper in my hands.

"Detective Bohannon said the other women the guy attacked were killed."

"I am sure Detective Bohannon didn't intend to upset you."

What a strange thing to say! I nearly retorted that I

imagined the families of the women killed were probably pretty upset too, but I held my tongue. I really didn't have the culture down well enough to express myself.

I looked back at the paper and the artist's rendering of my face. I wondered if whoever had done it had done it while I was asleep in the hospital? Civil rights didn't seem to be much on anyone's radar in this timeline. Nor the concept of invasion of privacy.

I looked again at Mary. She was a total enigma. Very generous but hardly friendly. And yet there was something about her—something just below the surface—that seemed somehow endearing or even ardent. I couldn't put my finger on what it was.

"I was thinking I might go for a walk to one of the squares," I said. "Isn't Forsythe Square near here?"

"A walk?" she said, startled.

"You know, to stretch my legs."

She glanced at my legs, and I remembered then that I hadn't put on the hose that she'd left for me either. As it was, I was so warm that everything I touched was sticky. I could only imagine how much worse it would be if I had on a girdle and hose.

"Would you like to come, too?" I asked, standing up.

She set down her magazine and looked around as if this was truly the most outlandish suggestion she'd ever heard of. I'm sure people back in the twenties took walks. Especially women like Mary who otherwise had nothing else to do with their time but flip through magazines that wouldn't serve them.

It was a long time between getting dressed, eating three meals and getting ready for bed again. Especially without television to break up the monotony.

"Yes, alright," she said, standing but not looking totally sure of what she was doing.

It was a relief for me to be in charge for a change, and I began to move quickly toward the front door.

"Let me tell Seamus we're going out," she said. "I'll get my hat. I'll get one for you too."

I nearly told her not to bother, but then it occurred to me that a hat might be nice against the afternoon sun.

13

We stepped outside and into the heat and humidity of a typical Savannah afternoon in June. Sweat clung to my hairline as I gazed around at the grand residential homes that fringed the beautiful old squares. The magnolia trees were in full bloom, their enormous white flowers sending off a fragrance so strong you could taste it. The brick streets and lush gardens of azalea, magnolia and crepe myrtle were impressive even to me, someone who has seen them every day since childhood.

I was astonished to see that Mary's townhouse literally faced Lafayette Square, a beautiful and famous old square where I have often eaten lunch on fine days.

Mary adjusted her hat, and with a measured, dignified pace she led the way down the block. She told me childhood stories and pointed out different architectural features unique to each house we passed or garden we visited.

As we walked, I found myself filled with admiration for her grace and poise despite the heat and her clothing which had to be even more constricting than what I was wearing.

Killing Time in Georgia

In spite of the fact that we were in a time in American history when it was more shameful than 2023 to be and unmarried woman, she seemed confident and content.

Her eyes lit up as she pointed out certain trees or shrubs as we walked along. It was almost as if these landmarks were her friends, and she was happy to see them again.

"You see the old Boxer Mansion there on the corner? They were friends of my parents. I heard that there used to be incredible parties here! Everybody dressed up in their finest, playing games like Hide and Seek, or Mingle and Jingle."

I loved that she was relaxed enough to share these details of her life with me.

"That sounds amazing," I said to encourage her.

"The Boxers were a prominent family in town. They were very wealthy and hosted huge parties. It was said that one time they even hired an opera singer from out of town to perform for them!"

"Wow. What about that house?"

I pointed to a giant house that frankly looked like it had been abandoned but was no less dramatic for that.

"That belonged to the Wilsons—a very eccentric family. They kept to themselves mostly but would occasionally throw the wildest costume parties late into the night."

"What kinds of costumes?"

"Oh, all sorts of things! You'd see people dressed up in historical costumes or ones from stories – like pirates or princesses. It was always quite a sight! And then there was the Richardson family."

She pointed to a house in a classic example of Victorian architecture.

"They were the first to move in and they were quite the wild bunch. Every summer they would host these raucous parties on their porch. Music would pour out until late into the night. Everyone in town knew it was a sure sign that summer had arrived!"

Of course, those families were long dead in my own time. But I couldn't help but look at the houses that had once rung with so much joy and music and laughter—families growing and moving away and then fading away—and not feel heartsick about all that had been lost.

I could hear the nostalgia in Mary's voice, too, and I knew she was remembering her own parents and growing up with her sister. She was quiet for a bit after that, and I hoped that her reminiscing hadn't made her sad.

Suddenly she glanced at me.

"What about you?" she asked. "You really cannot remember anything about your own people?"

"I know my mother must be so worried about me," I said.

"That is Mrs. Amanda Belle, yes?"

"Yes, that's right."

She glanced sideways at me.

"I am sure Detective Bohannon will have checked for a Mrs. Amanda Belle in Savannah," she said.

She was subtly telling me that nobody could find my mother. The upshot being that I must be either crazy, lying or misremembering.

"She doesn't live in Savannah."

Immediately, I was sorry I said it.

"Oh?"

I nearly groaned. If I told her my mother lived in Pooler and they tried to look for her there, they weren't going to find her.

"I don't remember," I said uncertainly. "It's all very muddled right now."

She reached out and gave my arm a squeeze.

"Don't you worry about it, Miss Belle," she said. "Things will come back in their own time."

I smiled gratefully at her.

As we passed by one garden Mary began relating a scandalous story about a secret affair between two rival families that had been going on for generations unbeknownst to anyone but the families themselves. I loved hearing her speak and it was impossible not to get lost in her story telling or be impressed at how she knew all these secrets hidden throughout her neighborhood's history.

It was during this stroll through Savannah's most beautiful residential squares that I began to see how much Mary loved the city. While she was particularly captivated by the architecture on our walk, she also nodded hello to various passersby, regardless of color, and I thought I could see she loved the city's culture and its people too. It was impressive —her acceptance of the city with all its flaws—social, racial and gender inequality, especially for the times.

We passed the Cathedral Basilica of St. John the Baptist, a magnificent structure built by Spanish missionaries in the sixteenth century and one of the oldest buildings in Savannah an imposing presence. It didn't look any different now than it did in 2023.

Soon we passed several squares and came to a park bench facing what I knew to be Oglethorpe Square—one of the original colonial squares of Savannah. As we sat there, I thought I saw Mary thinking it might be time to make our way back home but she surprised me.

"Care to go further into the city?" she asked, looking down the sidewalk toward the river, almost longingly.

"Sure," I said eagerly, in spite of the sweat dripping down my face. "The fresh air is doing wonders for me."

She looked at me as if not sure I wasn't joking but finally nodded and we headed on.

The simple fact was, I had more than fresh air and leg stretching on my mind as the reason I wanted to further our walk. I already knew I would only find more and more evidence of a Savannah that was totally foreign to me, but I also knew that if I had any hope at all of reversing what had happened to me, it wouldn't happen from inside Mary Thompson's townhouse.

"May I lead the way?" I asked. "I think this neighborhood is bringing back memories."

She frowned at first and then seemed to see the merit in the suggestion if I were trying to get my memory back.

"By all means," she said.

I knew exactly where I was. Johnson Square was directly ahead of us. It was a popular garden even in 2023 and just a few streets away from my workplace. While most of Savannah's squares are surrounded by row houses, Johnson is like a grassy oasis. It was flanked by two majestic antebellum mansions, one at each end. The only structure in the square not made of brick was the Lee House, a Greek revival. In my day, the Lee House was a popular stop for tour groups.

Everywhere I looked, it felt like I was walking through a Eugenia Price novel.

I set out at an energetic pace. To her credit, Mary adjusted her speed to match mine. By now I was full-on sweating, my underarms damp and uncomfortable, but I didn't see her looking anything but totally fresh and unfazed.

The sidewalks are cobblestones, worn to roundness by years of foot traffic. The red brick streets are wide and lined with trees, arching over the roads in a canopy of green. I was tempted to go to the street of my apartment building, but I reminded myself that it wouldn't have been built in 1923.

I found and stayed on Abercorn Street since it was a straight shot from there to the Olde Pink House, which I was curious to see before it became a tourist-favorite restaurant, but mostly because it was on the way to East Bryan Street.

"My goodness, you keep up quite a pace, Miss Belle!" Mary said breathlessly.

I turned to look at her and saw she was finally pink in the face. My ruse of taking an afternoon stroll was taking a hit as a result of my crazy speed walking.

I was clearly walking like a woman with a purpose.

I gestured to a nearby bench across from the Colonial Park Cemetery.

"Let's sit," I said.

Spanish moss hung in tattered sheets from the massive oaks towering over the graves. The path that wound through the centuries-old cemetery was overgrown with vines and weeds. Looking across the old tombstones, worn smooth by centuries of wind and rain, I could see how they leaned and tilted in uneven rows.

"Does this place remind you of something in your life?" she asked a tad breathlessly as she pulled a lace handkerchief from her sleeve to dab at her cheeks.

Does it ever, I wanted to say.

Jazz and I often came here to eat our lunch. I once smoked a joint here—in the days when I didn't worry about random drug testing—with a young man I thought might end up being special to me. So yes, this place reminded me of disappointments and lost opportunities. But I was pretty sure I didn't want to share that.

"I don't know," I said. "I keep thinking that maybe something right around the corner will tweak my memory."

"Tweak?" she said and wrinkled her nose before finally smiling. "That's a funny word."

I looked out over the cemetery, which if my memory served, had been created in 1789.

"Do you come here much?" I asked.

Her eyebrows arched in surprise at my question.

"Never," she admitted.

"Savannah is such a beautiful town," I said. "It's the ideal walking town."

She turned and smiled at me.

"You do talk so strangely," she said. "I hope you don't mind my saying so."

"Not at all," I said. "Have you always lived in Savannah?"

"My family has, yes. For generations."

"Is your house a family home?"

I didn't want to offend her. I know some people are a little touchy when asked about finances and I had no idea what the culture was about such things a hundred years ago.

"It is," she said. "When my parents died, and Eliza decided to go into the church…"

"Eliza?"

She smiled. "You didn't think my sister was born with the name, Beatrice, did you?" She shook her head in amusement. "But after she left to dedicate her life to God, I was left all alone. So here I am."

"You're not married?"

She blushed and began to straighten out the perfectly straight folds of her dress.

"Surely you have beaus," I said, realizing I had once more blurted out something inappropriate if not downright rude.

"Have you had enough fresh air, or do you want to walk on?" she asked as she stood up.

Killing Time in Georgia

I was sorry she didn't want to share anything more personal with me, but I think I understood why not. I guessed she was about my age. Unless she was a widow—except she couldn't be with people addressing her as "Miss"—she had never been married. That was a stigma to carry anywhere in the country in 1923, I imagined. But especially in the South.

"Just a little bit further," I said. "If you don't mind."

We continued our stroll down Abercorn Street, past the Owens-Thomas House and the Slave Quarters that what would one day be an antebellum house museum included in some of the most popular tours in Savannah. Then we made our way across East Broughton Lane to Reynolds Square.

"We are going to the river?" Mary asked, I thought a little timorously.

"Not quite," I said, feeling my excitement begin to mount. To my left was where the Bank of America Financial Center should be and directly ahead was Bay Street.

As I led the way across East Bryan Street and down the little alley—even now, too small to merit more than a smudged and unreadable street sign, I could sense Mary faltering behind me.

But I didn't care. I stood on the sidewalk and stared at the little antique shop—the very one I'd been in just two days ago.

14

I walked up to the shopfront as if I were in a trance. The picture window was cloudy but the display of violins, a hand-carved trunk and several antique beaded evening purses clearly visible from the street. The metal door was painted a dark green with stripes of rust collecting at the bottom.

I pushed open the shop door and stepped in, the sound of the bell over the door heralding my entrance.

The scent of wood dust, grease and stale air, with a hint of old paper and rusting metal filled my nostrils. A clock chimed loudly numerous times. The walls were lined with shelves of antique and curio artifacts, gold statuettes, crystal carafes, silverware and other paraphernalia. They stretched from ceiling to floor and wall to wall. The wall across from the counter was crowded with books. A grand, oak counter anchored the room. An elderly man stood behind it and looked up as we entered.

He readjusted the small gold *prince nez* on his nose.

"Good morning, ladies," he said.

I was too enthralled about my quest to even respond to

him. I walked past him, focused on the back wall. That's where it had been before. From where I stood, I could see the gilded frames hanging.

It has to be here!

I walked quickly down the aisles of heirloom fashions and shoes, of china dolls, shelf after shelf of porcelain figurines, old globes, antique side tables, water pitchers, and a wide selection of costume jewelry, including rings, brooches and pendants.

"Georgia?" Mary said behind me.

But all I could think was that the portrait was here. It had to be! It was my gateway back to my life.

As I walked quickly down the endless rows of bric-a-brac and cheap trinkets, a sense of intense anticipation seemed to grip me. I felt like a child on Christmas morning; as if something wondrous was waiting around every corner. I felt alive with anticipation, my heart racing and my eyes widening with every step.

I spotted the wall of frames on the far wall and my heart leapt as I raced toward them, my eyes skimming over each in turn. There were still lifes, landscapes, family portraits and sketches. I grabbed the corner of one painting leaning against the wall.

"Please don't touch the merchandise, Miss!" the man said loudly as he hurried toward me.

But I was beyond niceties. I pulled the portrait to look behind it, and behind that one and the next. The agony of knowing it wasn't here beginning to dawn on me until I could barely breathe.

It has to be here!

"Georgia, my dear, I think you should come with me," Mary said in a calm but firm voice.

The air felt heavy as if I had been holding my breath

without realizing it. Tears started to form at the corners of my eyes and a lump formed in the back of my throat, making it impossible to speak. I slowly turned around and looked at Mary who had followed me down the aisle and was now looking at me with genuine worry in her eyes.

"It's here," I said desperately. "I know it is. It has to be!"

"Miss, I must ask you to leave," the proprietor said as he arrived at my side.

My emotions were a tumult inside me. I felt gutted, anxious and so incredibly disappointed. With all my heart, I needed this portrait to exist.

I gazed around at all the artifacts in the old junk store. I had been so sure that it was here, tears streaming down my face. I allowed Mary to lead me out of the store. My last ray of hope died as I stepped out onto the street.

The full brunt of my disappointment settled heavily upon me like the fog rolling in off the river.

∽

Ten minutes later, Mary hailed a cab and we were being conveyed swiftly back toward her townhome. From the moment I'd burst into the antique shop and gone running up and down the aisles like a mad woman, Mary had begun to act as if she was seriously rethinking the wisdom of inviting me into her home.

I didn't realize that during my desperate search for the portrait that Mary had been nearly beside herself with panic at being out in the heart of the city—and in an alleyway no less! There was of course still a serial killer roaming around Savannah preying on women.

Heartsick, I climbed into the back seat of the car, which was very uncomfortable I have to say. There were no springs in the seat cushions, and hard, sharp metal protruded everywhere in the interior just waiting to drive into tender skin at the first hint of a fender bender.

And of course no seatbelts.

By the time the taxi pulled up to her townhouse, Mary was more in control of herself. I'm not sure what she'd made of my behavior at the antique shop. At this point I was so disappointed, that I didn't really care. I was also angry at myself for getting my hopes up. I'd had this insane idea from the moment I'd first laid eyes on Mary and realized that she was the woman in the portrait that it meant something. I stupidly thought that revisiting the shop—and finding the portrait again—might somehow prompt a reversal of what had happened to me. Like what? An opening to a time portal?

I clenched my jaw in disgust. How could I possibly get back to my own time if I didn't even know how I got here in the first place?

After Mary paid the driver, I followed her into the townhome and realized that, after such a long and chatty afternoon together, we hadn't said a word to each other in nearly forty minutes. I felt responsible for that, but I didn't know how to fix it.

As soon as we stepped inside, I had every intention of going straight to my bedroom to climb under the covers and wish or sleep away the last hour of the day.

A tall man with thick dark hair dressed in a butler's livery stood in the foyer, his hands behind his back. He gave me a suspicious look.

"Miss Mary?" he said, his voice a rich and rolling Irish brogue that clearly belonged on the stage. "You have a caller."

Mary sighed heavily which made me think that perhaps she too had been looking forward to a little alone time.

"Who is it, Seamus?" she asked, plucking her hat from her head and ruffling her hair with her fingers.

"Detective Bohannon," Seamus said, looking at me as if I was the reason for this disgraceful event. "Again."

I peeked into the parlor where I saw Detective Bohannon standing by the sofa, his hat in his hand.

"Miss Belle," he said formally.

Mary came up behind me and offered her hand to him I realized that I probably should have as well. I decided to use what everyone saw as my obvious mental deficits as my excuse. I pulled my own hat off and knew I must look a sight: flushed and damp with sweat.

"Detective," Mary said as she indicated for him to reseat himself. "Do you have news for us?"

"Possibly," he said as we all sat down. I saw that the butler had brought him an iced tea while he waited.

"Seamus," Mary said softly, and the man turned on his heel and disappeared on whatever mission Mary had quietly sent him on.

Sam cleared his throat and ran a finger around his collar. I could see that he looked hot too.

"We are narrowing our leads and hope that Miss Belle might be able to help us."

"Yes, of course," I said.

"I was wondering if you remembered anything more about the man who attacked you?"

He must be desperate, I thought, if he's asking me this same question three hours after asking me the first time!

Even so, I thought hard. The only person I honestly remembered attacking me was Jimmy White and that wouldn't help the detective. Neither would my describing

White. If anything, it would send him on a wild goose chase that would help nobody.

"I'm sorry," I said. "Not really."

"Can you remember why you accompanied him into the alley?"

I felt a flinch of guilt at that because he said it in a nearly judgmental way. If alleys in 1923 were synonymous with bad places to be—and definitely to go to deliberately—for any reason, then I was presenting myself, at least to Mary, as indecorous. Or even indecent.

Suddenly I felt a horror invade my brain.

Did he think I was attempting to sell my body?

I blushed and then hated that he could see me do it since it looked like I was admitting to doing something shameful.

"I have no memory of going into the alley," I said firmly.

"So you were dragged there? Because witnesses say you were definitely in the alley."

"Well. If that's what they say."

"Some new evidence has come to light."

I frowned.

"Evidence? Like what?"

"It was found by a child," Bohannon said, as he reached into his vest pocket.

"A child?" I said in surprise and confusion. And then I remembered seeing a couple of barefoot boys around eight years old as Mary and I had walked around today. I thought they were just playing in the gutter, but were they perhaps street urchins?

At that moment, Seamus came back into the room with a tray of teacups and a silver teapot. The detective did not withdraw his hand from his pocket. We all waited as Seamus set the service down on the coffee table.

"I will serve, Seamus," Mary said. "Thank you."

Seamus sniffed as if annoyed at being dismissed but left the room.

"Pray, what did the child find, Detective Bohannon?" Mary asked as she began to pour the tea.

Sam removed his hand from his vest pocket and pulled out a laminated card which he laid on the coffee table before us. I leaned in and then caught my breath and sat back quickly not at all sure I was going to be able to explain this.

It was my Georgia driver's license.

15

After that, it didn't take much for me to look as if I was about to experience a rather severe fainting spell. I'm sure my face went white when I saw my drivers license sitting there on the antique coffee table. I immediately began to fan myself with my hat which appeared to be a time-honored signal for anyone living in the South to assume that I was about to have a fit—or at the very least needed to lie down.

"Miss Belle?" Mary said with concern in her voice, "are you well?"

"No," I said, fanning faster. "I really don't think I am."

Mary stood up immediately.

"I'm sorry, Detective Bohannon," she said. "I must insist that Miss Belle lie down. I believe she's had a shock."

Sam stood up too, his face displaying guilt for having caused this reaction in me.

"Of course," he said.

Mary took my arm and led me to the stairs.

"Seamus, please show Detective Bohannon out."

As we climbed the stairs to my bedroom, my mind was

spinning with thoughts at the sight of the card and because I had been too rattled from my disappointment at the antique shop to think of a lie fast enough to make him happy.

How did my driver's license get in the alley?

Mary helped me get my shoes off and lie down on the bed before then going for a cold cloth for my head.

I was wracking my brain trying to understand how my license made it back in time with me but not my cellphone or wallet when suddenly I remembered that I only had my cross-body purse that day. Because we were all going out for drinks after the office party, I'd brought only my license and phone.

I could not help but wonder what Bohannon thought of it all. Being the Southern gentleman that he was, he of course accepted Mary's insistence that I be allowed to go upstairs and lie down instead of giving him a good reason for this very bizarre form of identification with my name, photo and a date one hundred years in the future.

Anybody else—Rob, for example—would've had me in custody and under the hot lights rather than walk away without a reasonable explanation.

What would he make of it? Should I affect not to know what it was? Say it wasn't mine? No, that didn't make sense. My photo was on the card.

Mary came back with a ceramic basin and a washcloth. She sat next to me and wrung out the cloth.

"You don't need to do this," I protested, trying to take the cloth from her.

"Please lie quietly, Miss Belle," she said firmly as she positioned the cloth on my forehead.

I watched her closely, wondering how much she'd seen of my driver's license. Surely, she had questions too.

"It was just the heat," I said.

"Of course."

"I'm fine, really."

She kept the cloth on my head but picked up the basin, her expression unreadable.

"I'll have Cook bring up a light supper," she said. "The walk was too much, and I take responsibility for that."

I sighed. I was sorry she saw my running around the antique store acting like a crazy person as something she had caused. And that she felt she'd somehow derailed my health progress as a result. I knew she felt as if she'd failed me, *and* her sister. At this point the best thing I could do for her was not argue with her.

"Okay," I said. "Thanks. That would be great."

After she left, I took a moment to reflect on where I was, how I got here, and how in the bloody hell I was going to get back.

16

I was glad to have the rest of the evening to myself. Once I was sure that Sam Bohannon had gone, I allowed myself some time to relax. I took off the heavy woolen clothes and hung them at the foot of the bed, then used the washcloths that Mary had brought upstairs to sponge off my neck and face.

When I sat down on the bed to try to figure out what I was going to do about my drivers license showing up, I decided to lay down just for a moment, but when I woke up it was dark outside.

True to her word, Mary had sent a tray up to me, a bowl of fragrant chicken and rice—like my mother used to make—and a side salad of cucumbers and tomatoes tossed with Vidalia onions. For dessert, there was a rice pudding, topped with a sprinkle of nutmeg and studded with raisins that made me realize how hungry I was. It also reminded me of my childhood.

I climbed out of bed and pulled a chair over to the desk by the window and ate every bite of the food on the tray and then instantly felt guilty. I could just imagine Cook returning the empty tray to the kitchen and reporting back to Mary that while I evidently didn't have the strength to eat downstairs like a normal person, I'd succeeded in licking my plates clean even so.

I opened up my door and listened in the hallway, but all was quiet. Returning to my room, I felt suddenly antsy, so I dressed again and picked up the tray. I decided I'd have a little snoop around and the empty tray would serve as a good excuse in case I was intercepted by Mary or one of the household staff.

The long carpet runner felt thick and soft under my bare feet. The staircase treads, banister and railing were all made of mahogany, and the corridor walls paneled. It felt unnaturally quiet as if all life had been extinguished in the house. I could hear my heart beating rhythmically in my ears and as I neared the landing, I heard the large clock in the dining room sounding the hour. It was ten o'clock. I was pretty sure that was too late for Mary to still be up.

A twin set of wall sconces in the foyer matched the glow of the chandelier overhead whose prisms made sparkles on the wall. The air felt dry and unusually cold. With nothing else to distract me, I noticed it was musty and smelled of furniture polish and wax.

As I walked through the dining room, I spotted another door that either led to the basement or possibly the kitchen. Balancing my dinner tray on one hip, I opened the door and saw a light and heard voices.

"We never had no problem until she came," a woman's voice was saying.

I assumed she was talking about me. I eased open the door and took my first step on the wooden stairs, praying it wouldn't creak and give me away.

"She's a pretty little thing," said a voice I recognized as Seamus's.

"Is that all that matters to you? Well, that explains a lot."

"What is that supposed to mean?"

"You know what it means! You don't have two cents to rub together."

"Bah! Woman, you don't know what you're talking about."

I made it halfway down when the step beneath my naked food creaked loudly and all conversation stopped. I sighed in resignation and made my way the rest of the way down the stairs to what was clearly the house kitchen as Seamus came to stand at the foot of the steps.

"Look who's here," he said in a voice that could have been friendly or threatening. It was impossible to tell. He took the tray from me.

"Good evening, Miss," Cook said, clearly the owner of the other voice. Her eyes darted back and forth in her head as she clearly tried to remember what I might have overheard her say.

"Good evening to you, too," I said. "A delicious supper. Thank you very much."

"You didn't have to bring the tray down," she said in an indicting tone.

"No trouble," I said. "I was hoping for a cup of coffee to finish things off."

"Coffee?" she said and looked around her spic and span kitchen.

"No worries," I said. "A glass of water will do."

She hesitated just a moment as Seamus put my dirty dishes into the sink while she opened a nearby cupboard and drew out a glass. She handed it to the butler, and he left the room.

"The cistern will be colder," she explained.

"How thoughtful," I said, seating myself at the kitchen table.

The kitchen was long and broad, with a large island of black granite for cooking on, with a ceiling that had been recently cleaned. The light off the white plaster was bright and clear.

On the floor was a gray and black hand-woven woolen rug. I couldn't find a refrigerator, but I saw a big wooden box, with a handle on top that I imagined was the ice box.

All very Downton Abbey.

"I'm sorry if my being here has caused you more work," I said.

"That is fine, Miss," Cook said. "I am sorry for your misfortune."

That was the opening I was looking for.

"Speaking of that," I said. "I don't suppose you've heard of anything, you know, around the neighborhood?"

Seamus returned with a pitcher and handed it to the woman. She snorted derisively.

"This neighborhood?" she said as she poured the water into a glass and handed it to me.

"Well, then, just around town," I said.

In my experience, it was the people not directly involved with certain crimes who heard things. Gossip and rumor usually had their roots in the truth. I know Rob would laugh at me for believing that kind of *People Magazine* mentality—and now that I think of it, he has done just that—but I stand by it. People hear things and especially when they don't have any skin in the game, they're open to sharing what they hear.

"The police think my attacker was a garden variety mugger," I said.

That wasn't at all true. Bohannon definitely thought my attack was linked to the two murders that had happened before me.

Both Cook and Seamus looked at me in confusion, so I had to assume that the term *mugger* had not yet been coined.

"You know," I said. "A robber."

"Everyone knows it's the Spinelli Family behind the attacks," Seamus said, seating himself at the table. His cheekbones protruded like an Irish wolfhound's, and his dark hair was slicked down the side of his head and perfectly parted over the top. He still wore a crisp white shirt, and waistcoat and polished leather shoes.

I turned to him.

"Who are the Spinelli Family?" I asked.

"Dago crime family," Cook said turning away to wipe down an already pristine butcher block table behind her.

Organized crime? I had no idea Savannah even had such a thing in the twenties.

"They own whole parts of Savannah," Seamus said. "Everybody knows that."

"What parts?" I asked.

He shrugged. "The newspaper, the police—"

"You don't know that!" Cook said, turning on him, her chin jutting out indignantly.

He appeared unruffled by her irritable reply. "Everyone knows that," he said.

"Why would a crime family want to attack women?" I asked.

"Why do they do anything?" Seamus retorted. "Probably to shanghai them into service to their dastardly desires."

"Then why were the women killed?" Cook asked. She

waved her rag in my direction. "Missy here is the only one not killed—nor kidnapped neither."

Seamus shrugged again. "Is there pie left?"

I thought that was probably my cue to leave, so I finished my water and thanked them for the conversation before making my way back upstairs. I know what I said about the average joe having information that could be beneficial in an investigation, but honestly, serial killers didn't typically kill for a reason. Or at least not a reason fathomable to anyone except themselves. They had no motive beyond their own demented pathologies.

As I made my way silently back up the stairs, I decided that while on the face of it, the information I'd learned tonight didn't appear useful, I wouldn't discount the idea that an organized crime family might be behind the attacks —for reasons that had yet to be revealed.

17

The next morning, I made my way through the French doors into the garden where Mary sat at a round wrought-iron table having her breakfast. a table filled with pastries and coffee, covered in a white linen tablecloth. The mouthwatering aroma of eggs and sausage hung in the air, as did the scent of freshly brewed coffee.

"So, you're up," Mary said as I took my seat at the table opposite her. She poured my coffee into a china cup decorated with violets from a silver coffee set.

I added a dollop of cream and a spoonful of sugar to my cup. I wasn't surprised when it was the most amazing cup of coffee I'd ever had.

Is everything just better a hundred years ago?

As I reflected on why food was so much better here, I filled my plate from the silver-domed serving plate of scrambled eggs and sausage links that looked as if they'd been handmade.

Mary went back to her newspaper for which I was grateful. I needed a moment to ease into my day, especially with all that I felt I had to process.

I wasn't sure what to make of Seamus's belief that the attacks had to do with Savannah's current organized crime family. It didn't make sense to me but if he'd heard something, it was possible there was at least a connection there worth checking out. The next time I saw Sam—after I figured out what to tell him about my driver's license—I'd see if I couldn't push him in the direction of at least questioning the Spinelli's.

At least it might get him to stop asking me about an attack that never happened.

I used a small silver spoon to spread marmalade on what looked like a homemade English muffin. It was pretty clear that it was the preserve was homemade too, and when I bit into it, that was confirmed. Slightly bitter but rich in flavor, it nearly brought tears to my eyes it was so good.

I can't believe these people eat like this all the time. It was enough to make me want to give up fast food forever.

Not for the first time I wondered what Mary's story was. Where did her money come from? How is it she was living here alone?

"Can I ask you why you wanted to go to that shop yesterday?" she asked, still looking at her paper.

I thought about lying to her, but it was so hard keeping all my fibs straight that I thought the more I could tell the truth, the better.

"I'd been there a couple of days ago," I said. "I saw a portrait, and I was hoping to find it again."

She frowned. "You didn't behave as if you were shopping for a painting."

I sighed.

"I can't explain my behavior," I said. "Is it okay if we leave it at that?"

Her eyebrows shot up and she was quiet for a moment, but

then she nodded. Honestly, I think she appreciated my directness, which I realized might not be a common trait in 1923.

We ate our breakfast silently after that, with only comments on the weather and the hydrangeas growing in hedgerows at the base of her brick wall. The scent of jasmine rippled on a gentle breeze. The branches of a nearby cherry tree were rife with blossoms, their petals falling like raindrops to the ground. Birds twittered in the white oak tree by the fountain as a sparrow flew under the eaves of the house with a nest-building twig in its beak.

"Your garden is so beautiful," I said. "Do you have a gardener?"

"I do most of it myself."

"Well, it's really beautiful."

"You are welcome to help me prune the climbing roses later if you'd like."

"Love to. One hundred percent," I said.

She looked at me in confusion. "Are you saying yes, you'd be interested?"

"One hundred percent," I repeated as I speared a sausage link and put it on my plate. "So how well do you know Sam?" I asked.

"Who?" She looked at me with confusion.

"The detective."

"I don't know him at all."

I realized she thought I meant how well did she know him *socially*.

"Is he single, do you know?" I asked.

She coughed violently for a moment as if she'd swallowed a prune pit. When she recovered, she turned in her chair as if to get a good look at me. I knew it was a question that probably was never voiced in this time. I'm not sure if she thought it was wildly inappropriate or simply mad to say it out loud.

"You really have no idea where it is you are from?" she asked. "Your people?"

I nearly laughed out loud because some things never change. As soon as I started to date someone my mother would immediately begin asking about "his people." I'm pretty sure it's a Southern thing.

I shook my head and smiled ruefully. "Sorry," I said. "Amnesia, you know."

"Uh huh," she said, still eyeing me suspiciously.

"So listen," I said. "I have an errand I'd like to run."

She looked at me as though I'd lapsed into another language. I pushed my plate aside and leaned forward across the table.

"Here's what I think, Mary. The guy who attacked me and the other women has a pattern of behavior, you know? If we can find the pattern, we can find him. Better yet, we can catch him in the act."

"I have no idea what you're talking about."

"Come with me. What else do you have to do today?"

She frowned and turned to concentrate on her fruit compote.

"What would this errand look like?" she asked.

I tilted my head to study her. In my view, her life was dull and dreary, but she wasn't a stupid person. I could only imagine how frustrated she had to be in her station. One can only pull so many weeds before you want to jump off a cliff.

"I would like to go back to the spot where I was attacked," I said.

When she frowned, I plowed ahead.

"After that, I want to go to the places where the other women were attacked."

Her eyes widened.

"But the police will have thoroughly examined those areas."

"I'm sure they have," I said. "But we wouldn't be there to look for forensic material. We would be there to see what *similarities* there were at each location. Trust me, the cops were looking for fingerprints and fibers, not why the guy might have chosen the place he did."

She examined me with wide eyes, and her eyebrows rose. A hint of interest flashed in her gaze and then disappeared.

"How do you know about these things?"

"That's a long story and I promise I'll tell you about it sometime," I said. "So, are you in?"

She frowned again uncertainly.

"Are you asking me if I want to go on this mad escapade with you?"

She flapped out her napkin and then folded it primly and placed it on the table.

"Look, Mary, I'm sorry if I—"

"Of course I'm in," she said standing up before pausing and looking me in the eye. "One hundred percent."

18

The cobblestone street of the historic district on Bay Street by the river is especially steeped in history. Even in my own time, I always enjoyed looking at the honey-colored buildings lining the road as they reflected the evening light, sometimes making parts of the street look as though they were on fire.

The alley where I'd supposedly been attacked was situated in the center of the historic district, but off the beaten path and away from all the noise—and from help, should that be required. I stepped into the entrance to the alley, peered inside, and then took a few tentative steps in. Rubble crunched under each step.

The old bricks of both walls were worn, the mortar crumbling in places. The pavement was cracked and strewn with litter. Puddles had formed from the morning's rain. The humid air reeked of garbage and motor oil.

I walked midway down and tried to remember being here. I tried to see if anything—the smells, the absence of air on my skin—anything might trigger a memory for me.

I'd been found in the early evening. At this time of year, it wouldn't have been dark yet.

Mary stood at the entrance of the alley gripping her purse tightly to her chest as if expecting someone to come and snatch it at any moment.

I could see she wasn't comfortable being here. I don't know if she had an overactive imagination that was prompting visions of what had happened here during the attacks, or what, but she kept looking around and over her shoulder like she expected a mad killer to show up any time intending to claim two more victims.

"So what do you see?" she asked, clearly eager for us to wrap up and leave the alley.

"Nothing really," I admitted as I glanced around. "I have no memory of being here."

"Good. Then let's go," she said, rubbing her arms as if she felt a chill—although at eighty plus degrees that was hardly likely.

The next crime site was a long walk away and, in the heat, we would've done better to have hailed a cab. Mary had known exactly where to go, though, making me think she was more interested in the lurid details of the murders than she'd let on.

The crime scene was another alley, this time about a block from the hospital. Both of the alleys' walls were covered in graffiti—none of the drawings or words made sense to me. Discarded newspapers fluttering in the corners where they'd been blown by the breeze.

Once more, Mary waited for me outside the alley. After exploring the alley, I rejoined her.

"No joy?" she asked, once more clearly ready to move on.

I shook my head.

"Do you know any details of the attack?" I asked. "Her name?"

Mary made a face as if remembering was distasteful.

"Alice Marshall," she said. "The papers said she was attacked on her way home from the cinema."

I looked around. There were no movie theaters in my time near this neighborhood but of course that could've changed.

"Do you know what was done to her?" I asked.

She deepened her frown.

"She was murdered, Miss Belle," she said sharply. "I assume you want to visit the last site?"

We continued walking down the street toward the hospital, both of us silent, involved with our own thoughts. The hospital was on the opposite corner of Abercorn and East Huntington. Mary stopped outside the wrought iron fence which enclosed the hospital garden. The black gardener I'd seen before was nowhere in sight.

"Here?" I asked in surprise.

Mary glanced toward the garden but made no move to enter.

"Do you mind if we don't go in?" she said, shivering. "It's horrible to imagine. Especially in a garden."

We stood on the perimeter looking into the garden from the streetside.

"Do you remember her name?" I asked.

"Mercy O'Gillis," she said. "She was found by the fountain."

"What time?"

Mary looked at me. "Pardon?"

"What time of day was she found?"

"Early morning, I think."

I looked back at the garden.

"So the police think she was attacked sometime in the night and found in the early morning?"

"I honestly don't know what they think," she said. "May we go now?"

"Sure," I said as we turned to walk back the way we'd come.

These two murder sites were nowhere near where I was attacked. Plus, I wasn't killed. I was beginning to think the police were grasping at straws by attempting to connect the three incidents.

"I wonder if I could get the addresses from Sam for the two witnesses who gave statements about my attack," I said.

"What in the world for?" Mary asked, her pace quicker now, clearly intent on putting distance between us and the two crime scenes.

"I'd like to ask them some of my own questions," I said.

"You don't think the police will have questioned them sufficiently?"

"It's not a matter of how intensely they were questioned, but more about what those questions were. Was the male witness a high-ranking member of the community or maybe even a police supervisor? If so, don't you think Sam would be hamstrung by social decorum? Perhaps even to the point of not being able to ask all the questions he might?

"And what about the female witness? She could be a veritable treasure chest of information. But because the attacker was a man—I can tell you right now that Sam would probably have hesitated to ask her pointed questions."

"I see what you mean. But surely you don't intend to ask the female for specifics of what she saw?" Mary blushed and focused on her clutch.

"Whoa, whoa!" I said. "Mary, I was not sexually assaulted."

"Oh, good Lord!" Mary pressed both hands against her chest and shook her head as if she could erase my words. "Must you say everything that comes into your head? Goodness!"

"I'm serious. There was none of that. If anything, it was a mugging gone wrong. At the very least, he didn't have time to do more."

"I cannot listen to a minute more of this."

"Okay, fine," I said. "I get that it's delicate, especially in 1923, but these are the kinds of questions that need to be asked."

We walked in silence for a while, and I regretted that I might have lost her as an accomplice. It had been nice to have a friend in this time period—even if I wasn't able to tell her the truth about myself.

19

The harsh clacking of a typewriter sounded in the background, and the staccato rhythm filled the air in the Oglethorpe Street police station. Deep voices bellowed from the back of the police station and reverberated off the hard walls and concrete floor. The detectives' wooden desks were lined up neatly. But the one Sam sat at had a stack of file folders and case notes covering the desktop.

He'd been trying to have a word with the lieutenant all morning. He knew he was on thin ice with him. A killer on the loose for three weeks and not a single arrest? As lead detective Sam knew he was probably hours from losing the biggest promotion of his career.

When Alice Marshall was killed, there were few in the department who hadn't seen it as a run of the mill slaying. Tragic, of course, but these things happen from time to time. Especially to women in Miss Marshall's line of work.

But then, a week later, when Mercy O'Gillis was found in the hospital garden, her throat slashed in exactly the same way, the mood within the department changed. Emergency meetings were called, statewide papers sent out stringers, Atlanta picked up the story and sent a photographer down. The tension in the office escalated. And with it the pressure to solve the murders as quickly as possible.

After that, it had been everything Sam could do to convince the Lieutenant to keep him in his role as primary detective on the case. Sam knew the bottom line—the only thing that mattered—were results.

Not sociableness or affability. Comradery and buying illegal drinks at the speakeasy off River Street was what you defaulted to, Sam thought angrily, when you didn't have the facts to make your case.

He looked around the detective's room observing everyone going about their business, laughing and talking amongst themselves. His gaze fell on Chester Hawkins. He knew the big detective was poised to pounce on Sam's back as soon he saw a break.

Hawkins would have no trouble finding a suspect to parade in front of the papers.

Guilty or not.

Sam straightened the folders on his desk and picked up the small plastic card he'd received from the boy the day before. He needed answers on this. Answers he was sure Georgia Belle had, regardless of how she attempted to say she didn't. He needed a win on these two murders which—now thanks to Miss Belle—were inextricably connected.

With a live victim who, if she could just remember what she'd seen, could give Sam the details he needed to catch this bastard, Sam would finally have the triumph he needed.

His thoughts went to the beautiful stranger. Georgia was so strange in ways he couldn't put his finger on. Even so, all he had to do now was get the information out of her that he knew was locked inside. And now he had a plan for doing exactly that. Compliments of his own Granny Winslow's favorite adage about luring a bee with honey.

He glanced at his watch. The shop he needed to visit for his plan to work would be open for another hour, but he didn't want to push it.

Just as Detective Chester Hawkins passed by, Sam reached for his jacket draped over the back of his chair. Hawkins's hip banged into Sam's desk, knocking the pile of folders to the floor. Hawkins turned and gave him a smirk before heading to the lieutenant's office.

Lieutenant James had just come out of his office to study the evidence board on the wall opposite it.

"We're wasting time," Hawkins said to him without preamble. "You need to take Bohannon off the case. We're laughing stocks in the papers."

Lieutenant James didn't turn from the evidence board which had photos of the two victims and reports on their cause of death as well as all clues discovered at the two crime scenes.

Sam walked over to the two men. He could see the lieutenant was seriously considering Hawkins' words. Sam clenched his fists.

"We are close to a lead, sir," Sam said. "I have a plan."

"We've heard that before!" Hawkins exclaimed. "We don't have time for this. We have to find this killer before another innocent girl is killed."

"And that's what I intend to do," Sam said, still addressing the lieutenant.

Hawkins waved a hand dismissively at him.

"You've been lead detective on this for three weeks and

we still don't have a suspect. You have no idea who the killer is!"

Sam forced his temper to stay in check.

"Sir," he said to the lieutenant. "I'm confident that I have an idea that can generate a lead in the case. The last attack on—"

"I have heard this before, Sam," his boss said wearily. "You've been working your ass off on these cases. No one can say different. But Chester has a point. We have to nail this bastard."

Out of the corner of his eye, Sam saw Hawkins grin and fold his arms across his chest.

"You've chased down every lead," the lieutenant said to Sam, as he put a hand on his shoulder. "You've made sure all the evidence was there, but now we need to come together as a team and find this guy."

"You need to let someone else lead the investigation," Hawkins said to the lieutenant.

Sam turned to face Hawkins, their eyes locked in mutual dislike. Sam could feel his heart pounding in his chest, both from anger and the adrenaline as Hawkins silently jeered at him.

"This isn't a therapy session," Hawkins said with a sneer. "You got problems from the war? You need to work them out some place where innocent women aren't being killed."

"That's enough, detective!" Lieutenant James said sharply.

Without thinking, Sam lunged forward and shoved Hawkins against the wall.

The big detective outweighed Sam by twenty pounds, and he was ready for him. Every barb, every insult had been calculated to provoke. The second Sam made his move,

Hawkins drove forward hard with an uppercut that caught him off guard and sent him flying backwards into some nearby chairs. Stunned but still seeing red, Sam leapt to his feet and charged again, the two of them now trading blows until a loud voice roared "Enough!"

Sam and Hawkins stood panting and glaring at each other as Lieutenant James came between them.

"I should write you both up," he said. "Hawkins, take a walk."

Hawkins hesitated as if he was considering disobeying, but then took a step back. Sam turned to the lieutenant.

"I need one more day," he said, before turning and spitting blood out onto the floor.

"A day won't matter," the lieutenant said.

"I have a lead," Sam said.

"Are you talking about the girl who was attacked in the alley off River Street?"

"Yessir."

"I thought she didn't remember anything."

"I think I know how to help her remember."

The lieutenant laughed.

"If you mean help her in a little more creative way, then I'm glad to see you are finally joining the team, son."

Sam's cheeks burned. No, he would not falsify evidence or witness testimony. But if working inside the system meant looking like he was playing their game, then by God, he would.

"Yessir," he said. "I think you'll find that my new idea is very creative."

"All right, son. One more week," the lieutenant said.

"Thank you, sir," Sam said turning back to his desk, his aching jaw set in determination. With a little bit of cooperation from Miss Georgia Belle, he was finally on the verge of snagging the one clue he'd been looking for—the one that would lead him directly to the man the papers referred to as *The Savannah Killer*.

One lead. And all he had to do to get it, was be a little creative.

20

It was nearly lunch time, but I could tell Mary wouldn't be comfortable going to a restaurant. Besides, I didn't have any money to contribute. We decided to return home for lunch which suited me except for one little thing.

In all the walking and talking and poking into alleyways, I had begun to remember something.

It wasn't much and I wasn't ready to make a big announcement about it yet, but the fact was, ever since we'd left the alley where I'd been found, I'd had a feeling in the back of my brain that I couldn't define.

It was like there was a certain melody of music that I was remembering. I glanced at Mary as we walked. I was sorry if I'd offended her with my questions, but I was glad for the silence that her pique afforded me so I could work out what it was I was remembering. It was about midway in our walk back to her town house as we passed near my own attack site, when the realization came to me.

"I think there was a bar or restaurant nearby," I said, stopping suddenly.

Mary turned and walked back to where I was standing.

"What do you mean?" she asked, waving a hand to indicate the street. "There are at least four establishments like that within shouting distance."

"I know, but that's not what I mean," I said, feeling the excitement build in my chest. "I remember smelling fish frying the evening I was attacked."

Mary wrinkled her nose.

"Savannah is a river town," she said patiently. "There are dozens of seafood restaurants along this stretch."

"Yes, yes, I know," I said, looking around me. "But not one playing music in the middle of the day."

She stared at me for a moment and then her eyes widened. The sounds of jazz music filtered through the noise of horse carriages, backfiring vehicles and people's conversations as they passed us on the street.

I looked around to try to find out where the music was coming from and then began to walk in the direction of the alley where I'd been found. Sure enough, the music became louder.

"It's here!" I said to Mary as I hurried down the street off the crossroads of Bull and West Harris Street. I felt a tingling up and down my arms. The music was close now.

I walked further down the street, aware of the sound of Mary's leather shoes behind me. I only had to walk past two storefronts before I came to a side road and the obvious source of the music.

In front of me was a plain wooden door meant to be missed. It was carved into the molding of the building, an entrance not intended to be easily seen. I glanced back at Mat Lane which branched off West Harris. It was a quiet enough street such that if you didn't know this bar was here, you'd never have noticed it in the shadowed recess in the brickwork.

The music had stopped. Mary came to stand beside me.

"Is this it?" she whispered.

I didn't answer because I didn't really know what I was looking for. All I knew was that my nose and my ears remembered this place. I reached for the door handle and Mary instantly grabbed my arm.

"Georgia, no," she hissed.

I turned to her.

"It's broad day light, Mary. We're a block from the police station."

She looked at me and then at the ominous wooden door.

"It's an illegal establishment," she said, dropping her voice. "A speakeasy."

"You don't have to come," I said. "You can wait for me on Bull Street."

She let out a gasp of exasperation. But she didn't walk away.

The door wasn't locked, and the little peep hole set in the middle of it was not manned. Evidently twelve o'clock noon was a little early for most drinkers. Even so, we tiptoed inside so we might have the element of surprise for whatever we might find.

The bar inside was a long and glossy bench of clear varnish with a long rectangular mirror above it. Prohibition, if I remembered my history correctly, had started a few years ago and had at least another ten years to run before the country gave up on outlawing alcohol. Places like this would be peppered all over Savannah—the long mirror over the bar would help give its patrons a heads-up in the event of a police raid.

The wood paneling and art-deco lamps seemed out of place to me against the rough-hewn rock walls. Small round tables with red-checkered tablecloths surrounded the dance floor where a couple of men stood fiddling with their musical instruments—likely the source of the music we'd heard. The far end of the bar featured a pair of double doors leading to another exit. The whole place smelled of body odor and booze.

A man stood behind the bar staring at us. He wasn't washing beer glasses or in any other way behaving like a normal barman but only watched us as if we were unwelcome apparitions.

"Good day, Sir," Mary said, nodding pleasantly at the man. "We were wondering if you could help us."

"You're lost," he said with a curl of his lip.

"No," I said, approaching the bar. "We're looking for someone."

He snorted in a very ugly fashion, and I realized he thought we were wives looking for our wayward husbands. That was fine with me. I love it when people—especially men—underestimate me.

"We ain't open yet," he said.

"We can see that," I said pleasantly. "I'm looking for a Mr. Havington. He's a tall man—"

"Don't know him."

I frowned.

"It doesn't seem like you gave me much of a chance to describe him," I said. "Perhaps if you'd allow me, you *would* know him."

"I need to ask you...ladies...to leave," he said, a wolfish grin on his face.

I felt Mary stiffen beside me and I silently willed her to stick with me a little bit longer.

"How about a Lydia Bartram?" I said. "Do you know her?"

The look on his face—startled and afraid all at once—

told me that he *did* know her and there was little use in denying it. Except he didn't care if I knew he was lying. Not one little bit.

"Get out now," he said. "Or I'll lay hands on you."

Mary was already turning to leave and since I thought we'd pretty much drained this cistern as dry as we could, I was right behind her.

Outside, we both kept moving until we stood once more on Bull Street. I put my hand on her arm.

"Are you okay?" I asked.

She turned to me, her face flushed with a small, exhilarated smile on her face.

"One hundred percent," she said.

Suddenly an elderly man shoved past us, the alcohol fumes steaming off him. Mary instinctively took a step back to avoid contact with him. But she wasn't the one he was aiming for.

"You need to know," he said to me, his breath blasting into my face like an aerosol assault.

"I beg your—" I started to say as I pivoted to avoid him.

His gnarly fingers pinched into my waist, fumbling and poking, before he turned and hurried back down the alley away from us.

"Georgia, did he hurt you?" Mary asked, hurrying to my side, her hand on my shoulder.

I watched the old man stumble back down the alley, in the direction of the speakeasy.

I looked down at my waist—my belt, to be more precise—and at the folded note the old man had jammed there.

21

I hurriedly opened the note and read the words written in a shaky scrawl:

L B is sil to Mario S. B crful

Mary looked over my shoulder and then tugged me away from the opening of the alley.

"It's gibberish," she said. "Old sot. He should be arrested."

I tucked the note into my straw clutch. It wasn't gibberish—at least not totally—but I could understand why it didn't mean anything to Mary. As we walked back to her house, Mary went over and over the barman's strange reaction to Lydia Bartram's name.

"It was clear he knew her," she said.

"I agree," I said, distractedly, my thoughts still on the note I'd been given. "We need to find out who she is. My guess is she goes to that speakeasy, perhaps in the company of the mysterious Mr. Havington."

"Agreed. Why else would the two of them be so near where you were attacked?"

We walked a little bit further. The shoes I was wearing didn't fit me wonderfully and I was beginning to develop a multitude of blisters such that before long, I was hobbling.

Now that I'd essentially called into question one of the witnesses to my assault, I decided to do a little acrobatic brainstorming and see where I came out. And to see how far Mary might go along with my crazy theories.

"You know, Mary," I said. "I don't remember seeing my attacker that night."

"That's not surprising," she said.

"Maybe not," I said. "But let me ask you this: what if there was no attacker?"

She stopped short and turned to look at me, her brow wrinkled into a frown.

"Explain, please," she said.

"Let's just say, for argument's purposes," I said, feeling my way along, "that I fainted. I wasn't attacked at all."

"You weren't attacked?" She looked unconvinced.

"I think the heat got to me and I swooned."

"And the helpful Mr. Havington and Miss Bartram came to your aid," she finished.

I beamed at her. I was delighted that she was willing to switch courses and imagine a different scenario from the one the police had been painting. And one that cast suspicion on my two dubious witnesses, too.

"Well, it would explain why I wasn't killed," I said. "Because the man who attacked the other girls, killed them."

Mary frowned and turned to continue on toward home.

"And it would explain why your mystery card was not found by the police after your attack," she said.

"Yes," I said. "It would mean that Havington and Lydia were not who they told the police they were."

She flashed me a questioning frown.

"You think they were thieves planning on robbing you when you were vulnerable?"

I pulled her off to the first park bench we came to and pulled the note out of my clutch bag.

L B is sil to Mario S. B crful

"I'm thinking LB means Lydia Bartram," I said. "I'm sure the old man heard us asking about her."

"I agree," Mary said. "But what does *sil* mean?"

"My guess is sister-in-law."

She looked back at the note. "Mario S."

"Do you recognize the name?"

She looked away and for a moment I didn't think she'd answer.

"He's the head of a...a family in Savannah," she said. "A very powerful family."

"Spinelli," I said, the realization suddenly dawning in my brain.

She looked at me in surprise.

"I had a little conversation with Seamus and your cook last night," I said.

"I heard."

That surprised me but I was glad that her servants weren't keeping secrets from her.

"Seamus said word on the street is that the Spinelli family was involved in the attacks."

"Seamus is a terrible gossip."

"That doesn't mean it's not true," I pointed out.

I still didn't believe it likely that a crime family could be involved because of the whole pathology about serial killers. Now, if the women had disappeared, I might believe it, since they could be kidnapped to be used for human trafficking. I'm almost positive that was a thing during this time, but just not called that.

"Is it possible that *Mr. Havington* is an alias?" I asked.

"For Mario Spinelli?"

"It's just a thought."

"What would his motive be?" she asked.

I really liked Mary. Maybe because she wasn't from my own time where people tend to overthink the simplest notions, it was refreshing to see her go right to the heart of the problem. It made me trust her reflections because they seemed so straightforward.

"That's the million-dollar question," I said. "An organized crime family usually centers its business around whatever criminal activity makes them the most money—or possibly power—but neither of those are in the offing from randomly attacking women."

"Perhaps the attacks were not as random as we thought," she murmured as if to herself.

After that we walked in silence, each of us lost in our own thoughts. It was a lot to process. If the local crime family *was* involved in the murders, then that was a question I'd at least have to entertain. The team of Havington and Lydia was another question. What were they doing there when they saw me fall? Had they been at the speakeasy? Who was Havington, really?

We were a block away from the townhouse when I spotted the now familiar form of Sam Bohannon, standing at the foot of Mary's house steps.

"We have company," I said.

"So I see. Will you tell Detective Bohannon you're not sure you were attacked?"

She really was beginning to amaze me at how perceptive she was. She'd actually gotten to that question before I had.

"I don't know," I said as we neared the house.

As we approached, I saw a large wicker hamper on the ground beside him.

"This is unexpected, Detective Bohannon," Mary said pausing on the brick steps to her townhouse.

"I was hoping to see if you and Miss Belle might be convinced to take a walk with me," he said. "To discuss the case."

Right when I thought this was the strangest attempt by a police officer to get a victim's statement, I realized that in this time period it might mean something else. Mary clearly was one step ahead of me in that regard because she walked past the detective to her front door.

"I have an appointment I am already late for," she said. "But I'm sure Miss Belle is free to walk with you." She turned to me. "Georgia?"

She was clearly urging me to go with Bohannon. We both knew I would get more information out of him if I was alone.

"Yes, of course," I said, smiling sweetly. "I would love to."

22

The picnic spot that Sam led me to was in Monterey Square three blocks from Mary's townhouse. He spread out a red-checkered wool blanket on the grass and, as I seated myself, he began to unpack the hamper. Up until then, very little had been said between us. I figured this was his party, and I would wait to see what he had in mind.

I looked around the square. I'm sure I've never seen anyone have a picnic directly on the ground in this square in my own time, but we weren't the only ones today who'd had the idea about a picnic.

A warm summer breeze rustled the leaves of the elm tree above us. Daisies peeked out from under the blanket. Sam laid out cucumber sandwiches with the crusts cut off, a plate of scones, a jar of strawberry jam—clearly homemade—and a flask of sweet tea.

"I hope you don't feel like you're being ambushed," he said as he handed me a plate with a sandwich and macaroni salad. "That's not my intention."

"Not at all," I said. "I've got some questions for you, too."

"Oh?"

He poured tea into a glass and handed it to me.

"Well, for one," I said, "how come nobody's mentioned the Spinelli family in all this? From what I hear, they've got their finger in every piece of crime happening in Savannah."

He looked at me, his hand poised in midair as he was in the act of pouring his own tea.

"How in the world would you know something like that?"

"Servant hall gossip," I said with a shrug. "But they usually have their ear to the ground. It's not evidentiary, but it's not nothing."

He looked at me curiously.

"Plus, Mary and I just got back from the alley where I was…found…and also the two places where Mercy O'Gillis and Alice Marshall were killed," I said.

"You what?"

"But the place where I was found—which, of course you know was nowhere near where the others were—as I'm sure you know—was within a half-block of a speakeasy off Bull Street. Mary and I stepped inside to ask a few questions and guess what we found?"

He looked at me, dumbfounded.

I pulled out the note that the old man had given me and showed it to him.

"We discovered that the female witness to my assault—remember her? Lydia Bartram? Turns out, she's the sister-in-law to the head of the Spinelli family. A Mario Spinelli. Did you know that?"

He took the note and read it, and then ran an agitated hand through his hair. I saw him start to say something then think better of it, before finally answering me.

"We are aware of the connection, of course, Miss Belle,"

he said. But from his reaction, I was pretty sure he'd had no idea of the connection before now. He began to look around the picnic area for something, more likely to get his thoughts and feelings together.

"Well, don't you think that's a pretty big coincidence?" I asked. "That the sole female witness to my so-called assault is connected to organized crime? What was she doing there? Was there a reason why the serial killer—if he was actually there—didn't go after *her* instead of me?"

"Please, stop," he said tightly.

His brown eyes searched my face in frustration, his mouth was drawn in a straight line.

"Miss Belle..."

"Please call me Georgia."

"Georgia. I need to ask you to refrain from trying to do my job. If you can be patient, I promise we will find the man who attacked you and...the others. I promise you that."

I frowned because this sounded like some major BS to me. It's certainly not the kind of thing any modern law enforcement officer would ever dream of saying to a victim. I accounted for the historical time difference and gave him the benefit of the doubt. Because whatever I'd thought before now, I was beginning to think that Detective Bohannon was completely stymied by this case.

In fact, I would bet money that he didn't have a single lead on what had to be the most notorious crime committed in Savannah in the past one hundred years.

Somebody wasn't going to keep their job for long, I thought. Or if they did, they were going to have to find a viable suspect. Fast.

"I was hoping to find out something more about you," he said, turning to face me on the blanket.

He was handsome with his dark hair and smoldering

eyes, but those eyes held a hint of something else—a sort of deep, lurking sadness. At the moment, there was a bruising around one eye and his lip was split. It just made him all the more alluring to me, wondering how he got them.

"What do you want to know?" I asked, picking up one of the peeled hard-boiled eggs from my plate.

"First, if you could kindly tell me about the card that was found when you were attacked."

I knew this was coming and I had only a very imperfect explanation for it.

"It didn't look familiar to me," I said.

If he'd been just a little more open to accepting the idea that his witnesses weren't on the up and up, I'd have told him I didn't think I was really attacked. But he wasn't, so I wouldn't.

He frowned and waited.

"It's possible," I said hesitantly, "that it was some kind of identification card that I'd had made."

"It listed your birthday as December 10, 1982."

"Well, obviously that must be a typo."

"A what?"

I cringed at my idiocy. Even though they had typewriters in 1923—I think—I was pretty sure the term typo had yet to be coined.

"A misprint," I said.

"It listed your address as 54 Barnard Street, Savannah."

I held my breath because it was clear he'd gone to that address. Since I hadn't bothered going there myself in this time, I had no idea what was there now. Most likely not a series of mid-range apartments.

"There's only a small grocery store at that address," he said.

I laughed weakly. "Gosh, did they at least get my sex right?"

As soon as I said it, I saw the shocked look on his face. Evidently the word *sex* was inappropriate in any context in this decade. Why hadn't I said *gender*?

"It also says the license was issued December 1, 2021," he said.

How many times can I punt to typographical errors?

"That is indeed a mystery," I said. "I can only assume the person who created the card for me was completely incompetent."

"Or a writer of science fiction novels," he said.

I laughed again. "Good one."

"It appears to be a license issued by the State of Georgia," he continued. "A license authorizing you to drive a motorized vehicle."

"Well, I know how to drive," I said.

"I have never seen a license of this kind before. Certainly not in Georgia. I have to say if it is a counterfeit attempt of some kind to—"

"Look, I don't know what to tell you, Detective. It's not fake, if that's what you're—"

"No, no, I'm not accusing you of anything. But so you do recognize it?"

I held my tongue. I have a habit of speaking too much when I'm in trouble and that always—without fail—makes the problem about a thousand times worse. I gave a helpless shrug that I hoped he would interpret as a typical female combined with amnesia victim and just let the whole driver's license thing go.

Whether or not he would revisit the question of the mysterious, typo-ridden, illegal license later on, he seemed amenable to letting it go for now. Thank goodness.

He handed me a cloth napkin.

"I was hoping you might remember something more from the time before your attack," he said.

I felt for him, I really did. If all he had in the way of a lead was a victim who survived—but couldn't remember anything—then he really was barking up the wrong dogwood tree. Me telling him I wasn't actually attacked would likely be the last straw for him. He had nothing. And in me he had less than nothing.

"I remember I had some kind of job here in the city," I said. "One that I enjoyed and that gave me satisfaction."

"You worked at a job?" He looked at me with surprise.

"I did. But don't ask me what because I can't remember that."

He nodded but smiled at me, his eyes crinkling in the corners and his dark hair glossy in the sunlight. I know it's corny, but I swear I felt a spark of electricity between us—almost like we were sharing a secret.

As we talked—mostly about nothing and certainly nothing that could help him in his investigation—I realized I felt more alive than I had in a long time. I ended up telling him how much I loved doing puzzles and reading murder mysteries—especially Agatha Christie. At first I panicked, not sure she'd been published yet, but he nodded as if he knew her. I even told him that I thought I might like to be a writer like her.

That part wasn't really true, but I knew I couldn't tell him I wanted to be a detective myself. I thought massaging the truth to fit the times was the best way to keep him engaged. It shocked me when I realized how much I really wanted to do that.

He listened thoughtfully, his head slightly cocked as he took in my words. He wasn't listening like a detective taking a statement from a witness, but like a man who might be interested for other reasons. Other, more romantic, reasons.

"You know," he said, "real crime isn't like fiction."

It was my turn to smile then. I knew I had to allow him to patronize me because I simply couldn't tell him the truth. But I still wanted to connect with him, even if there were only a few acceptable levels I could do that on—that wouldn't get me committed to a 1920's mental hospital.

He reached out and took my hand.

"I just want to ask," he said, "if there's anything at all that you can remember about your life before the attack, I believe it would be helpful."

I knew what he wanted, and I knew I couldn't give it to him. Not the truth he wanted anyway. I could tell him a different truth that, while it wouldn't help him, at least wouldn't be a lie.

"I know I have a mother," I said. "A mother who loves me very much, who makes macaroni salad and devilled eggs just like these. A mother who I know is very worried about me."

As I spoke, I thought of my mother and wondered if she was sitting beside my comatose body in some hospital in Savannah or if time had telescoped such that my mother didn't even know I was missing.

Or maybe I was dead. I obviously hated to seriously entertain that theory, but under the circumstances it was no less unimaginable than the idea that I'd gone back in time a hundred years.

Well, perhaps a little less unimaginable.

23

Sam watched Georgia as she spoke and was amazed yet again at how much she affected him—more than anyone he'd ever met. She seemed to look right into his soul and coax out the slivers of pain and memories that he tried so hard to keep hidden.

How unbelievable was it that she would go to the crime sites? On her own? And she clearly felt that going would give her information that she wasn't getting from the police.

Who is this this fascinating girl?

As she spoke, he noted her flashing eyes and her hair—thick but cut short as was the current style. He felt a stirring in his gut as he watched her and reminded himself that he should be extra vigilant to guard against developing feelings for her. It was making him doubt whether or not he could do his job properly—let alone his plan to relax her with a picnic and some pointed questions.

"Oh, cake!" she said with delight at seeing the confection on par with what Sam would have expected from a precocious child.

"You have a sweet tooth?" he asked with a smile as she sliced a large wedge for herself.

"I do," she said.

As he watched her eat, spilling crumbs and clumps of fudge onto the blanket, he thought back to the fact that she'd actually tracked down the identity of one of the witnesses to her attack.

How is that possible? Lydia Bartram is connected to Mario Spinelli?

How is it *he* hadn't uncovered that?

Even more extraordinary than the fact that he'd missed this major connection was the way that Miss Belle had revealed it to him. He ran the memory again in his head as she licked bits of fudge from her fingers. She'd actually presented the information quite delicately—as if she knew he should be ashamed not to have discovered the information himself. She was being considerate, even circumspect.

Horribly, embarrassingly circumspect.

Who is this girl? How does she know what she knows?

And why wasn't he able to get more out of her than the fact that he wasn't doing his job properly?

"You didn't bake this cake, did you?" she asked with a grin.

"There's a bakery on West Broughton," he said with a smile.

"Ah," she said. "Just one of the many weapons in your scabbard. I guess you use rum when your suspect is a hardened seaman and chocolate cake when she's an amnesia victim."

He knew she was joking but she was too close to the truth for him to laugh.

How does she know such things?

All of that aside, the fact of her strangeness, and her

boldness in going to the attack sites, especially when impaired with amnesia—aside from all that, Sam felt a nearly irrepressible need to hurry back to the department so he could dig further into the nugget that she'd just handed him about Lydia Bartram.

He was startled to realize that in spite of his plans going slightly awry this afternoon, this was the first time he'd felt like he'd had a real honest-to-God lead since Alice Marshall was killed.

≈

As we ate, I watched the sun inch its way down toward the horizon, casting a warm orange hue over our picnic.

Every time I asked Sam a question about how he got into the police department or where he went to school, he seemed to clam up. I honestly couldn't tell if his constraint was something specific to him or just the way men were back in these days. It made me think of Rob. Not that I haven't had plenty of experience with men in my life, but Rob has been on my romantic radar ever since I started at the Savannah police station with his ice-blue eyes, blond hair, and body of an underwear model.

He wasn't a jerk, not at all, but unlike Sam, I could see how much he loved talking about himself. It occurred to me as I'd watched Sam pack up the picnic and hand me a cloth napkin to brush crumbs from my dress, that I'd been giving Rob the benefit of the doubt for being boorish and self-focused because of the job he does. The whole reason I couldn't make it as a police officer had made me admire Rob all the more—for his bravery and quick thinking. All things I lacked.

But here was Sam doing the same job as Rob—arguably

a harder one because Rob had never tackled a serial killing before—with many fewer resources and he seemed to have hung onto his manners and his morality while he did it.

I watched him stand and shake the blanket out before reaching for my hand to help me to my feet.

It was definitely something to think about.

24

That afternoon, I sat with Mary by the fireplace where we had our tea and I told her all about my picnic with Sam and the fact that I'd told him about our discoveries today.

"But you didn't tell him your theory about fainting instead of being attacked?"

I sighed.

"He didn't look open to hearing it."

"Do you think he felt what you did tell him was helpful?"

Mary's forehead wrinkled with doubt.

"You mean about Lydia being related to the head of the crime family? I do. Not only that, but I got the distinct idea that it was the first real lead he'd had in a long time."

"So you believe he's stalled in the investigation?"

"Don't you? The paper talks about the crime and how the police are investigating it but there's not been a single arrest. That's pretty weird for a serious crime series like this."

"True," Mary said. "I imagine when the police show up,

people stop talking. Especially the guilty people."

"Which is an argument in favor of us asking around," I said. "Nobody is threatened by a couple of women."

"That is certainly true," she said.

"How is it you live alone, Mary?" I asked abruptly.

In my day it wouldn't at all have been an inappropriate question but when I saw Mary stiffen, I knew things were different here.

"I just do," she said.

"How did your parents pass?"

A flinch passed over her face.

"In a motor accident a few years ago."

"I'm so sorry." I hated hearing that. It was bad enough to lose your parents one by one.

Her face softened at my words, and I saw a glimmer of emotion in her eyes, but she quickly regained control of herself.

"I was taught to be self-sufficient," she said.

Nobody is taught to live without family, I wanted to say. But if she needed to keep that lip stiff in order to carry on, I wouldn't make it any harder to do so.

"What about you, Georgia?" she said. "Can you truly not remember your own parents?"

She seemed so fretful about my lack of memory—and personal history—that for a moment I desperately wanted to tell her the truth. I caught myself in time. I gave a helpless shrug which she seemed to accept, and we both turned to stare into the fire.

The wood in the fireplace gave off a pleasant scent, something like flowers and a mixture of green leaves and clean bark. The tea set lay on the coffee table. Even the tea ware itself was a reminder of days long past. Each cup—its edge delicately scalloped and rimmed in gold—was a jewel of refined living. Even the handle of the teapot which mimicked a graceful swan arching its neck over the lid, made me think how so many basic practices and simple rituals in this era were used to enhance any given moment.

The fire snapped and popped, crackling as it ate the aged wood. I sat back into the damask covered wing back chair, the exquisite teacup in my hand, and tried to remember when I'd last felt so relaxed—even with all that was going on. There was something about stopping in the middle of all of it and taking a tea break that seemed to settle and help ground me.

I'm not sure when Americans stopped having tea breaks, or when we decided that walking with to-go coffee cups made more sense than sitting by a fire or in a garden and relishing every sip. I get that I have a busy life back in 2023—and I pray I'm able to get back to it—but these moments of reflection had their place too.

"I was wondering if you were up for another outing tomorrow?" I asked.

"I'm listening."

"I think I need to talk to Mr. Havington."

"I'm game if you are," she said with a shrug.

I think, to a certain extent, she was just trying to relieve her boredom. But I couldn't help but see her nascent interest in puzzles. How terrible to have to suppress those passions that might normally make us soar into our complete selves.

After that, we both grew quiet, content to stare into the fire and focus on our private thoughts. Mary wasn't the most demonstrative friend I'd ever had but I could tell she was glad of my company. Until now it hadn't occurred to me that she might be lonely. That was a shame too. She was smart and had a good sense of humor.

I remembered that in this decade, the Great War had recently ended. I know that didn't impact the male population here in America as badly as it did in England, but it probably still put a dent in the available men with whom Mary might have been matched up. I was sorry about that. She would've made a great catch for someone. In any decade.

There was a sudden, loud knock at the door, and I nearly dropped my teacup, it was so jarring in the peaceful setting. Mary frowned and looked in the direction of the door. Clearly, early evenings visitors were not the norm.

Seamus appeared as if from nowhere and glided to the door. I looked at Mary who was listening to the sounds of voices on the doorstep and I wondered why she didn't just jump up and go see who was calling. They certainly weren't there to see Seamus.

But there was protocol, I suppose, or maybe habit and Mary was clearly going to observe the rules. She waited, frowning slightly, until Seamus came into the room.

"A Police Detective Hawkins to see you, Miss," he said.

"To see me, Seamus?" Mary asked, her glance going instantly to me.

"No, Miss."

"Show him in, please."

But the man in question was already striding into the living room, his eyes going to the cozy set up of tea in front of the fire. He stood beside Seamus and put his hands on his hips.

A large man with hooded eyes and a double chin, Detective Hawkins wore a cheap, ill-fitting black wool suit, the lapels already outdated, the vest straining against his paunch. He eyed me up and down, curling his lip into a sneer.

"Miss Belle?" he said to me. "I need you to come with me, please."

This I had not expected. Especially since up to now my sole contact with the police department had been Sam.

"Me?" I said. "Why? Where is Detective Bohannon?"

"Detective Bohannon has been reassigned," he said in a deeply patronizing tone. "Get your hat, please."

Mary stood up and so did I.

"You won't be needed, Miss Johnson," he said curtly to Mary. "Just Miss Belle."

"Miss Belle is a guest in my home—" Mary started to say.

"My man is waiting outside in the car," Hawkins said.

"But why?" I asked. "What's happened?"

"We need you to come down to the station to identify the man we have arrested in your attack."

"You've arrested someone?" My mind was flying all over the place. Since I hadn't really been attacked, this was very bad. Should I say I tell him I hadn't been attacked? And that I definitely couldn't identify the person because I hadn't seen him?

"Miss Belle?" said the detective as he took my hat out of Mary's hands and roughly shoved it into my hands. "Now, please."

"Have you arrested someone?" I asked as I jammed the hat on my head and followed him to the front door. I turned to give one last helpless glance back at Mary who stood by the fire, her arms hugging herself, a worried look on her face.

"He was seen leaving the alley after your attack," Hawkins said as he held the door open for me. "We're confident he's the one who killed our other victims."

25

A thick haze of cigarette smoke hung in the air in the police station.

I strained to see if Sam was in the office. I didn't know if he had his own office or was in the bullpen with everyone else. The way the brutish Detective Hawkins prodded me through the station, it was a wonder I kept my feet, let alone locate Sam.

There was a peculiar odor in the place—body odor and cigarette smoke mostly—and from the few poor unfortunates I saw handcuffed to chairs, a smell of despair too. Hawkins led me down a long nondescript hallway to a small room. Inside two other men waited. They wore plainclothes and both smoked. When I walked in, they stood up but openly leered at me.

I don't know whether they were just so used to only seeing prostitutes in the police station that this reaction was their default mode with women or if they genuinely didn't care about openly disrespecting me. I was astonished so see the behavior code that Sam and Mary seemed to live by so totally ignored by these men.

On one side of the small room hung a large window and it took me only seconds to realize it was a one-way mirror. Through the window stood seven men. They stood on large black numbers painted on the floor. Four white men—all smoking—and three black.

Each man in the line-up was dressed in a different outfit. The three black men were wearing suits, one white man was in overalls, and the other three white men were in police uniforms with their standard-issue weapons holstered on their belts.

I looked at Hawkins, incredulous. Was this a joke? Did he really think I'd believe that suspects were allowed to stand in a line-up *armed*?

Detective Hawkins was watching me closely for my reaction to the lineup. I looked closer at men and saw that one of the black men was the hospital gardener. I was astonished.

That's who they think is the mastermind serial killer? The hospital gardener?

I indicated the lineup with a wave of my hand.

"The man who attacked me was white," I said.

Hawkins' face screwed into a thundercloud of annoyance.

"I thought Bohannon said you didn't see his face," he said.

"I saw his hands. He was white."

"The doc said you have amnesia. I don't think you remember what you saw."

"Then why did you bring me down here?"

"I'm asking myself the same thing, darlin'."

I turned to look at the men in the lineup, the ones who were clearly policemen were laughing and cutting up. The other men stared silently at the ground until instructed by Hawkins to look up or turn this way or that.

The look on the gardener's face was enough to turn my stomach. He looked terrified. He looked hopeless. I was looking into the face of a man who knew he didn't stand a chance.

"I thought the eyewitness said my assailant was blond-haired and tall," I said.

"Just tell us if you recognize any of the men in the line-up," Hawkins said.

"None of these men," I said in frustration.

He snorted as if he expected nothing better from me and then spoke into a cumbersome mouthpiece attached to the wall to order the men to exit the room in single file. I watched the gardener and the other two black men, their shoulders sagging in defeat, turn and head to their unknown fates. I was sickened by what I was seeing although I could hardly be surprised at the rampant bigotry in the South during this period.

"My sergeant will give you a ride home," Hawkins said to me.

I was pretty sure that was the last thing Hawkins wanted to offer me, but he probably didn't want to be the reason I got mugged on the way home either. Or maybe that was giving him way too much credit for being a decent human being.

"I'd like to speak to Detective Bohannon," I said abruptly. "It is my understanding that this is his case."

"Is that your understanding?" Hawkins said with a sneer. "Well, that explains a lot, especially since he ain't on the case anymore. You'll be dealing with me from here on out."

As he turned and left the room, his words echoing in my head, I couldn't help but think how close to a threat they sounded.

26

The next morning, Sam climbed the steps to Mary Johnson's massive, two-story Victorian house which loomed in the gloom of the overcast day. The small front lawn was fronted by massive magnolia trees and flanked by holly bushes in full bloom.

It was Georgia herself who answered the door, although the Irish butler was right behind her with a look of frustration on his face.

"Sam," she said, reaching out and tugging him into the house by his sleeve. "I'm so glad to see you. You're not going to believe what happened."

"I heard," he said, smiling slightly as he came into the room.

As he'd noted on his prior visits, the interior was lavishly decorated. The wallpaper in the foyer was floral yet elegant. A piano sat in the corner of the salon where Georgia led him, its surface polished to a shine. Ornately framed oil paintings of landscapes lined the walls, the frames worn to a dull patina from years of polishing.

"How can they do that?" Georgia asked as she led him to one of the two brown leather sofas in the parlor. "That's profiling in the worst sense."

Not for the first time, he wasn't sure what her words meant. He sat down opposite her.

"I wanted to tell you in person," he said. "I've been taken off the case."

"I know," she said, her face scowling. "That ogre Hawkins told me. But why?"

The butler Seamus stepped into the room.

"Would Miss like for me to bring in tea?" he asked eyeing Sam with suspicion.

Georgia glanced at him with surprise at the interruption.

"Sure, okay, thanks," she said.

Sam waited for the butler to leave before rubbing his face wearily with his hands. He clenched his jaw in frustration.

"Well," he said, bitterly, "a man is running around Savannah killing women. And I didn't make an arrest."

"You mean you didn't find the first vulnerable person who couldn't fight back and pin it on him!" she said heatedly.

"Henry Pickett doesn't have an alibi," he said.

"That's the hospital gardener? I'll bet half the men in Savannah don't have an alibi for that night! Does Mr. Pickett have any prior arrests?"

"No. But these sorts of killers are typically not habitual thieves or home breakers," he said, impressed in spite of himself at how she continued to insist on having an opinion about matters she could not possibly know about.

Was it the arguing or the passion that he found so alluring? It didn't matter. In any case he'd never met anyone remotely like her in his life.

As Sam sat in Mary's living room telling me how Henry Pickett totally fit the profile of a serial killer, I was doing everything I could to keep my temper. As soon as he mentioned that these sorts of killers weren't habitually picked up for petty crime, I wanted to retort that neither were they usually black either.

Statistically, serial killers were unmarried middle aged white men. They were often the last people you'd suspect because they kept a low profile, were usually affable and inoffensive and sometimes even social. But if I trotted all that out, I was pretty sure Sam would expect me to cite my source. And naturally I couldn't do that.

As Seamus brought the tea service in and set about pouring, I had time to watch Sam's face. I could tell he was frustrated and I'm sure it was hard to come here today to tell me that he'd been taken off the case. That had to be humiliating. I also didn't blame him for the lack of forward movement on the case.

As far as I could see, crime scene analysis in 1923 consisted of physical evidence and witness testimony. Period. There was no DNA analysis, only primitive fingerprinting, and no voice or facial recognition software to help identify the culprit.

It was all just shoe leather and having a good nose for a lead. But when you mixed racial bigotry into the stew, the inclination to accurately detect weakened. Why bother knocking on doors or digging through trash when there were all these built-in victims lying around to redound to your glory?

I hated thinking that about Sam. I liked him. I could see he was a product of his time. But that didn't mean he didn't have a heart or a conscience. Or a brain. Maybe he just needed someone like me to give him a gentle push in the right direction.

I took my teacup and sat back on the couch with a large, shortbread cookie. Mary was visiting an old friend a couple of streets over and I was glad to have the place to myself for a change. As I watched Sam drink his tea, I realized that if I wanted him to trust me and be open to hearing the things I could teach him, I needed to get a little closer.

"Where in France were you?" I asked.

He looked surprised and for a moment it looked as if a shade had come down over his eyes.

"Verdun," he said simply.

Verdun was bad. I didn't know much, but I knew that.

"Are you in touch with your comrades in arms?" I asked more gently.

He looked at me as if I were speaking Greek. I knew a lot of people had died in the Great War. For my generation, that conflict got significantly de-emphasized due to World War II. But I knew it had been terrible.

"Not much," he said.

Suddenly the handle of the delicate teacup snapped in his fingers and the cup fell to the carpet. Sam jumped to his feet as if a starter's pistol had gone off and I felt sick with the series of memories my questions must have generated.

Naturally PTSD wasn't a thing recognized back in this time. But that didn't make it any less real. I was sure he'd seen terrible things—horrific things. And lost friends. Too many to bear maybe, and with no help at all when he came back to the States and tried to pick up the threads of his psyche and begin life again.

"Don't worry about it, please," I said, reaching for a

napkin to blot the tea out of the carpet. "I'm sorry. That is my fault."

"Of course, it isn't your fault," he said sharply.

I knew he was angry at himself and his sudden lack of control. Seamus came into the room and looked at the mess on the floor and then at me.

"Another cup, please, Seamus," I said as if I'd been ordering servants around all my life and not just the occasional Starbucks barista.

Seamus left the room, and I moved to the sofa to sit next to Sam. I can't imagine that that was going to calm him, but I couldn't stand the divide between us. I needed to distract him and maybe in the process, get the information that might help us both.

"I was wondering if you could tell me," I said, "since you know how interested I am in mysteries, how it is you go about solving a mystery in the first place?"

His eyes were bright as if he could tell I was trying to distract him, but to his credit, he allowed it.

"We sift through evidence at the crime scene," he said. "We look for clues."

"What kind of clues?"

He stared out into middle space as if thinking about what it was he did. I was glad. It meant he was moving away from the memories of his time in the war.

"Well, fingerprints," he said. "And footprints. Any kind of physical evidence, too, like clothing or weapons. And we question witnesses."

I nodded. It was clear that detection in 1923 mostly had to do with visual cues, physical evidence and witness statements.

"How do you know witnesses aren't lying?" I asked. I was pretty sure lie detectors had yet to be invented.

"Sometimes you can tell," he said. "After years of doing this, you develop a sort of second sense."

"And other times?"

"Other times you're fooled," he admitted.

"What happens when all your evidence and eyewitness statements don't lead you to a suspect?"

He shrugged. "The case goes unsolved."

Case clearance rates in 1923 were likely to be every bit as important as they were in 2023. Maybe more so.

"And if you have a viable suspect?" I pressed. "With only circumstantial evidence to indict him? What happens then?"

He scratched his head.

"Well, if we can't prove the guy did it and his lawyer can't prove he didn't," he shrugged. "Stalemate."

I frowned. "Does *stalemate* mean the guy goes free?"

He seemed to snap out of his reverie as if suddenly realizing I was hanging on every word.

"No, he doesn't go free," he said tightly.

"What about his civil rights? What about due process?"

"He'll be judged fairly."

There was no doubt we were both talking about Henry Pickett now.

"The suspect you have in custody is already not being judged fairly!" I said hotly. "It's racism, pure and simple. You admit you have no evidence, no eyewitness, no—"

"Georgia, stop," Sam interrupted, agitated himself now. "We have a *witness*."

At his words, my thoughts seemed to tangle in confusion as I struggled to comprehend what he'd said.

"What are you talking about?" I asked in frustration.

"A witness has come forward who has identified Henry

Pickett as being the man fleeing from the alley after your attack."

27

There really didn't seem much to say after that.

I wasn't willing yet to admit I *hadn't* been attacked and Sam wasn't ready to say that Henry was implicated in the other killings. Unfortunately, thanks to this new eyewitness, Sam was convinced that Henry was guilty of assaulting me. He was also convinced that justice was going to be served.

I think he read the room pretty accurately once Seamus came in with another teacup because he declined to have more tea. He stood up and abruptly made an excuse and left.

How could I tell him that there was no assault? How could I rewrite what I'd led everyone to believe up to now? Was I going to have an *aha! moment* as if my memory had just come back and realized I'd only fainted after all?

Would that make a difference for poor Henry?

The whole reason I'd let people believe I'd been assaulted in the first place was because I *had* been assaulted —just not in 1923—and because, at the time, it had seemed easier than trying to explain why I was talking so strangely and couldn't remember any details that would illustrate who I was.

After Sam left, I paced the living room for a bit, frustrated and unsettled. I hadn't been able to get out of him the identity of the new eyewitness. But from what he said—*the witness rethought her testimony*—who else could it be but Lydia Bartram?

I couldn't believe that people were just allowed to say whatever they wanted—for any reason—in order to implicate whoever they wanted. And, if the party in question was black in 1923, they just got arrested and that was all the evidence necessary.

Up until this morning, I think there were moments when I'd found myself wondering if living in 1923 could possibly work for me—especially if I wasn't able to find my way back to my own time.

But his visit this morning reminded me that this was a dark, even backward time I'd landed in. I could only imagine that I'd surely wither and die under its rampant racism and oppression of women.

∽

A few hours later, Mary returned from her social visit looking vaguely dispirited but immediately suggested we make a visit to the hospital. It seemed she had a habit of going there once a week or so to visit the patients who didn't have family. I was impressed. I guess I got the idea that all Mary did with her time was arrange flowers, have tea and… no, that's about it. So I was pleased to see she reached out to the less fortunate in this way.

She insisted I change clothes for the excursion which I hardly thought necessary, but I was learning not to sweat the small stuff during this time. If she thought I should dress a certain way—or not wear my sitting in the garden clothes to the hospital, I wouldn't argue with her.

I bathed again and put on the outfit that she'd laid out for me on my bed. The only servants Mary had were Cook and Seamus and I couldn't see either of *them* hand selecting my clothes so it must have been Mary.

It was still hot of course and maybe that was partially the reason for the costume change. The clothes I had been wearing were already damp with perspiration. I put on the twill suit that she'd laid out and put the same ill-fitting shoes back on, wondering if I was going to be in 1923 long enough to justify asking Mary to buy a pair that actually fit me.

I was grateful when Mary called for a taxi to take us to the hospital. The walk a few days earlier with Sister Beatrice hadn't felt long at the time, but three days of wearing ill-fitting leather shoes had made me dread the long walk. The taxi was some kind of antique car—or would've been in 2023. Actually, it looked new as we climbed into it and settled into the leather seats, uncracked yet by time and use.

Mary turned to me as soon as the taxi pulled away from the curb.

"Seamus said Detective Bohannon came to tea today," she said.

"He came to tell me what I already knew," I said. "That he'd been taken off the case."

"Are you sure it wasn't a social call?" she asked as she looked out the window at the passing scenery.

I blushed a little, but I was secretly pleased that she thought so. I had to admit, I thought he liked me. It was hard to tell with all the 1923 formalities and odd manners—

not to mention him interviewing me for details about a serial killer—but I did think there was something more there.

"He might be just doing his job," she said.

"If you say so," Mary said. "But I don't think I've ever had a policeman look at me the way he looks at you."

I can't say I didn't like the idea of Sam with a crush on me. He was a total dish and so strait-laced. I found myself wanting to mess up his hair a little. But since I didn't know how much of that was proper in this time, I decided I'd better play it cool.

"Do you visit the hospital a lot?" I asked, ready to change the subject.

"I suppose so," she said. "Many of the patients don't have family or at least none that visit."

She leaned back against the seat, watching the landscape outside blur by. As for me, I took the brief ride as an opportunity to get my thoughts together. Mary wasn't wrong about Sam. He definitely appeared to be interested in me. I got a tingle of anticipation when I thought of that. But also dread.

It was unusual, having so many secrets that needed to be kept from him, and still feeling alive when I was with him—even when I was frustrated with him.

It was almost like I thought all the secrets and occasional lies didn't matter because of my situation.

I should have reminded myself that lies always matter.

28

It felt so much hotter inside the hospital ward than out on the street.

Mary and I stood by the bed of a young woman who was having gall bladder surgery in a few hours. Unlike the three other beds we'd just visited, this woman—Anna Wilkins—had her husband and her parents by her bedside. She looked terrified.

The sterile white curtains swished from the breeze made by a small fan that was completely insufficient to combat the summer heat. Anna lay in a single metal framed bed—one of ten in the ward—each made with a pressed white sheet with a woolen hospital blanket folded at the bottom.

Anna's husband and parents sat on folding chairs beside her bed, holding her hands. The old woman wiped tears from her eyes with a lace handkerchief.

There was a faint smell of mold in the ward. A hushed murmur of hospital staff occasionally walked past, the squeak of their leather soled shoes. I was so impressed with how Mary came right up to the patients' beds and found all the right words to say to ease their suffering. All the families of the patients seemed grateful for this breath of sunshine. I don't know what compelled Mary to do it, but she was a natural.

I hung back while she talked, unsure of what to say to help make the experience less painful or fearful for the patients.

"Hello, Mrs. Wilkins," Mary said to the young woman. "Are they taking care of you?"

"Oh, yes, Miss," the young woman said. "They surely are."

"You know I was in this very hospital when I was younger," Mary said. "Burst appendix. I can tell you, that was a day!"

She smiled reassuringly at the family. I could see she was trying to tell them if *she* could be here, hale and hearty after an emergency operation years ago, then they had little to fear.

I smiled at the little family and said a prayer for them too. I'm sure surgical procedures in 1923 weren't like the stone age, but still, I did remember that Sulfa drugs weren't invented until the early 1930s. Penicillin wasn't around until the 1940s. If you got an infection, there was a good chance that, assuming your body didn't fight it off, you were going to die.

Simple surgeries often led to infections as there was nothing to give patients afterward. Sepsis was a common result of unsuccessful surgical procedures as was peritonitis.

I saw the clipboard hanging from the end of Anna's bed with the big red mark that indicated she was slated for surgery today. I couldn't help but notice that there was a tray of food on the table next to her.

I hoped it was a snack for her family and that Anna hadn't just eaten a hearty meal.

Dr. Clay Ryan, the physician walked in and stood at the foot of Anna's bed, looking severe and distant. He carried a clipboard and tapped his pen against it in a rhythm of impatience. His salt-and-pepper hair was slicked back from his forehead, giving him an untouchable aura.

The frown on his face made me feel uneasy; it was obvious he wasn't happy with what he was seeing.

He wore a white lab coat over a wool suit. I thought he must be baking. Suddenly, I noticed the paperback book sticking out of one of his coat pockets. The lab coat was made of a thin material, but I couldn't read the title. I didn't know they had paperbacks in this time. I thought they were all leather-bound hard backs.

A few minutes later, after Dr. Ryan left without speaking to the family, I excused myself and went out into the hall. I knew it was useless asking the doctor for an update on Anna's surgery. Even without HIPAA, he wasn't likely to tell me anything. But I found myself worried about her. And her prospects.

∽

I stood out in the hall gathering my thoughts when all of a sudden, I saw the brutish hospital orderly Gus Jones. He was standing near the entrance to one of the patient's rooms, leering at someone inside with his beady eyes. I marched over to him.

"What are you doing?" I asked.

He looked startled, as if he had been caught red-handed doing something he shouldn't. His eyes darted around the hallway before settling on me. I grew more suspicious by the second.

"What are you doing here?" I asked him sternly, folding my arms and narrowing my gaze.

Gus cleared his throat before stammering out a response.

"I, uh, was just checking on one of the patients," he said without much conviction in his voice.

I pursed my lips.

"At this time of day? Does the hospital usually employ you to check on patients?"

His face reddened. "I wasn't hurting nobody."

I leaned in close.

"Well, I'm watching you," I said. "Just to make sure of that."

He began to back away. But before he turned, he winked at me.

"I think there's going to be a time for you and me someday, duck," he said. "You know?"

"You're disgusting," I said.

"It's not against the law to like what you see." He dragged his eyes over me from top to bottom.

"Get away from me," I said in a threatening voice. "Or I will see what hospital security has to say about you."

He snorted derisively and walked slowly away. I watched him go and I realized I felt shaken. It was clear that he was not at all worried about losing his job. White men in the south were all-powerful. In 1923 women had only recently gotten the right to vote—and then only white women—and civil rights violations were an accepted matter of life for any and all non-white, non-male citizens.

As I watched him go, I wondered if he could be the monster killing vulnerable women in Savannah. I know at this point his only real qualification was that he was creepy and unstable. That was hardly professional, thinking someone who makes my skin crawl might then logically be a serial killer.

But I still thought it was worth thinking about.

29

As I watched that little worm run back to wherever it was he came from inside the hospital, I reminded myself that I would have little to no support for any complaint I made against him were I to report him.

I needed some air. I turned to make my way to the entrance of the hospital and stepped outside instantly feeling the famous Savannah heat like a boiling washcloth to the face. I shuddered when the heat hit me. But I needed a moment away from the sickness and despair in the hospital. I made my way to the hospital gardens.

The irony wasn't lost on me that I was finding peace in the garden—the domain of poor Henry Pickett who was under arrest for having assaulted me. How could I clarify that to the police when I couldn't even do it with Sam? And from what Hawkins said yesterday, they no longer cared about him accosting a woman who'd survived. They were laying both murders at his feet. If I were to say I hadn't been assaulted, it would make no difference for Henry's case.

The garden was neatly manicured with an eye to design

and form. The pathways weaved and wound around a stone fountain in the center of the garden. The rippling water somewhat cooled the hot summer air. The walkways were lined with camelias, azaleas and gardenias.

It wasn't long before I realized I didn't have the stomach to return to the hospital. I decided to walk back to Mary's house and call the hospital and leave a message for her telling her what I'd done.

The fact was, I was shaken. I don't know whether it was that creature Gus Jones or the fear that I'd seen in poor Anna Wilkins' eyes as she waited for her surgery. There were a lot of things to terrify you in this time in history.

I set out for Mary's townhouse. Sometimes, back in my own time, I would go for a run when my thoughts began racing around my head and threatening to overwhelm me. When you're running, you have to be mindful of not tripping or getting run over. It's a great way to force yourself out of your own head. I wasn't fool enough to consider jogging down the sidewalk to Mary's house, but a brisk walk would do just as well.

The cobblestone streets were lined with oak trees draped in soft strands of Spanish moss which gracefully swayed in the warm breeze. The ancient buildings that lined the streets were majestic but inviting, the stucco walls painted in soft pastels, each window adorned with intricate ironwork. Everywhere, there were gardens filled with flowers of all sorts, making the air heavy with their sweet scent.

I walked as quickly as I could without causing undue attention to myself, my eye caught movement down one of the side streets. It was a very cute, small shaggy dog. I hesitated and then rerouted down a side street. I hadn't seen a collar on him. Perhaps he was lost?

The sun had already begun its descent towards the horizon, casting its fading light onto the cityscape. The buildings loomed high above me, hemming me in, the shadows of their windows and balconies stretching out like giant fingers in search of something. I kept my eyes peeled for the pup as I passed alleyways, the sound of my footsteps echoing off the walls as I went further into unfamiliar territory.

I noticed pieces of trash scattered here and there and even the occasional sleeping homeless person tucked away in a corner. I thought I spotted a furry shape darting around a corner but when I went to check, there was nothing.

When I finally decided to give up the hunt, preferring to believe that he'd made his way back to his home by now, I realized I'd gotten turned around. I hurried back to what I thought was the main street that I'd just left and when I got there I stood, my breath coming in quick pants, as I looked in every direction and realized I did not know where I was.

I reasoned that I'd only gone off trail for about ten maybe fifteen minutes. I had been walking quickly to try to catch the dog, but surely I couldn't have gotten that far off course? I recognized nothing around me.

The street sign said Laissez Street, which was not a street I recognized. Not in 1923 and not in 2023 either. I was furious with myself for having gotten so turned around. A tiny needle of fear had begun to inch into my chest.

I began walking quickly toward what I thought might be Drayton Street, my heart thumping in my chest as I tried to recognize something of my surroundings. As I passed an alley, I glanced down and saw a busy avenue at the end of it. I hesitated to enter it.

There was every reason to believe that that street was Drayton—or perhaps one of the streets that ran parallel to the river. I didn't know much but I knew if I could just get to a square—any square—I could find my way back to Mary's. Yes, it would be the long way around, but it beat racing down a street and not knowing if I was even going in the right direction.

I entered the alley and instantly the sound of horse hooves clopping, and traffic dimmed. I looked up at the fire escapes that hung over the alley. Everything was silent. I increased my pace suddenly doubting the wisdom of my plan.

I was halfway down the alley and just thinking about running the rest of the way, when I heard a noise behind me.

Too close behind me.

Praying it was only a rat, I whirled around.

He was medium height and not ten feet behind me. And wearing a mask.

There was no time to turn or run. Or even think. He was too close for any of that.

I opened my mouth to scream but nothing came out.

He charged me and I just stood there, frozen in horror, waiting for it.

30

My heart raced as I watched him come, my terror ramping up. All at once, the sky spun around me, and the smell of garbage flooded me. My vision dimmed. I felt like I was standing at the edge of a cliff, one misstep away from falling into an abyss.

I felt my assailant jerk my bag from my hands. By then, my entire body was shaking uncontrollably, until I felt myself falling.

Until finally my whole world went blessedly black.

∼

I don't know how long I lay there. I felt disembodied, my body unconnected to my mind and its ability to make it move. It was just me, and the vacuum of space. Like a silent spray of bullets, bits and pieces of light and discordant images whirred into my brain like embers in a blender. I felt my chest tightening painfully as if oxygen was being sucked from my lungs.

I opened my eyes to a silent, muffled world. My head was vibrating with pain as I tried to orient myself. I was still in the alley and the man who'd loomed over me to grab my purse was gone. I heard the sounds of traffic humming in the distance.

I sat up slowly, not wanting to rush things or to alert my attacker in case he was still in the area. I took in a long breath and let it out and when I did, I noticed the pile of trash close to my hip. I inched away from it and was just about to stand up, using the wall behind me as support when my eye fell on something in the trash pile that shouldn't have been there.

A crushed jumbo Slurpee cup.

I turned my head and saw the tall, stately oaks at the mouth of the alley, a thick layer of moss cascading down their trunks. The pavement beneath me was cracked and caked with dirt and leaves. The scent of the nearby river was thick in the air.

A small moped zipped by the alley entrance followed by a gaggle of laughing teenagers. My heart began to pound.

I'm back.

I sat there, my brain buzzing, unable to land on a single thought for longer than a second until I crystallized the thought that had been slowly throbbing in the background of my mind:

Why am I not in a hospital?

I'm supposed to be in a coma dreaming everything that happened to me in 1923!

I glanced around the alley, now seeing that there was no mistaking it for any time but my own. I struggled to my feet.

I wasn't sure what it meant that I was here in this alley, and not vegetating in some ICU ward. I walked cautiously down the alley and stepped onto the main street. The noise of my surroundings seemed so loud and threatening. It felt as if a hundred cars and trucks were coming straight for me.

It was almost dark but there were tourists still out and I could see the lights of a restaurant down the street. I felt a throb of anxiety as I realized that if it was true that I'd been gone for three days—and I *wasn't* in a hospital bed, then my mother, my work, and Jazz would all be beside themselves with worry.

I hurried down the street, very aware of my outlandish garb as it now seemed to chafe with every step. As I ran, all I could think was: *It wasn't a dream.*

It was real. Mary was real. Sam was real.

Tears sprang to my eyes, and I gulped for air to try to quell the hysteria that was building up inside of me. I took long, deep breaths, careful not to hyperventilate, as I hurried toward my neighborhood.

By the time I turned down my street, I felt somewhat recovered, until I saw my mother's car and my heart went into my throat. I could only imagine what she'd gone through these last few days.

What was I going to say? Was I going to default to amnesia in this timeline too?

I ran into the courtyard of my apartment building and instantly saw Jazz coming out of my apartment with a bag of garbage in her hand.

She screamed and dropped the garbage and just stood there, staring at me with her mouth open.

The door to my apartment wrenched open and my mother came out and put a hand on Jazz's shoulder before following Jazz's eyes to what had made her scream. Then my mother clapped a hand to her own mouth, her eyes filling with tears.

I ran to both of them, and they grabbed me, pulling me in tight as we all began to sob.

"I am so sorry," I said. "I'm so sorry."

"Lord help us," Jazz said, squeezing me so tight I couldn't breathe.

I turned to my mother but all she could do was shake her head and cry as if the wonder of having me back from the dead was too much to process.

"I'm sorry, Mom," I said.

"What happened to you?" Jazz said as she shook me. "We have been going crazy! Oh! I've got to call Rob and tell them we found you!" She gave me one last squeeze and ran into the apartment.

Tears of joy still streamed down my mother's face. She looked at me as if she was afraid to blink. Afraid when she opened her eyes again, I'd be gone. My heart wrenched for the pain she must have endured while I was gone. How stupid and thoughtless I'd been—thinking she'd been by my bedside all this time. Never for a minute imagining what she might have been going through.

Inside, my apartment was tidier than I've ever seen it— evidence I suppose of my mother living there for three days.

"Are you hungry?" she asked, still hanging onto me as if afraid I'd disappear again if she let go.

"A little, yeah," I said, knowing that she needed to feed me more than I needed the food.

She gave me a hard, painful squeeze and turned to the kitchen.

"You just sit there, Georgia Rae," she said from the kitchen. I soon heard the sounds of pots and pans shifting in the sink. In a moment the scent of garlic and onions drifted into the living room.

Jazz was on the phone, watching me as she talked.

"Yes, I know!" she was saying, her eyes on me as I sat on the couch. I looked everywhere at once, seeing things I'd not seen before but had always been there.

The automatic can opener, the glowing screen of the NEST temperature indicator. The LED light from the microwave oven.

"I haven't had a chance to...." Jazz smiled at me and appeared to be listening to the person on the other end of the line. I wondered if it was Rob.

"Yep, okay, will do," she said.

She hung up and came over to throw her arms around me again. "I'm so glad you're back safe."

I hugged her tight and then pulled back.

"Is everything okay?" I nodded at her phone. "Who was that?"

She frowned and tilted her head.

"Georgie, you've been gone for *three* days. Where were you? We thought you were kidnapped or killed and thrown in a landfill."

Her voice broke on the last words, and I noticed she dropped her tone so my mother wouldn't hear.

"I...I was attacked at the grocery store parking lot," I said, having had at least a moment to get my thoughts together.

"By Jimmy White, right?" she asked eagerly. "They picked him up. They had the two O'Deckie sisters who said he assaulted you, but they didn't know where you went after that, and White kept saying he didn't move you."

"That's right," I said, licking my lips. I noticed my mother had appeared in the doorway of the kitchen, a dish towel over one shoulder, listening.

"I...I...after he hit me, I guess I blacked out," I said,

wondering at what point Jazz might know something I didn't know.

"The sisters said they saw you go down," Jazz said. "But by the time they ran over to you, you were gone."

This was going to be tricky.

"Where were you, darling?" my mother asked in a quiet voice from the kitchen. "Who gave you those clothes?"

I looked down at my dress. This was going to be impossible to explain.

"Y'all," I said wearily. "Do you mind if I only explain this once?" I turned to Jazz. "I assume that was Rob you were talking to?"

"He was out," she said. "It was Jen and she's on her way over."

I felt a wave of disappointment that it wasn't going to be Rob hearing my story—he'd be more inclined to believe it than Jen would.

"Okay," I said. "If you don't mind, I want to take a quick shower and change clothes."

I stood up but so did Jazz.

"Do you think you should?" she asked, tentatively.

I put a hand on her shoulder and gave her a light squeeze.

"I wasn't raped, Jazz," I said. "I promise. I need to change clothes."

She stepped aside as I moved down the hall to the bathroom. Things were going to be hard enough explaining what had happened to me without sitting in a dress only my great grandmother would've worn.

31

My apartment living room was sparsely decorated with a single inexpensive couch, two armchairs, and a couple of mismatched end tables. A few framed photos hung on the walls. Looking at it all now, I was suddenly struck by how shabbily I lived. I made decent money. I didn't have to live like this. There was no art, no design, no style, no purpose or joy in any item my eye fell on.

When I thought of how Mary lived—among treasured curios and tea trays by the fire—I was astonished that my idea of living could be so...meagre.

In the center of the room was a low coffee table with a small spread of food that my mother had put out: cheese and crackers, deviled eggs, a spiral-sliced ham, egg salad and an assortment of cupcakes.

Jen Turlington showed up just as I was pulling on jeans and a t-shirt. I had no idea how she was going to accept my cock-and-bull story but since I was almost positive that I'd broken no laws, I tried not to look or sound too guilty.

I stepped into the living room and my mother beamed

when she saw me, as if afraid I might have disappeared out the bathroom window. Jen stood in my doorway in her full cop's uniform, the utility belt sitting high on her waist and her hands resting on it as she studied me from top to toe.

"You have got to be kidding me," she said with a sneer.

I had no idea what that meant so I chose to ignore it.

"Darling, come get it while it's hot," my mother said as she gestured me over to the small coffee table.

"Hey, Jen," I said as I walked into the living room. "Oh, Mom, this looks amazing." That was when I realized I was starving. I sat down and didn't know where to start first. Fortunately, my mother leaned over and began preparing me a plate of sliced ham and various salads.

"What the hell happened to you, Belle?" Jen said harshly as she stepped into the living room.

Jen had a perpetual sneer on her face as if she were sucking a lemon at any given time. Today was no different.

"Kindly do not speak to my daughter that way, Officer," my mother said tartly.

I saw the expression change on Jen's face. She wasn't used to people defending me. And she wasn't used to the epitome of Southern gentility correcting her either. I don't think Jen is from the South so while she didn't say "Yes, Ma'am," she at least knew not to argue with my mother.

I scooped up a huge forkful of corn pudding—my favorite and I have no idea how or why my mother had the ingredients on hand—and motioned to her that I would begin talking in a moment. Finally, I swallowed and turned to my mother first.

"This is amazing, Mom," I said. "Really what I needed to make me feel human again."

My mother beamed and turned away to bring in a large

pitcher of iced tea. I'd have preferred a beer, but cold tea sounded good too.

"I was just telling Jazz and my mother," I said to Jen, "that after I was attacked by Jimmy White—and oh, I hear you got him? Well done."

Jen blinked, clearly not prepared for a compliment from me. She pinked and then frowned as if I'd caught her in a delicate situation.

"Anyway," I said. "After he hit me, everything went black. I don't know how long I was out but when I woke up..." I bit into one of my mother's amazingly buttery buttermilk biscuits. I know she drizzles butter on top of them when she pulls them out of the oven, and they just melt in your mouth.

"For crap's sake, Belle!" Jen said and then looked quickly at my mother who scowled at her.

"I woke up," I said, dotting my lips with a cloth napkin, "in a sort of storage room. It was dark and cold, and I was on the ground. My head was killing me and after a few seconds, I must have passed out again."

My mother and Jazz both pulled up chairs to listen.

"The next time I woke up, there was a bottle of water next to me. Oh, and a bottle of ibuprofen."

"Maybe White had a confederate?" Jazz asked with a frown.

"Maybe," I said with a shrug. "So I drank and took the ibuprofen and then I slept some more. I think at one point I tried to see if I still had my cellphone, but I couldn't find it, and I was so tired."

"That was due to the concussion, no doubt," my mother said nodding knowingly as if she'd been saying it all along.

"I feel like I slept forever. I woke up one more time with food this time and water next to me and I was feeling a little better but maybe there was some kind of sedative in the water? Because then I got really tired again."

I prayed Jen wasn't going to insist I take a drug test. The idea of being drugged had just come to me and I probably shouldn't have gone with it but it was too late now. How would it look if I refused a toxicology panel?

"And then?" Jen said sarcastically, making it as clear as she could that she didn't believe any of this.

"Then I woke up about an hour ago," I said, spearing a ham slice, "and I was no longer in the storage closet. I was in an alley."

She frowned. "Which alley?"

There was no point in fabricating this part of it. She was welcome to go dust the crap out of that alley.

"It's the one to the south of Telfair Square," I said. "So wow, I was gone for three days?"

I looked from Jen to my mother to Jazz. I could tell that my mother and Jazz still had questions—mostly related to the outfit I'd been wearing—but that would wait.

"More like four," Jen said her thin lips twisted into a sneer. "It was like you disappeared off the face of the earth. And White never mentioned any accomplice."

"Well, he wouldn't, would he?" Jazz snapped.

Jen didn't even honor her with a glance.

"So, what about White?" I prompted Jen. "You got him, right?"

"We did. And his complete stash of counterfeit phones. And the two old ladies said they'd make witness statements."

"That's great," I said. "I'll bet Rob was thrilled."

She snorted in derision.

"Yeah, I told him you'd reappeared, and he said to give you his regards."

I felt a stab of disappointment at her words. I don't know what I was expecting but at least a phone call if not a personal visit. I'd been missing for four days *and* solved his case for him, and he couldn't even come see me?

Sam would've come.

After that I felt much more tired than I ever remember feeling. Jen took my statement and left, and after a while so did Jazz. I could only imagine the agony that she and my mother had gone through these last few days. I felt terrible about that because while I'd been in 1923, I had only peripherally thought of either of them and never about what they must be doing through.

Part of that was because I assumed I was lying in a hospital bed somewhere with them on either side of me holding my hands. The possibility never once occurred to me that I'd just vanished as far as they were concerned.

After Jazz left, my mother and I curled up on the sofa to watch television, more as a distraction from the intense emotion of the day than anything else. My boss Dennis Gibson called but I let my mother talk to him. He basically called my return a miracle and to please take the rest of the week off with pay.

I wondered uncharitably, if that was because he was afraid I'd sue the department even though technically it had happened on my own time.

In any event, I was glad for the time. I really think the last thing my brain was capable of at the moment was processing emergencies happening to random people—in any century.

32

The next morning, my main task was to convince my mother that I was fine and that she could go back home to Pooler and resume her life there.

We bought lattes to go at Starbucks and walked to Franklin Square which was near where she'd parked her car. As we walked, I was remembering my walk not far from here with Mary. Everything looked so much dirtier and older today. We sat down on a nearby park bench to watch the birds and a few small children playing while their various minders watched them.

"And you're sure you're going to be alright?" my mother asked, her brows knit together in concern.

"I'm fine, Mom. Honestly."

"Georgia, darling," she said hesitantly. "The outfit you were wearing..."

I sighed. I'd known this was coming.

"My own clothes were...soiled," I said carefully. "So when I woke up, those clothes were there for me."

"Left for you?" She wrinkled her nose.

"I think whoever it was," I said, "was trying to be helpful."

She snorted.

"Being helpful would have been calling the police when they found you," she said.

"Good point. But I'm home now and I'm safe."

"It just seems very strange."

You can say that again. But I only nodded in agreement.

After that I walked her to her car and waved her off, promising I'd call that evening. As soon as I left the parking lot, I walked toward West Bryan Street, knowing I was going there nearly from the moment I ended up back in my own time. I'm not sure what I was looking for or hoping for, but I knew that whatever the key might possibly be to my three-day excursion into the past, it would be found at that antiques shop off East Bryan Street.

∾

The small brick townhouse-turned-antique shop looked no different today from when I'd visited it four days earlier, and in fact not that much different from my last visit there with Mary. I stepped inside and a young black woman, her dark hair twisted into long dreads, smiled at me.

"You're back," she said.

That startled me for a moment until I realized that of course she meant nothing more by it than a greeting to a repeat customer.

"I am," I said. "I was thinking about that painting I found last time I was here. You know, the one of the woman portrait done around the time of World War II?"

She frowned and got up off her stool from behind the counter, but I waved her back.

"Don't worry," I said. "I know what I'm looking for."

"If you're sure." She took her seat again and went back to the book she'd been reading.

As I walked down the aisle, feeling the excitement building inside me, I wondered how much the painting was, if I could afford it, or if upon second inspection I'd find it really was of Mary. And more importantly than that, what the artist's signature on the bottom right hand of the portrait would read.

I was almost positive that it would say *G. Belle.* I normally dated my canvasses on the back—back in the day when I used to paint. I was particularly eager to see if the artist had written the *date* on the painting.

I moved down the aisle of the store, my eyes darting from one item to another. I went slowly, running my hands along the dusty shelves and peering into murky corners, looking at every painting, every display case, every shelf. My heart sank as I rounded the last corner and came face to face with the realization that the painting wasn't here.

I went back to the counter, and the woman looked up at me expectantly.

"Didn't find what you were looking for?"

"No," I said. "It was a portrait of a woman, with brown hair, big eyes, and wavy hair to her shoulders like they wore it in the nineteen forties."

She frowned.

"I'm sorry. It doesn't sound familiar, and I do know our inventory pretty well."

"It was here just four days ago. Do you think someone bought it?"

She frowned.

"Well, I have an assistant who sits in for me when I'm

away from the shop, but he would've written it down if he'd sold an oil painting."

I waited while she pulled a heavy leather ledger from a shelf over the counter and drew a finger down the columns. I knew what she was going to say before she did.

"Nope. Sorry. Are you sure it was my place you saw the painting? There are some actual art galleries on Bay Street. I'm really more of a curio shop."

My shoulders slumped in disappointment. It was bad enough that the painting was gone, but for it not to even be remembered?

Had I imagined it?

I must have looked distraught because the woman asked me if I'd like a cup of tea. I shook my head.

"I guess I just had my heart set on it," I said.

"Are you a painter?"

"I used to be, I guess."

She laughed. "That's not a very definitive answer."

"Well, it's certainly not my day job," I said with a weak smile. "Do you paint?"

"No, but my auntie does. She teaches at SCAD. I don't think she does oils though if that's what you like. More like watercolors."

"That's cool," I said. "Well, I better get going."

Just before I left, I reached over to take her business card out of the holder on the counter—if for no other reason than to make her think I might be repeat business. She had been kind to me.

"Have a good day," she said. "Sorry about the painting."

I smiled and walked out the door and was just about to tuck the card into my pocket when my eye fell on the name.

Antiques and Things
Alisha Pickett Marlow, Proprietor

I stared at the card and felt my heart began to beat faster.

I have to say that *Pickett* is not an extremely unusual name in the South but still, it did seem a bit coincidental. Without realizing I intended to do it, I went back inside the store.

"Yes?" she asked.

"I was just wondering," I said. "Your aunt who teaches at SCAD. What's her name?"

"Elise Pickett," she said with a smile. "Thinking of taking an evening class?"

I smiled wanly. "Something like that."

33

When I left the antique shop, I wasn't sure exactly what I was going to do with the information about Elise Pickett. There was no reason to believe beyond the fact that she was black and from Savannah that she might be related to Henry Pickett—the poor black scapegoat sitting in a jail cell in downtown 1923 Savannah—or more likely long moldering in his grave.

But I couldn't stop thinking about it. At the very least I needed to pull the thread to make sure the ends didn't connect with Henry. For some reason, it was just really important to me to see if this woman—and Alisha at the antique store—were somehow connected to the poor man I knew in 1923.

But first, I was hungry. I went from the antique shop to a pop-up kiosk that sold pizza by the slice. I bought a pepperoni pizza slice, and a cold beer and went to Franklin Square to eat and think about what had happened to me.

I'd had no trouble sleeping last night—probably out of pure exhaustion—but now my brain was in overdrive, and I had about a million different things that seemed to be demanding my attention.

One of them was Detective Sam Bohannon. I'll admit to looking him up straightaway this morning on Google, but I found no trace of him. Bohannon is a Southern name but unlike Pickett, it's not that common. I don't know if not finding anything on Sam meant he'd never married or just never had children. I felt sad at the thought, but also relief. Don't ask me why.

As I was eating my lunch, it occurred to me that I should check in with Jazz, but I didn't have my cellphone. I'd asked Jen about it last night—had White scooped it up after he attacked me?—but she said there was no sign of it in the evidence locker.

I thought that extremely odd since I know I didn't have it with me in 1923. Just forming that sentence in my head made me laugh out loud which scared a few pigeons near me. After I ate, I tossed my wrappings away and headed to the first electronics store I could find to buy a new phone.

After that, now once more fully connected with the world at large, I headed in the direction of the alley where I'd awoken the day before. I'm not sure what I was looking for, perhaps evidence of some kind. But what other kind of evidence did I need than that 1900's frock hanging in my closet right this very minute?

I found a bench and called Jazz.

"Hey, you," she said, answering. "Got a new phone?"

"I do. But I can't figure out why nobody found my old one when White hit me."

"It's a mystery. Listen, be glad you're not in the office. The temp that Dennis hired to fill in for you is a total suck up. She's definitely after your job."

I wasn't sure how I felt about that. Up until I'd gone back

to the 1920's I would've said that I loved my job. But strangely, I didn't feel at all threatened by the idea of someone else sitting in my chair hoping to fill my shoes.

"Any other news?" I asked.

"No, just the usual."

"Have you seen Rob?"

"Girl, will you get over that? He's working some tourist fraud case or something. Has he called you to see how you're doing?"

"No."

"Well, see? Let him go."

I knew she was right. In fact, four days ago, I would've defended Rob. But somehow, I didn't feel like it. Somehow, I felt that it was a pretty jerk move not to at least call me after I'd been missing for four days.

We talked for a few minutes more and then disconnected. I walked across the street to the alley where I'd woken up back in 2023, but where, more specifically, I'd been in fear of being attacked. I looked around, trying to remember what the space had looked like a hundred years ago when I'd stepped into it. But there was nothing that jumped out at me. Figuratively or literally.

As I was leaving the alley, I decided to walk over to the spot where White attacked me and look around for my missing cell phone.

I walked six blocks before cutting over by way of a dirt path which sliced through to the strip mall, most of whose businesses had long been closed. The chain link fence encircling the area was wrapped in unbroken wire, and weeds were everywhere.

I glanced over at the Indian couple's grocery store. I saw it was open, but I knew the couple had probably been questioned by the police, and from what Jazz had relayed to me, hadn't seen anything. I passed a man sitting on the sidewalk with his eyes closed, resting from a day of hard drinking.

After searching the ditches on both sides of the sidewalk, I felt myself getting frustrated. Usually when that happens it's because I have allowed myself to get hungry. But since I'd just eaten, it had to be something else.

There was something unresolved buzzing in the back of my brain. I knew from experience that until I isolated and identified it, I would feel edgy and ill at ease all day. I've learned that sitting down to try and figure out what the problem is almost never works. My best shot was to go on with my day, find a task—preferably a mindless one—and then whatever it was that was bothering me would present itself.

I turned to head back in the general direction of my apartment. I passed a Starbucks store that in 1923 was an old Singer Sewing store that shared space with a fabric store. I was stunned to realize I'd looked in that store display window not one day ago. The memory of it was so vivid as to take my breath away.

When I came to Drayton and Liberty streets, I realized that Mary's townhouse was only a few blocks away. Suddenly I was desperate to go there. I walked so quickly, I was practically running, and I had to keep reminding myself that Mary would not be there.

When I turned the corner onto Abercorn Street, I saw that so many of these beautiful homes had been renovated and restored back to their former glory—in fact the glory that had been on full display in 1923. As I walked down the street, my excitement welling up inside me, I wondered if this was the thing that had been nudging me all afternoon.

I went straight to Lafayette Square but ended up walking a full half block past the townhouse before I realized I needed to turn around. When I did, my steps slowed as I saw Mary's townhouse.

It was a wreck.

The beautiful Victorian townhouse that I had come to know literally sagged on its cornerstone. Years of neglect and abuse had left the front of the mansion stark and gloomy. Its shutters hung crooked on the windows, paint peeling off the walls, and the gutter surrounding it was nothing but a stretch of rusting iron rods stuffed with dead leaves.

I stood transfixed in front of the house. No one had come through that door for so many years that moss had actually begun to grow in the cracks of the front steps.

Tears welled up in my eyes as I looked at the townhouse, a place that had given me much-needed refuge just a few days ago, a place where I'd sat with Mary in the garden and schemed and planned—and felt alive for the first time in my life. That thought surprised me, but it was true.

I let the tears roll down my cheeks and thought of Mary. I don't know what happened to her but looking at this wreckage made me think that nothing good had happened after I left.

34

I lifted the kettle from the stove and poured the hot water into a mug my cabinet. The words had worn away after years of being put in the dishwasher. I dipped the tea bag into the hot water. I don't know why I was expecting the scent of jasmine or perhaps lavender. But there was no scent. This was just basic black tea, nothing more, nothing less. I dunked and swirled the bag a few times before tossing it in the sink.

I looked at the tea in the mug and was stabbed with a longing that I couldn't explain. Maybe it was because I knew that in 1923 a cup of tea would've been a restorative ritual, almost an act of spiritual devotion. And the benefits it gave could cure heartache as well as an upset stomach.

All I wanted from it today was an occasion to stop, take a breath, and maybe appreciate a moment of life's small pleasures. As I drank the tea, I couldn't stop thinking of Mary. Or Henry for that matter. And of course, Sam. How I wish it *had* all been a dream, that these people were only figments of my imagination.

I finished my tea and rinsed out the mug, deciding that I

would never use it again. It wasn't much—a single cup of tea and a moment of reflection—but it occurred to me that that moment deserved a bone china teacup with a beautiful scattering of flowers on it.

I glanced at the clock in the kitchen and decided to call Mom early. That way I'd confirm that she got home okay and tick the box for letting her know I was fine. I did feel terrible for the pain my absence had caused her. It occurred to me that the fact that I'd assumed I was having some kind of coma-induced dream that had landed me back in 1923 meant that adjusting to the truth—that I'd really gone back in time—could account for why I was at sixes and sevens now. I put the call in to Mom.

"Yes?" she answered warily.

"It's me, Mom. I got a new phone."

"Oh, darling! I wondered if this was you since the number was the same. Did you have a good day?"

"I did," I said. "Very pleasant. And I'm having a lovely cup of tea now and relaxing."

This of course was only partially the truth, but I knew it would ease her mind.

"I'm so glad, darling. Well, you enjoy yourself. Can you come for dinner over the weekend?"

"I don't see why not," I said, feeling a little sad about the fact that I had no reason for why I felt so listless. I realized that my life, when it didn't include work, tended to be as flat as a stomped-on johnny cake.

After hanging up with my mother, I went to my laptop and booted it up. First, I googled for *Mary Thompson*. I think I was hoping I wouldn't find her, at least not by that name which would mean she found someone and married. But no, she was there. Her photo came up, fuzzy and in black and white, and a lump formed in my throat when I saw her.

There were no articles on her except one when she was briefly vice-president in charge of her neighborhood garden club. I thought of her garden and how much she loved it.

The only piece of information was Mary's obituary and I cringed when I read the date. October 1992. I stared at that date a long time, thinking of what I'd been doing then when she was here in Savannah in a nursing home for three years before she passed. I wondered when she'd sold or lost the home on Abercorn Street and if she'd seen it fall apart. I prayed not.

She was born in 1898 and died at ninety-four. I swallowed hard and felt my eyes burn. She'd lived another sixty-nine years after I knew her. But they were sixty-nine lonely years. She'd died an old maid with no family around her. I thought about that all the rest of the day, wondering what had happened to Cook and Seamus, imagining they probably got old themselves. Did they have families? I never learned Seamus's last name or Cook's first name.

I felt an ache in my chest at the thought of them. That buzzing in the back of my brain was still there so all my effort to distract myself had not helped in revealing what it was that was bothering me.

I got up to make myself a plate from the leftovers of the feast that my mother had made. I heated it up in the microwave, marveling at the fact that Cook had been able to create such extraordinary delectables without the aid of modern cooking equipment.

I ate quietly at the table before turning on the television set to listen to the evening news. The news had nothing much going on beyond the usual and I found myself wondering how everyone back in 1923 could stay so well informed without TV or social media. There was the radio—or the wireless as they called it. Suddenly my brain put together the fact that news didn't get around as fast as it did today as evidenced by the fact that when I was there, they were dealing with a serial killer and didn't even know it.

I rinsed out my plate and reached for my laptop again. I googled *serial killer Savannah 1923* and not surprisingly nothing came up. They didn't know that term back then and so would never have described it as such. I tapped my fingers lightly on the keyboard trying to think. Then I typed into the search window: *suspicious attacks on young women 1923 Savannah*.

A series of newspaper articles appeared. And with them, almost immediately, Sam Bohannon's name.

~

I scoured all the newspaper articles for any shred of information about Sam, either things he'd told to the paper —or was loosely quoted on—or efforts he was making. I saw when he was pulled off the case and after that all public information about the murders seemed to dry up. Clearly, Detective Hawkins wasn't giving interviews.

I also didn't find any reporting on my own assault beyond the vague piece I'd already read in the *Bugle* in Mary's living room. That in itself disconcerted me briefly since it made me doubt—just for a moment—that I'd actually gone back in time. But of course, how would I know Sam and Mary if I hadn't been back there? How would I know about the attacks on Mercy and Alice? No, I didn't know why my own attack wasn't covered, but that was irrelevant.

I scanned all the articles until the last one which appeared to be an admission of failure by the Police Department. There was a line in one of the articles that referenced the "Negro" held under suspicion of murder.

I sat and stared at the reference to Henry Pickett on my computer screen. It was possible that this was why there was no mention of my assault or any assault after mine. Presumably it would be tricky to justify pinning a murder on their prime suspect if it occurred while he was in police custody. I cursed the fact that I hadn't bothered to visit the *Savannah Bugle* when I'd been back in 1923 but I reminded myself that I hadn't had any control over my leaving.

That thought stopped me in my tracks.

The fact was, up to this moment I'd believed that I'd had no control over going to 1923 *or* coming back. But now that I thought about it, *both times had been triggered*.

That didn't exactly give me control over moving through time, but it at least gave me an idea of what might have caused it.

I got up to pour myself a glass of wine. When I came back, I sat down and typed into the search window: *Spinelli crime family*. Nothing specific to an actual crime family came up—not even in the newspapers back then although that might not be a surprise if the publisher was in their pocket. There was a little information on the family itself. Not much and hardly enlightening, but at least it proved that they'd existed.

By the time I'd finished my wine I felt discombobulated and unsatisfied. It wasn't until I re-read the *Savannah Bugle* articles that I'd printed out on my home printer and reread the sentence about Henry Pickett that I felt a few things click into place.

The next thing I did was go online and find and print out a list of characteristics for the typical sociopath. I sat staring at the paper in my hands.

Lack of remorse or guilt, impulsivity, the need to control, predatory behavior, antisocial behavior, manipulation, torturing animals.

I swallowed hard. There was no doubt in my mind that I was looking at a checklist for finding a serial killer in 1923 Savannah.

And as I stared at the list, I had a creeping sensation that I'd met him.

35

That night I couldn't sleep. I must have laid there in bed for hours staring at the dark ceiling, wondering what had really happened to me.

Finally giving up on sleep, I got up and made myself a cup of cocoa and got my laptop out again. This time I went online to research Candler Hospital. I was not disappointed with the amount of resource material. Currently a historic hospital on Reynolds Street, it had originally been founded in 1804 as a seamen's hospital and a poor house and by the time I landed there, it was Savannah Hospital just off Abercorn.

I was surprised to see that today it was considered the second oldest hospital in America in continuous operation. I thought of the smoking doctor and Sister Beatrice. It took me another two hours of intense research before I found her.

I found a photograph of a nurse—very fuzzy and of course black and white—standing in a group of other nurses—all dressed in religious garb. The picture was too poor to say for sure that it was Sister Beatrice. There was no caption, but I knew it was her. Amazingly, it was while I was sifting through page after page of research material for the hospital that I finally found Sam.

It was a photograph of him standing in a hospital ward, ramrod straight and looking very serious. My eyes welled at the sight of him. There was no way I would've recognized this man's face if I hadn't met him. Hadn't *known* him.

It wasn't a dream. Sam had been real.

I wiped away my tears and the very real sorrow I felt that he hadn't been able to solve his case, and that he'd eventually lost or walked away from his job as this photo seemed to indicate. The article referenced without naming them, the three women murdered that year.

Three women.

I closed my laptop, finally tired enough to try to sleep. As I made my way into my bedroom, I thought the buzzing feeling was a little less fuzzy. I'd found something in my research that I couldn't yet put my finger on. It was something having to do with Henry—or maybe his descendent Elise, if she was his descendant—that I needed to explore further.

That is, if I had any hope of ever getting a decent night's sleep again.

∼

The next morning, after several hours on the Internet, I had enough information to piece together a sketchy outline of the Spinelli crime family's activities in the early twentieth century. It seemed they were involved in smuggling, extortion, and prostitution.

In later years, they branched out and became more diversified, with interests in gambling, racketeering, and drugs. It wasn't until I went down to the courthouse off Martin Luther King Jr Boulevard and asked for records under the Freedom of Information Act—that I was able to get a better glimpse into the world of the Spinelli's. I found very old court records detailing a few arrests, but no indictments, or convictions. I was able to see how they operated their criminal empire, and I got an idea of the kind of power they wielded.

Although they didn't seem to exist now in Savannah, I could see that the Spinelli's had been a powerful family in 1918. I searched for any mention of them from the early twentieth century in old newspaper articles. It turned out there were a few reports of criminal activities and arrests, but it was difficult to tell how many of these were related to the Spinelli's and they quickly began to fade from view. Either the family got better at hiding their crimes and their connections to them, or changed their name, or had simply died out.

I reread the articles and cross-referenced them with other sources. I read books about organized crime in the area and searched for mention of the Spinelli's. By the time I finally closed out of my Internet search in early afternoon, it was clear to me that the Spinelli family had become a nonentity by 1930—just seven years after the Savannah murders.

Before I quit for the day, I decided to Google *Elise Pickett*. I read her online dossier, next to a photo that showed an attractive, middle-aged black woman with a steely gaze and an erect carriage to her shoulders.

She was a master builder of art, creating beautiful pieces that were both modern and timeless. Her paintings were a combination of real life and abstract fantasy, while her sculptures depicted abstract forms with precise mathematical shapes.

After receiving her Master's degree from Tennessee's Belmont University Watkins College of Art she had taught at the Savannah College of Art and Design for twelve years. It was a very impressive dossier for a woman who was clearly academically gifted as well as an artist in her own right.

I looked at her photo again. Unless I was imagining it, I thought I saw something in the tilt of her chin that reminded me of Henry Pickett.

At the end of one article on her, I found a mention of her father Henry Pickett III which was hyperlinked. I drilled down and found a picture of a handsome if angry looking young man who very much resembled the man I'd known in 1923.

What I read in the photo caption made me drop my jaw in astonishment.

36

Colonial Park Cemetery is basically an asphalt park with a pond, a greenhouse, and a winding walkway lined with flowers and trees. And of course, lots of headstones. It also features an iron fence as old as the civil war, surrounding the place, separating the living from the dead.

I sat on a bench staring at the graves and remembering when Mary and I had sat here—just days ago. The sun hid behind a curtain of gray clouds and silver raindrops that made puddles on the grass. I ran my hand over the wooden bench and wondered if it could possibly be the same one.

I reflected on my night's work and of my online discoveries. I had taken a screenshot of the story I'd found about Henry Pickett III—the grandson of the man I knew in 1923 who had been falsely arrested. Every time I looked at the photo of Henry Pickett III and read the caption, I felt sick to my stomach.

Henry Picket III was still alive today.

Alive and serving a life sentence for murder in Chatham County Prison.

I felt a wave of emotions come over me, my mind filled with questions about the man in prison just a few miles from where I sat and also the man a hundred years earlier awaiting trial for a crime he didn't commit.

What did this mean? Maybe Henry III was just a bad seed? What about his father? Henry Jr? Was he still alive?

My emotions swirled uncomfortably, the questions in my head more insidious with each passing moment. How was the present-day Henry's criminality connected to his grandfather? I stood up, suddenly agitated. It was starting to sprinkle, and I was getting nowhere sitting on a bench staring at a two-hundred-year-old cemetery looking for answers. I walked slowly back to my apartment.

I arrived home, sopping wet and discouraged. In 1923, getting wet meant a lot of extra work for servants—if you had them—to dry and press your linens. And of course it meant getting dressed again which was not as simple as it is today. Even if you eschewed the girdle and hose, there was still all the work getting your hair just right. People back then didn't believe in pulling it back into a ponytail and calling it done. Or if they did, they made sure nobody saw them in public.

I shed my wet clothes in a pile on the bathroom floor and took a hot shower, washing my hair until it squeaked. Then I toweled off and put on a terry cloth robe and went into the living room where I'd left my laptop plugged in.

I decided I might qualify for being slightly obsessed since I could not stop thinking of the people I'd met a few days and a hundred years ago. I didn't know where they were or if they truly existed since I was becoming less sure that I'd actually gone back there with each day that passed. But since so many of the people that I'd dreamt of seemed to have actual biographies traceable in 2023, I couldn't stop researching them to see what happened to them.

Which might tell me what had happened to me.

I made myself another cup of tea—using the same mug I said I wouldn't use again since I hadn't replaced it yet—and opened up my laptop.

First, I googled for *Henry Pickett 1924* but found nothing. I searched for a Henry Pickett Jr. but also found nothing. Then I typed in *Henry Picket III 2001* and found the same arrest picture I'd found earlier of an angry looking young black man. He'd be in his seventies today—and in prison for the past twenty years.

After that, I deepened my search for *Elise Pickett*. When I did, a series of articles popped up. She even had her own Wikipedia page. She was an artist and a teacher, in her mid-fifties. There was no mention of a husband or children.

I felt a surge of resolution and before I closed my laptop, I found a list of the SCAD faculty directory and Elise Pickett's email address. I debated how much to tell her until finally settling for a simple request for an interview to get an impact statement from her on the arts in a post-pandemic world. It was pretty weak, but if she had any ego at all she likely wouldn't see past the ruse. I hoped for both our sakes that that was the case.

A knock on the door startled me as I was certainly not expecting anyone. I jumped up to peek through the blinds to see none other than Rob Lockwood standing on my doorstep.

37

He wasn't in uniform, but his hair was wet, so I guessed he'd just come off duty. My heart started pounding at the sight of him. I hurried to the door before I realized I was still in my bathrobe.

I opened the door and he looked at me and grinned, his handsome face lighting up at the sight of me.

"Well, this is a nice surprise," he drawled.

"Rob, hello," I said, not inviting him in because it hadn't crossed my mind that he was interested in coming in. "How nice to see you."

"Be nicer on your side of the door," he said, teasing.

"Oh! Of course!" I said, opening the door wider and stepping out of the way, one hand clutching at the neck of my robe.

"Give me one second," I said, "to throw some clothes on."

"Don't go to all that trouble for me," he said with a wink.

I motioned toward the couch which didn't look too disheveled.

"I'll be right back," I said, hurrying off to the bedroom.

I shut the door behind me and quickly pulled on underclothes and a pair of jeans and a thin cotton blouse. I hated that I didn't have a smidge of makeup on, and my hair was still wet, but I was afraid he'd leave if I took too long.

I hurried back io the living room and saw him sitting on my couch, one ankle crossed over a knee as he looked around my apartment. He'd never been here before. To see him here now felt totally foreign to me.

I took a deep breath, determined not to let my rampant insecurities get the best of me.

"Can I offer you a coffee?" I said. "Or tea?"

"Coffee, tea or you?" he said with a laugh. "Got a beer?"

"Yes, of course," I said breathlessly.

Is he coming on to me?

I went to the kitchen and pulled out two beers from the fridge and then hesitated. Did he want his in a glass? Should I offer? I glanced at the kitchen sink where every glass I owned was now sitting. That settled that. I came back to the living room and handed him his beer and sat down.

"I'm so glad to see you," I said.

"Well, I had to come see what all the fuss was about, didn't I?" he said, taking a long swig of beer. "So what happened to you?"

My mind raced as I tried to remember what I'd told Jen. I'd been so busy in the last couple of days, my head was stuffed with facts from Henry Pickett to the Spinelli crime family.

"You know," I said. "It's hard to remember. But it's all good now."

"Glad to hear it," he said, his eyes dropping to the unbuttoned gap of my blouse.

I was a little surprised he accepted my answer so easily. Almost as if it didn't matter.

"Work's been a bear lately," he said. "You heard I solved the White case, right?"

I nodded, wondering if he'd truly forgotten it was Jimmy White who'd assaulted me and which was the whole reason he'd got himself arrested.

Does he really not know I was involved in that?

"That was a tricky one," he said. "The guy's a wily bugger but I nailed him."

"That's great," I said, feeling my stomach begin to do something queasy and unpleasant.

"You know how Jen kept screwing up the Davison case?"

I nodded, although I didn't really.

"Well, she bested herself last week when she lost the key to the ladies and had to climb out the bathroom window. Man, the whole shop cracked up!"

"I'm sorry to have missed that," I said, smiling. I loved hearing him laugh, loved him making *me* laugh and just then when our eyes met, I felt a spark of electricity shoot through my body that left me breathless.

"I know they're missing you in the dispatch pool," he said. "Dennis says you're the best."

"That's nice."

"When you coming back to work?"

"Oh, soon, I think. I just took a little time off."

"Yeah, taking some time is good."

He looked into my eyes and licked his lips. I got the impression he did the same thing when he sat down to a plate of fried chicken.

"Sorry I didn't come by as soon as you came back," he said. "Killer week."

"No, sure, of course. I get it. Absolutely."

"But I missed you, Georgie. I kept looking for you in the office."

"Did you?"

He leaned in closer, his gaze lingering on me like he was attempting to hypnotize me. In some ways it was working. I definitely felt like I was under a spell.

"Sure would go a long way to making me feel better if I could get a hug," he said.

I felt a warmth infuse my body at his words. I couldn't believe this was happening. I scooted closer to him. He put his beer down and snaked an arm around me and pulled me close. His other hand cradled my bottom. He held me so tight, I was having trouble breathing.

I had waited for this moment for so long that I couldn't believe it was finally happening. My skin literally tingled with anticipation as I settled into his embrace. But he pulled back and found my lips with his.

It was our first *real* kiss. I melted into him, reveling in the moment, when he suddenly pushed me over on my back onto the couch, his body covering mine, his insistent desire pulsing off him like warning lights.

I squirmed as his mouth covered mine again. His hand went to my blouse and he tugged at the buttons.

"No, Rob, wait," I said, gasping and struggling to sit up.

He paused but didn't immediately get off. I got the impression he was having a brief but definite battle with himself. Finally, he sat up, his eyes going to my now unbuttoned blouse. He licked his lips again.

"You know, this has been great," I said, feeling flushed and used and sick with disappointment. "It was so great of you to come by. But my mom's due here any second. I'd love for you to meet her."

A panicked look flashed across his face, and he leaned away from me on the couch.

"Yeah, I really should be going," he said.

It occurred to me that he wasn't even going to bother coming up with an excuse for leaving. Maybe people as sexy and desirable as Rob never had to. Maybe they could just take what they wanted and walk away from what they didn't without a backward glance.

"I'm, sorry," I said, feeling my heart sink into my shoes at his words. I smiled so he would know what a good sport I was and how—if it was any other time—I'd be game. I don't know why I needed him to think that.

I wasn't game. Not ever. Not with him.

He wasn't looking for a long-term connection–he was looking for a moment's release with no strings.

As I walked him to the door, my heart pounding in my chest, I couldn't help but wonder if that was the very clear message I'd been giving him all these months.

38

The Savannah School of Art and Design is comprised of a series of campuses throughout Savannah but the one where Elise Pickett worked was situated in an old building on the edge of town. The school was founded fifty years ago, so nowhere near 1923. Because its campuses include more than sixty buildings, it wasn't surprising that every time you turned around in Savannah you were facing a part of the school.

Where I was headed today was Poetter Hall which was the first building established in the school campus and the school's first historic restoration project.

The whole time I walked to Bull Street to my appointment with Elise Pickett, I kept thinking about Rob's visit last night. It was true I'd felt manipulated and tricked but also like I'd led myself down this path. I'd clearly given him the impression that I was so enamored of him that I'd be happy to jump into bed with him—even though we hardly knew each other.

He hadn't bothered asking about brothers or sisters or what my major was in college or if I had any hobbies or a favorite color. He was used to being able to dispense with all the social niceties that the rest of us need to employ so people don't think we're selfish jerks.

Did he not care if the world thought he was a selfish jerk? Was he just too handsome to worry about that?

I was embarrassed for anyone I knew—mostly Jazz—who had seen me act like a mooning schoolgirl over this lout. Needless to say, the thought of how Rob stacked up against Sam was instant and indelible. Let's just say it wasn't a fair comparison. At all.

I stood in front of Poetter Hall on Bull Street. While it was true that SCAD hadn't existed in Mary and Sam's time, this building certainly had. Poetter Hall faced Madison Square and, according to last night's Internet research, had served as many different things over the years—a hospital, a high school, even a National Guard unit headquarters.

I'd seen a photograph of the building taken in 1902 and when I did—even though I'm sure I never went by there in 1923—I swear I had a flashback of memory of it. Or maybe it was just the sight of the horse drawn carriage on the street in front of the building.

It's a beautiful old building, designed in the Romanesque Revival style. Unlike a lot of the Victorian style homes in the mid nineteenth century, Poetter Hall has simple lines and non-ornate embellishments as well. It would definitely have stood out in 1923.

The waiting room I stepped into was painted a bright yellow. There was a small couch, a few chairs, and a coffee table in the room. Framed artwork by students were showcased on the walls. There was a faint scent of wood, paint, and fresh coffee.

As I waited for my appointment, I heard soft piano

music being played somewhere in the building, along with the sounds of shuffling feet and the occasional cough and doors opening and closing.

My questions for Elise would be round-about to start with. I didn't want to upset her or make her think I got the appointment under false pretenses, although of course I had.

Suddenly, the door opened and a middle-aged black woman appeared. She was dressed in a zebra faux-fur jacket with a brightly colored Hermés scarf around her throat. Her graying hair was pulled back into a bun at the nape of her neck with long dangling earrings. Her eyes had a distant gleam to them as if, as an artist, she was already seeing the possible in everyday things.

"You must be Ms. Pickett," I said as I extended my hand. She smiled warmly as she shook it, seemingly sizing me up before speaking.

"Please call me Elise," she replied as she led me down the hall to her office.

I sat in the chair opposite her desk and tried to get my thoughts in order.

"Now, Miss Belle," she said. "How can I help you?"

"Call me Georgia," I said.

I started off by asking Elise how long she had been teaching and what kept her inspired during times when students didn't respond well to criticism or failed to take direction. Although it wasn't easy to affect sincerity while dodging around the topic that I really wanted to get to—her father's incarceration, I listened as she spoke earnestly about how teaching motivated her each day.

When we'd been chatting for a few minutes, I thought it was time.

"Elise, I do have a few questions that are not related to

academia. You see, I'm writing a broad-strokes book on travesties of justice, and I thought, from my preliminary research on your family that your father might be a case I should include."

Her face hardened immediately and for a second I was sure I'd blown it. I'd gone over several different scenarios to present to her but there were none that were going to smooth over the fact that her father was serving a life sentence for murder. I could only hope she would be able to see past my blundering. Although *why* she might be interested in helping me write a book about her father, was anyone's guess.

"I see," she said. "I guess I don't need to ask you what you think you already know about my father."

"I know almost nothing," I said. "Just that he's serving life in prison for murder. I'm trying to find out if his case has been reviewed recently or if there are any new details concerning his conviction."

The room was silent as she processed my words and then slowly nodded her head.

"No," she said softly averting her gaze, "there will be no appealing my father's conviction. Anyone who knew him, knew he was guilty."

I frowned.

"Can you tell me what happened between him and his victim that resulted in this life sentence?"

Elise paused for a moment glancing out the window which looked out onto Bull Street with a view of the beautiful Madison Square before she turned back towards me with cold eyes.

"His victim was my mother," she said. "My father was a brutal man. He was a troubled young man, and a bitter old man. He didn't appeal because I stopped his lawyer from trying. Henry Pickett needs to stay where he is, so I don't go to jail for *his* murder."

I felt a knot in my stomach at her words.

"I'm so sorry," I said.

"Don't be. Other people have worse stories than mine."

I honestly didn't think that was true.

"And as a child?" I asked.

She tilted her head and looked at me as if curious about me. I suppose it was an odd question.

"My grandmother told me my father was normal growing up," Elise said.

"And your grandfather?"

I'd tried all the ancestry links prior to our meeting but could find nothing on Henry Pickett III's father.

"Henry Picket Junior," she said, nodding. "I remember him a little. Very dour, very nervous man. Died in prison."

My stomach lurched at the news.

"Do you mind telling me…?"

"Armed robbery," she said. "He killed a white store owner."

"How did he die, if you don't mind my asking?"

"I don't really know." She shrugged. "Prison is a dangerous place."

After a moment of reflection, she spoke again.

"I have a brother," she said. "Correction. *Had* a brother. He killed himself. He was a very unhappy man. But at least he and Xiomara made Alisha before he died. My niece is a constant source of joy for me."

I reminded myself that Elise never married.

"What happened to your family seems like a pattern," I ventured gingerly, hoping she would fill in her own speculation for what I was seeing.

"My grandfather was born angry," she said. "And

ashamed. It was a curse he passed down to my father. And he to my brother. I've talked it over with Alisha before—we're the only ones left if you don't count my father, which I don't.

"Our theory is that the men in our family had this anger that could never be requited because the source of the anger could never be avenged. Alisha and I have taken that anger and, instead of internalizing it as the men in our family did, we've turned it into a stimulation for productivity and creativity."

"This anger that has plagued your family...?" I prompted, tentatively.

"I believe it is the reason why my grandfather died in prison and why my father will do the same."

Did I dare ask her what the source of that anger was? Was there any reason on earth why she would tell me?

"Look, it doesn't matter anymore, Miss Belle," she said, her eyes hard and unrelenting. "It was a crime committed on our family a long time ago. It literally perverted the trajectory of my whole family for generations."

I edged forward in my chair and held my breath, knowing she was about to tell me, afraid she would stop, and I'd never know the truth.

She smiled sadly at me, but the smile never reached her eyes. Elise Pickett was bitter in her own way. And angry.

"In April 1923," she intoned, emotionless and flat as if reading from a well-known script, "because there was a lack of evidence to try him for murder, my great grandfather Henry Pickett was dragged into Oglethorpe Square and lynched."

39

I had to go back.

Not just for Henry Pickett's sake but for his son and his grandson and even for Elise who never knew her great grandfather but who knew the anger and the shame of what had been done to him.

"And all because there wasn't enough evidence to try him legally," Elise had said of her great grandfather's murder before walking me to the door.

The more I thought about it, the more I knew I couldn't just stay here and do nothing. I didn't know how long before Henry was murdered but I knew I didn't have time to waste. Something terrible was going to happen and I was the only person who might possibly, conceivably, be able to stop it.

Before I could even imagine if it was possible—and what might be involved in my attempting it—I had to clear the decks as far as my mother was concerned. I couldn't have her worried about where I was. Nor Jazz either. Of course, I couldn't tell either of them the truth. 1923 wasn't the only time with insane asylums and loving family members who thought they were doing the right thing.

I spent about twenty minutes online finding a retreat on Skidaway Island not far from Savannah. They had weeklong retreats and promised a complete respite from the outside world. No cellphones were permitted.

Once I'd decided on it, I sent an email to Dennis Gibson telling him I was going off to have a rest and expected to be back next week. He responded instantly that that was fine with him.

Jazz and my mother would both require phone calls, but I knew they would be easily convinced that a good long rest would do me good.

I called my mother first since she'd be the hardest sell. I caught her on her way out the door to her bunco group.

"Everything okay, darling?" she asked.

"Yep. I just wanted to tell you I've decided to do a week at Skidaway tomorrow. It's like a spa type retreat."

"Oh, darling, that's wonderful! Although personally, I don't think you're a bit overweight."

"It's not that kind of retreat, Mom," I said. "But there's no cellphones or contact of any kind from the outside world. Just reading and nature walks."

"Well, it sounds perfect, dear. Let me know when you get back."

"Will do," I said. "Love you."

"Love you, too, sugar."

After that, the rest was easy. I emailed Jazz what I was doing, and she called me instantly for the details. But she was a good friend and if I said I needed this, she was on board.

"You'll call as soon as you get back home?"

"I will," I promised, wondering for the first time if any of this was going to work out such that I actually did get back home.

I quickly chased my doubts and fears from my mind. I'd cleared the runway for takeoff. Nobody will be freaking out if they don't see me for a couple of weeks. I'd worry about getting home later. One step at a time.

First, I needed to scrape together the tools I would need to solve the crime. Then, I had to figure out how to go back —if it was even possible.

I didn't own a gun, so I didn't have to worry about that, but I did have a Taser, so I packed it with four darts and a charger. 1923 wasn't big on electricity but some places had it —including Mary's house.

I knew I wanted to bring a medical kit with antiseptic, painkillers and a round of antibiotics. Fortunately, I had an unfilled script for amoxicillin, which is pretty mild, but I figured in a world that had no antibacterial resources whatsoever, it would be a super drug. I was hoping so anyway, for Anna Wilkins' sake.

I found a set of walkie talkies, put new batteries in them, a set of binoculars with night vision capability, and a pair of UV sunglasses. And of course, my cellphone. I knew it would be useless except for its flashlight, audio and video recording capabilities, and camera function. I brought a charger with me and researched online any adaptor I might need for 1923, then I found a cellphone store on Bay Street that sold odd adaptors. The worst that would happen would be that I'd fry my cellphone. I'd take the chance.

I ordered a selection of adaptors from Amazon that might work and could do overnight delivery. The rest of the stuff I was able to pick up around town. I'd already dropped off my dress at the one-hour dry cleaning so that was ready. I went to the DWS store on West Oglethorpe and found a pair of leather shoes that looked the part but that fit me better.

The last things I ordered on Amazon were a dozen battery-powered fans. 1923 Savannah without air conditioning was boiling hot.

I sat in my apartment with my purchases and items I was bringing back with me in a large newsboy bag that I thought would fit in back then.

Now came the hard part.

I had a general idea of how I was going to do this—but it terrified me even to think of it. So I dedicated this night to research on other ways—any other way—imaginable.

I spent the entire night on the Internet poring over ancient texts, obscure quantum theories, and some very peculiar hypotheses from fringe theorists without any formal training in physics or mathematics. The key seemed to be a combination of several ingredients that on their own were useless but when mixed properly would create an energy field capable of warping the space-time continuum.

I knew none of it would work. At least not without a lab and a few hundred quantum physicists working full time to try to create it. The fact was, if there *was* a formula for time travel, wouldn't I have heard of it? Wouldn't it have been mentioned on social media?

I closed my laptop, discouraged but satisfied that I had at least done my due diligence, I had tried every way imaginable before approaching the only other way I knew that was remotely open to me.

The way that scared me to death.

I stood up and shook out the pins and needles in my arms and feet and was instantly gripped by a sudden urgency. I knew that Henry Pickett's days were numbered. I'd dearly have preferred getting one last good night's sleep in air conditioning before I went back. But I reminded myself that Henry didn't have air conditioning. And when

I put it like that, I wasn't going to be able to enjoy it anyway.

I figured I'd go back to near the same spot where I'd "jumped" last time. Not that there was anything special about the location. But nighttime was key, even though it hadn't been dark last time because darkness was an element that tends to terrify me.

And terror *was* key.

Both times I'd "jumped" time locations, I'd been as afraid as I've ever been. I don't know what else was going on with me on a deeper psyche level, but that much I know.

So that was what I would need to utilize.

I dressed carefully in the outfit I'd brought back with me from 1923, now laundered and pressed, and put on my new shoes. My fingers trembled as I did up the buckles. I loaded up all my purchases in the newsboy bag which was much heavier than I'd expected. I gave my apartment one last look, turned off all the lights and locked the door behind me.

The streets of Savannah were cloaked in shadows, and a chill ran through my body as I walked to the western edge of town, an area that I know tends to be dangerous. The warm night air carried the aroma of fried fish, and the cobblestones echoed with the sound of my footsteps.

Like most towns, Savannah was a different creature after dark.

I spotted a narrow alley up ahead off to my right. I walked to it, the dim light of the streetlamp casting a faint glow in the deserted lane. The night air had a chill. I wrapped the shawl I'd brought tightly around me.

An eerie silence permeated through the cobbled streets. Streetlamps flickered and the shadows of the old buildings loomed in the darkness. I took in a breath to give myself

Killing Time in Georgia

courage and turned down an alley that appeared to stretch endlessly into a murky abyss.

I stood a few feet into the alley and shifted the weight of my bag on my shoulder. The problem was, without an assailant threatening me with my life, there was nothing inherent in these alleys that would help facilitate my return.

Both times before, my time jumps were triggered by extreme fear or trauma. So clearly *fear* was my ticket to ride. As I stood there, staring around the bleak, graffiti covered walls of the alley, it was not lost on me that the whole reason I couldn't make it as a cop was that I was too afraid of everything. Amazingly, it's that very fear that's the reason I'm able to time-travel.

I narrowed my eyes to see better and took a few more steps into the alley as I watched the shadows deepen. My stomach tightened. I was doing the most unnatural thing I could think of—deliberately going toward harm. The first rule they teach you in police academy: go toward harm. It was the main reason I washed out.

I tried to imagine what I could threaten myself with to trigger the time jump. The fact was, if I was going to do this, I had to put myself in real danger—not just a sham to trick my mind—but real peril. Otherwise, I'd know there was nothing really to fear.

As I stood there in that alley watching for any change in shadow or movement in my surroundings I drew on my imagination, envisioning the most horrifying scenarios I could think of that might be waiting for me in this alley. Then, after a deep breath, I began to walk further into its darkness.

I walked slowly, looking everywhere at once. But even in the dark, everything appeared benign and even pedestrian. I heard the sound of scratching further into the alley's deepest recesses. I saw something move in the shadows and I felt my heart begin to pound in my throat.

I stopped walking. I didn't have the nerve to keep going but I could at least force myself not to turn and run. I anchored myself to the spot and thought of Henry.

Slowly, a figure morphed out of the shadows by the wall. My heart nearly stopped, and visions flashed before my eyes —a man attacking me with a knife or dragging me away from the light and torturing me for days.

I swallowed hard and took a step forward into the abyss.

40

I stood nervously at the edge of the portal, looking around at the unfamiliar sights, sounds, and smells of 1920's Savannah. I could see the outline of a cobblestone road, lined with old wooden buildings. Lanterns flickered on each side of the road, casting a soft light over the street. I heard the chatter of people walking by, the clop of horse hooves, and the low chatter of voices from the nearby shops.

Dear God, I'm really back.

The man I'd met in the alley had dissolved back into the shadows as quickly as he'd appeared, leaving no trace but my terror behind. And my terror was all I needed.

I took a deep breath, trying to steady my nerves and pulled myself to my feet. I leaned against the alley wall for a moment, getting my bearings. It had felt different this time, like a sensation of a wave of energy passing over me.

I looked around at the buildings, noting their age and architecture. I smelled the aroma of roasted meats and baked pastries, nearby. I gave myself a little shake, reminding myself that the serial killer was still on the loose and I was standing in an alley in an unsafe section of town. In the middle of the night.

I picked up my bag of antibiotics and supplies and stepped out of the shadows at the exact moment a tall, dark shadow filled the alley entrance.

"So, what do we have here, little pigeon?" the man drawled nastily. "Out for a late-night stroll, are we?"

He was dressed in a pair of loose-fitting work jeans and a checkered shirt. The menacing look in his eyes sent chills of dread down my spine. He took a step towards me.

My first instinct was to run, but he was blocking the mouth of the alley. I didn't have time to dig out my Taser. He lunged at me, suddenly grabbing my arm and wrenching it behind me.

"What do you want?" I gasped between gritted teeth, trying to sound brave.

He leaned closer and whispered in my ear "What do you think?"

My heart raced as he tightened his grip on my arm so powerfully that tears sprang to my eyes. I could feel the cold metal object he was pressing against the small of my back – a knife - sending even more terror coursing through me.

"You there! What do you think you're doing?"

My attacker froze. I turned to see the burly form of a policeman standing at the mouth of the alley. All at once the man released his grip and ran off into the darkness leaving me shaken.

The cop marched towards me with determined steps, and I was astonished when he grabbed my arm.

"Hello, girly. Solicitation on these streets won't be tolerated! You'll be coming with me."

Shocked, I stumbled after him.

"I wasn't doing anything wrong, officer!"

The police officer's expression hardened as he glanced in the direction my assailant had gone.

"No? Then why are you here?"

He scrutinized me from head to toe with his flashlight. Now that he was closer, I noticed he wore a crisp navy-blue uniform with fancy brass buttons and an embroidered badge. His shoulder patches identified him as one of the local police on patrol. His dirty-blond hair was combed close to his scalp, and his sharp blue eyes glinted dangerously in the dim lighting.

I realized immediately that he had mistaken me for a prostitute. Instinctively, I reached out to explain myself but froze when he reached for the handcuffs hanging from his belt. I felt a rush of adrenaline course through my veins. With a desperate swing of my heavy bag, I caught him full in the face knocking him back on his heels.

I turned and sprinted down the alley in the same direction my attacker had gone, my heart pounding. The policeman's whistle pierced the air like a relentless siren behind me, heralding my escape and calling for assistance.

41

I ran.

I darted to the end of the alley, leaping over an overturned trashcan and raced to the only exit—into another darkened alley. I couldn't determine how close the policeman was behind me. He hadn't looked like much of a runner, and I prayed he wasn't.

I also prayed that my earlier assailant wasn't waiting for me somewhere in the shadowed corners of the alley. On impulse, I flattened myself in the dark recesses of the alley wall to try to take stock of the situation. Aside from the sound of my own panting, I heard nothing.

Had he given up?

I took off my shoes, hating to, but needing to. I didn't need the sound of me clomping down the cobblestone street alerting anyone else besides the two who were already after me. I stuffed the shoes into my bag, withdrew my Taser just in case, and readjusted the bag on my shoulder.

I crept silently from my hiding place and made my way to the street. I looked both ways before venturing out, the hissing of the streetlamps overhead provided a menacing soundtrack for my escape. There was a horse drawn wagon and a couple of cars on the street but not nearby. I glanced up at the street sign. East Gaston Street.

I felt a rush of relief.

I wasn't far from Mary's townhouse. Six blocks at most. I determined to stay in the shadows, ready to zap anybody foolish enough to interfere with me and set my sights on Drayton Street.

I arrived at the townhouse and stood for a moment breathless in the bushes by the door. I didn't think the cop knew who I was to track me here, but I was taking no chances. I secured the Taser back in my bag, put my shoes back on and knocked on the door.

Seamus answered the door and looked at me with surprise.

"Miss!" he said before letting me enter after a brief hesitation.

"Who is it, Seamus?" Mary called out.

"It's Miss Belle," Seamus said, reaching out for my bag which I did not allow him to take.

When I entered the parlor, Mary was already standing in the middle of the room with her hands balled into fists. She did not move to greet me as I placed my bag on a nearby chair. The fireplace was crackling, but her gaze was piercing enough to ice my very soul.

"Mary," I began, a little unnerved by the look on her face.

I'd left her at the hospital without a word and then disappeared for four days. She wanted answers, of course she did. And she deserved them.

"I'm so sorry for not telling you where I was going," I said. "But I suddenly remembered about my mother, and I went home to visit her. In Jacksonville."

I hated lying but what else could I do?

"I am so sorry," I said.

But she wasn't ready to listen.

"You cannot simply disappear like that!" She exclaimed loudly.

"Mary, please understand," I said, taking a step towards her in an attempt at closing the gap between us both physically as well as emotionally.

"My mother is older now and becomes ill often. She hadn't heard from me in three days. Of course, she was beside herself with worry."

Mary seemed to soften then but only slightly. She still had her arms crossed and there was still a hint of disappointment in her eyes. I needed to move her off her anger long enough to help Anna Wilkins.

"While I was gone," I said, "I went to Saint Augustine where there's a sort of shaman who has amazing restorative powders."

Now she was looking at me as if I'd lost my mind and I imagined I did sound nuts. But how else was I going to explain being able to save Anna from a fatal infection? Nobody in this time knew about antibiotics but everybody knew about home remedies.

"I would've gone straight to the hospital," I said. "But I wanted to relieve your mind as soon as I could. But now, please, Mary. I need to go to the hospital. I have a...an elixir that I think can help Anna Wilkins. Will you go with me?"

Mary stared at me and that's when I saw the last vestige of anger fade from her face. She returned to the couch and sat down.

"You look terrible," she said. "Have you been sleeping in those clothes?"

"Mary..." I approached her. "We need to act quickly if we—"

"Seamus, bring a tray of dinner up to Miss Georgia's room. She'll eat after she's had her bath."

"Mary!" I said firmly. "I don't have time for that!"

"Yes, you do," she said, her eyes sad.

I read her face.

"Oh, no," I said softly, feeling despair flood my body.

"I'm sorry, Georgia," she said. "Miss Wilkins survived the surgery but succumbed this morning to an infection the doctors were not able to stop."

I sagged into a chair, enveloped in a sudden, overwhelming emptiness. I slammed my fists against my knees in frustration. Anna would still be alive if I had only come sooner.

"You could have done nothing, Georgia," Mary said. "Regardless of your magic potions. The doctor said the infection was too powerful."

I swallowed hard. All I could see in my mind was Anna's heartbroken husband and parents. I shook the image away. It didn't help. My regrets didn't help them or Anna. What had happened was a mark of the times. Anna had always been slated for early death—as so many people were during this time.

"Go to bed, my dear," Mary said tiredly. "You look exhausted."

I nodded and found my feet.

"I'm sorry, Mary," I said. "For running off."

Before Mary could answer, my eyes fells on the open newspaper on the coffee table. The headline shouted out at me:

The Savannah Killer Strikes Again!

42

Between the news of Anna Wilkins and a third murder believed to be the work of the Savannah Killer, I had trouble sleeping that night. There was no time to waste in trying to work with the Savannah police to solve these murders. At least this had to mean that Henry Pickett would be released. That was something.

I waved off breakfast the next morning, to Mary's consternation. Ever since I'd disappeared out of the blue, she was understandably worried I might do it again. But on the other hand, she also seemed more confident that I could handle myself on my own too. I told her I needed to talk to the detective on the Savannah murder cases and she surprised me by offering to come too.

I was pleasantly surprised at that, but I had a feeling I needed to be on my own today. Not just because I had things to process but every time I behaved naturally or normally—for me—it ended up upsetting her in some way.

I grant you that anyone running up and down an antique shop aisle like a mad woman might be cause for consternation even in 2023, but I had other things I wanted to focus on today and I didn't need somebody observing me closely as I did.

I made my way to the Savannah police station on Oglethorpe. It was a brick building with large windows and ornate ironwork on them. It had a big wooden door that looked sturdy enough to withstand a battering ram.

I marched up to the reception desk and asked to see Detective Bohannon since I was almost positive that Detective Hawkins wouldn't see me. But also, because I wanted to see Sam. Much like the last time I was here, the station smelled like body odor, coffee, and cheap cigars.

One of the many things I'd done when I was home in 2023 was do a little research on the Savannah police department itself in 1923. I think the most astonishing thing I learned was the fact that the station I was standing in now had only been created twenty years earlier. Less surprising to me was its history of corruption and malfeasance.

As I made my way through the station to Sam's desk, I thought I felt a shift in the atmosphere. Everybody seemed to be on edge.

And why wouldn't they be? They thought they had their killer and then boom! another murder. I wondered if this might mean that Sam would be reinstated on the case.

I found his desk and he was waiting for me, his arms folded across his chest, his gaze piercing and angry.

His expression reminded me of that of an old soldier who has seen too many horrors in war—distant and vacant, yet vigilant for any sign of trouble that may arise.

He crossed his arms.

"Why are you here, Miss Belle?" he asked gruffly, a far cry from the friendly tone he'd always taken with me before.

"I need your help, Sam," I said.

"May I assume this visit means you have remembered something of your assault?"

It wasn't just his body language that gave away his displeasure; there was something in his eyes too, like he was disappointed in me.

I took the seat by his desk and primly crossed my ankles to wait him out. He deserved his pique, same as Mary. I could only imagine what must have been going through his mind during those four days I was gone - worry over my well-being, confusion over my continued seemingly unexplainable behavior, anger for leaving without so much as an explanation – all of it written plain on his face.

"I apologize," I said. "I can't imagine what you must think of me."

"You left without a word," he said.

The ache of sadness deep inside me intensified at the proof of the breach I'd created. We'd gotten close, Sam and me. Not secrets-sharing close, but we'd had a definite connection. I'd ruined that.

"I'm sorry. If I told you that it couldn't be helped, I'd hope you could believe me."

He frowned at my words. "Where did you go?"

"I remembered where my mother was. So I went to Jacksonville to see her."

His eyebrows shot up. "Jacksonville? How did you get there?"

I'd thought this part out ahead of time and was glad I had. As long as he didn't try to track my ticket stubs or anything, I should be safe.

"I took the Orange Blossom Special to Jacksonville," I said. "I don't need to tell you that my mother was beside herself with worry."

He softened then and grunted. "Of course. You could have called though."

"Except I never got your number. I'm sorry. I didn't think I'd be gone so long." I needed to move us off this and get to the point of why I was here.

"Sam, I think you and I need to work together on the Savannah Killer case. I read that there has been another murder."

His reaction to that sentence was hard to describe. On the one hand he looked gratified that I wanted any kind of relationship with him. On the other hand, he certainly couldn't take seriously the idea of working with me. And then there was the fact of the third murder.

"What can you tell me about it?" I asked.

His frown deepened.

"Nothing. As you know, I am not on the case."

He glanced in the direction of an open file folder on his desk that seemed to outline a series of snatch and grabs in the tourist district of town. Even I could see it was very rookie stuff.

I looked around the bull room. The attention I'd garnered when I entered had dissipated. Nobody was looking at us now.

"Can I ask if Henry Pickett has been released?" I asked.

"Pickett?" he asked. "No. Why would he be?"

I looked at him and blinked, completely flabbergasted.

"Because a third murder happened while he was in police custody," I said slowly.

"That doesn't mean he didn't kill the first two," Sam said. "Or attack you come to that."

I knew telling him that I had not in fact been attacked would only distract from the bigger point—that a man arrested as a serial killer who didn't kill the last victim might not be the right suspect. I took in a breath and tried again.

"Sam, I fear the trajectory of Detective Hawkins's case is going off the rails."

"I have no idea what you just said."

"I mean, Detective Hawkins doesn't seem interested in finding any real evidence in order to track down the person actually involved in these murders!"

"Look, Miss Belle," Sam said stiffly. "I understand you didn't get on with Detective Hawkins and I don't blame you. The man is rough trade. But I cannot listen to this when I know the difference between a real murder investigation and a novel by some obscure English author."

"Do you?" I asked, knowing I wasn't helping my case but not being to help myself either. "Do you, really? Because even in a novel, there are plot holes that need to be plugged or the story won't make sense. Can you tell me what part of *this* story makes sense?"

Sam stood up.

"I'm sorry, Miss Belle," he said formally. "I'll walk you to the exit."

I stood up too.

"Sam, listen, please. Work with me. I have some ideas. Ideas based on real investigative principles. Do you *want* Savannah to be the nation's laughingstock?"

I seriously don't know why I kept saying things that were guaranteed to piss him off and ensure he wouldn't want to work with me.

"Well, we will just have to hope for the best," he said, his anger seething behind his words.

"Is that the Savannah police department's motto now?" I said as I allowed him to lead me though the room of now openly gawking detectives to the exit.

"Goodbye, Miss Belle," he said between gritted teeth as he prodded me into the waiting room and then turned on his heel and disappeared back into the bull room, the door slamming shut behind him.

I stood in the waiting room, my chest heaving with indignation and disappointment, close to tears and furious at myself. I couldn't understand why Henry Pickett wasn't being released immediately.

For a moment it occurred to me to ask to see him as a visitor. Perhaps I could give him some hope that the whole world was not against him. But I quickly abandoned the idea.

I was pretty sure a white woman visiting him in jail would go a long way to making things even worse for him than they were right now.

43

Outside the police station, a cooling drizzle fell and pooled over the cobblestones. The air smelled metallic and sweet to me, like fresh asphalt in a new parking lot.

I decided that if Sam was content to take witness statements for victims of pickpockets on Bay Street, then fine. It had been asking a lot to imagine he would partner up with me and do some real detective work.

I would just need to do it on my own.

I walked west on East Oglethorpe. In the course of my research on the Spinelli family, I'd found property tax records that gave dates and addresses that I'd then printed out. I couldn't imagine what anyone might think if they were to find these documents on me—they were dated April 2023—but they were going to help me find Mario Spinelli.

Oglethorpe turned into West Oglethorpe and then diffused into a series of roads that I'm not sure even existed in my own time. I turned south on West Turner Boulevard until I hit Louisville Road and saw a giant mansion on the street that matched the address I'd discovered. My research told me that the structure was a warren of several apartments shared by the Spinelli family.

I considered knocking on the front door for about a half minute, but figured there would likely be significant security that I didn't want to deal with. After living with Mary, it occurred to me that many of these big houses afforded easy access through their gardens.

I walked down the block keeping my eye on the trees over the tall brick wall that seemed to demarcate the grounds of Mario Spinelli's main house. And because every garden needs a way for wheelbarrow refuse to get in and out, I soon came to the wooden door in the wall that was my way in.

The garden was unkempt and wild with no visible effort to keep the weeds at bay. Even so, the sun shone on the chaotic beauty creating a picture of messy blooms and ferns. Among the wildflowers was none other than Mario Spinelli himself—a heavy-set middle-aged man—sitting in an Adirondack chair smoking a cigar.

With a deep breath, I stepped inside the garden. Immediately a young man I hadn't seen before materialized to my right. His face was hard as he narrowed his eyes at me.

"Stop," he said calmly.

Mario turned his head to see what was going on.

"Mr. Spinelli," I said to him. "I need to talk with you. I am not armed."

I wished I was. Why hadn't I thought to bring my Taser?

Mario turned in his chair to look at me and then waved his man away. He motioned for me to sit in the chair opposite him. I came over to stand in front of him.

"I know you lied in your eyewitness statement about my assault," I said. "I'm just here to ask why."

Mario leaned back in his chair with a look of amusement on his face.

"Is that so?"

"There was no assault that day," I continued, feeling a little braver but still on guard being in the presence of a powerful syndicate boss. "But for some reason, you said there was."

Up until this moment, I'd only guessed—because of the Lydia Bartram connection—that the mysterious Mr. Havington and Mario Spinelli were likely one in the same. It made sense if Lydia Bartram was his sister-in-law that he might be in her company that day.

The question I needed answered before I left today was, *why was he in her company?*

"Why did you say you saw an assailant?" I asked. "My guess is you saw me faint. I woke up and started yelling and so you had to improvise."

Mario raised an eyebrow but did not seem at all disturbed by my accusation. Instead, he leaned back in his chair with a smirk on his face.

"So, what if I did?"

I shook my head at his nonchalant attitude.

"You gave a false testimony to the police," I said. "Worse, you dishonestly identified yourself."

"Is there a question in there?" he asked, propping an elbow on the arm rest of his chair.

"No, just a need for clarification," I said. "Will you admit you were with your sister-in-law Lydia Bartram?"

"I admit it."

I was surprised he would admit it so freely. But it gave me the courage to press further.

"My source tells me Miss Bartram is more than a sister-in-law to you," I said.

I had no such source of course. I was trying to wipe that smile off his face at the same time I got some confirmation.

And boy did I get it.

Mario sat stock still, his face suddenly rigid with fury and indignation. His mouth was clamped shut in a tight line. He looked at me, and his eyes were stone hard.

"My wife Mable is ill," he said. "She suffers from a nervous condition that makes her... unable to perform as a proper wife. She doesn't live with me."

I wondered if where Mable lived was more along the lines of an institution. I decided that was probably better than the alternative or wherever it was where old mafia don's wives go when they're no longer useful.

"You found my driver's license," I said.

He frowned in confusion.

"Your what?"

"It's a small, laminated card. I'm sure I had it with me when I...fainted. You must have taken it. You or Miss Bartram."

"Ah, yes." He nodded. "Was that yours?"

"Well, since you found it next to my body, let's assume it was mine. You took it, didn't you?"

"I found it in the street," he said with a shrug. "I gave it to my little brother as a fun oddity, thinking he might like to keep it in his collection of bizarre artifacts. But Davey wasn't comfortable with the idea that it was connected to a violent attack. So he handed it in to the police."

I watched his face and felt he was telling the truth. There was no reason for him to lie at this point. I'd already made up my mind that he and Lydia Bartram had taken the license and probably my cell phone too.

At least the mystery of the drivers license was solved. The only possible fly in the ointment at this point was not had he been trying to rob me when I collapsed?—because clearly he had. No, the ointment spoiler was in fact the nebulous feeling that had been nagging at me ever since I'd entered his garden.

And that feeling was the result of the moment when I recognized the powerful stench of Mario's lemony aftershave.

The one that perfectly matched that of the man who'd snatched my purse in the alley four days ago.

44

My visit with Mario Spinelli came to an abrupt end after that when the young man who'd confronted me when I entered the garden appeared again to escort me out of it. I never saw the sleight of hand from Mario that called his goon over, but I was ushered out of the garden nearly faster than I could walk. When I was once more on the other side of the wall, I heard the sound of the gate latch being thrown.

I turned to walk down the street to try to digest all that I'd learned from the family crime head.

Once I recognized his scent as being the same as the man who'd accosted me, I realized that he of course knew exactly who I was. He must have gotten a private laugh out of the fact that I didn't seem to know that it was *he* who'd snatched my purse. That of course mattered less than the fact that I now could either view Mario as innocent of the Savannah Killings—since he didn't kill me when he had the chance—or I could keep him on my suspects list believing that since I'd vanished in front of his eyes when he attacked me, it meant he just hadn't gotten the chance to slit my throat.

In any case, I couldn't eliminate him from my list of possible suspects. As I walked away, I did consider it very odd that the head of a crime syndicate would be doing his own purse snatching but I filed that away in the back of my brain to deal with later.

I had enough on my plate for the moment.

After walking for several minutes, I found a comfortable bench near the Harper-Fowlkes House not far from Pulaski Square which was a favorite place of mine in 2023. I was happy to get off my feet. My new shoes were a definite improvement over the old pair, but they were still dress shoes and not great for all the walking I was doing.

I was enjoying the feel of the midday sun on my face when I looked up and saw none other than Lydia Bartram striding down the sidewalk opposite the square. She was wearing a flowing dress that twirled around her as she walked. Her honey brown hair hung in waves to her shoulders, topped off with what looked like a velveteen cap.

She glanced at me as she neared but I could tell she didn't recognize me. I was on my feet and hurried to block her way on the sidewalk.

"Good afternoon, Miss Bartram," I said. "Fancy running into you here."

Lydia's face twisted in confusion, her lip curling.

"Get out of my way," she said. "I don't know you."

"Maybe you don't know me with my eyes open," I said. "I was the unconscious body you told the police had been attacked in an alley a week ago."

"What are you talking about?"

But I could tell she knew me now. I met her gaze with an even stare.

"I'm talking about your attempt to rob me when I was unconscious in the alley," I said.

For a moment, Lydia seemed to waver under my gaze, but then her expression hardened again, and she squared her shoulders.

"You're crazy," she said.

"Well, your boyfriend Mario Spinelli just admitted it, so I'm not that crazy."

"Now I know you're lying," she said, but I saw a flash of fear pass across her features.

"Which part? About him being your boyfriend? Mr. Spinelli confirmed that too," I said.

Of course, he hadn't really. But she didn't know that.

"Does your sister Mable know about you two?" I asked.

Lydia crossed her arms defensively, her face contorted in rage.

"What do you want from me?" she snarled.

"Just an answer to a simple question. That way I don't have to go to the police to say you lied about what you saw. That's a crime, you know, lying to the police. I'm surprised Mario didn't mention that to you. A crime with prison time attached to it."

Lydia clenched her jaw.

"Ask your question. But then I'd lock your doors if I were you. Once I tell Mr. Spinelli about this disrespect, your life won't be safe anywhere."

I knew it was just a boastful threat, but I still felt shivers rattle through my body.

"You gave a statement to the police that you saw Henry Pickett leave the alley where I was attacked."

"So?"

"So, he could go to prison based on your word alone."

"Well, maybe he'll think twice next time someone asks

him to move his wheelbarrow off the sidewalk when he sees them coming."

I literally could not believe what I was hearing.

"You...you...implicated Henry Picket in my assault because he didn't move his wheelbarrow out of the way for you?"

"You must be new here, Miss," Lydia said with a sniff, pushing past me on the sidewalk. "Because if a Negro blocking the path of a white woman isn't a crime in Savannah, I do not know what is."

I watched her leave, her head held high, her shoulders haughty and proud. Lydia Bartram was the very picture of someone who would happily hang a man for spite.

45

After that, I was ready to go home and call it a day. I'd had just about the most unproductive, ineffective day imaginable. I'd literally risked my life—twice—to get information that I was almost certain would do me—or Henry Pickett—no good whatsoever.

As I walked back to Mary's I noticed the sun had edged downward toward the horizon and I was shocked that the day was nearly over. Plus, I'd skipped breakfast and forgotten to eat lunch. I was feeling lightheaded as I made my way down Whitaker Street.

Suddenly, my stomach tightened at the sight of the man waiting for me on the street corner before I recognized it was Sam Bohannon.

"Fancy meeting you here," I said, guardedly as I approached.

"Got a minute?" he asked, nodding toward the square ahead of us.

We walked across the street to a bench that faced the Sorrel Weed House. It's beautiful any time of day but maybe even more so as the sun was fading, casting a dying glow against its beautiful Victorian facade. Of course, it's supposed to be desperately haunted.

As we sat, Sam pulled out a flask and offered it to me. This was a surprise since alcohol was illegal at this time, but I readily accepted it. The liquid that coursed down my throat was harsh and I did end up coughing which for some reason, seemed to relax Sam. I suppose I've been acting so odd compared with most women in this time period that it was reassuring to him to have me act normal for a change.

"Look, I'm sorry about back there," he said. "At the station."

"You were angry," I said. "You were entirely within your rights."

"I don't know if I was," he said. "I do know it was terribly ungentlemanly."

"Well, it's fine," I said. "Consider it forgotten."

"I told you I fought at Verdun," he said suddenly.

I felt a surge of relief that he was sharing this with me. I held my breath, praying that he would continue.

"Before the war, I was in veterinary school," he said. "I had an idea of how my life would play out."

"How?" I asked.

He was silent for a few moments.

"I grew up on a farm in South Georgia," he said. "We had horses and I always loved working with them, riding them. To me there are few creatures on earth more beautiful."

I could tell by the way Sam talked, he was beginning to connect with me again, despite whatever had happened while I was gone. His face lit up when he spoke of horses and it made me so happy to see it; to get a glimpse into who he'd been before the war.

"My grandfather told me when I went to France that a

passion like I had would always stay with me. It was the reason I decided to go to veterinary school when the war ended."

"Your grandfather sounds like a wise man."

He nodded.

"He was. And he was right that my passion for horses would save me. It kept me sane during the darkest days at Verdun. When I thought I would lose my mind, I'd remember riding with my brothers on the farm in summer. Even in the killing fields of France I could feel the Georgia sun beating down on me. We'd race to the old pond and swim. Perfect summers."

He looked out over the square, seeing the years unfold in his mind.

"I think in some ways those memories helped me survive the war. I know that sounds mad."

"Not at all," I murmured.

I watched how the memory of those boyhood summers made his face relax, like a beacon of hope amidst all that darkness he had experienced during battle. The memories were something good and pure, untouched by the horrors he had seen.

"It wasn't until I came back," he said solemnly, "that I realized that everything had gone wrong in the world. Things that were supposed to be sweet were acrid and rotting."

He shuddered and let out a deep sigh before continuing,

"But after I saw what I saw in the war, after a while, I couldn't get back to the place where I'd been before," he said. "When I came home, going to school felt like a waste of time."

My heart ached for him because of all the violence he

had seen in war, leaving him unable to pursue what once made him feel alive.

"You know Sam," I said, placing my hand over his, "I think helping animals is still one of the purest forms of love there is."

He looked at me in surprise and then let out a soft chuckle.

"Yeah," he said calmly, finally smiling again, the sadness seeming to fade from his face. "Maybe."

I felt terrible for him, but I also found myself moved by something in his affect that seemed to retain a shard of hope despite all the cruelty he witnessed. I took his hand in mine.

I was so sad for him, not just because of what he'd experience in the war, but also because of the incredible life-altering hardship it had created for him afterwards. Here was this man who had gone through unspeakable horrors, yet despite it all had kept a good heart. I could never imagine what it must have taken for him to live each day with these demons haunting him still.

"Your brothers?"

He stood up as if to stretch his legs.

"Both killed in the war," he said. "Shall we walk on?"

It was fully dark by the time we reached Mary's townhouse. I was grateful for his company, especially after dark. I hadn't felt so vulnerable right after talking to Mario. But once Lydia Bartram threatened me, I began to be more aware of how dangerous it was for me to be out after dark.

After Sam had revealed so much to me about his past, I hated keeping the kinds of secrets I had from him. At the very least I wanted to tell him that I was never attacked.

Unfortunately, I'd have to lie about suddenly remembering that fact, so I wasn't sure the lie didn't cancel out the truth-telling.

I hoped he might come in for a nightcap, but it was clear he was ready to be alone. He nodded goodbye to me on Mary's threshold, and waited for me to step inside, before turning and disappearing down the dark street.

As I watched him go, I couldn't help but wonder what kind of real intimacy was possible when one person had to keep the biggest secret of her life from the man she was beginning to care about—or risk being committed to a nineteenth century insane asylum?

46

Dinner that evening with Mary was such a comfortable affair that it wasn't until I was upstairs in bed that I realized I'd become so accustomed to having her to talk with. I didn't tell her the full content of what Sam had shared with me—I was pretty sure that was private—but I did relate how it had made me feel to be with him. A diary just doesn't cut it when you're trying to decipher the actions and feelings of a new man in your life. Sometimes, you just need to talk to your BFF.

As I snuggled down into the comfortable bedding, I felt the trials of the day finally fade away. I hadn't yet started feeling guilty about eating Mary's food and sleeping in her guest room without paying rent, because I was confident I was going back to my own century soon.

Although that of course just triggered a whole different feeling of guilt.

The next morning, I made a point of having breakfast with Mary because I saw how rude it was for me to have dashed off the day before. Plus, I ended up nearly fainting for lack of food.

The weather was dampish this morning, so breakfast was set at the big dining room table. There were only two place settings and Seamus had put a fire in the hearth in the room. The scent of bacon, fresh brewed coffee and baking bread hung in the air as I took my seat opposite Mary.

"Did you sleep well?" she asked, putting her linen napkin across her lap.

"I did, thank you," I said. "Wow, this looks amazing."

"What are you plans for today?" she asked as she spooned scrambled eggs onto her plate. "I was thinking of going to the hospital again if you think you'd be interested."

I hesitated. I did want to go. If for no other reason, than to locate some poor soul who might benefit from the antibiotics I'd brought with me. But I was worried about my progress on the Savannah killings.

I didn't know when that mob was coming for Henry. But I knew they were coming.

"Can I take a raincheck?" I asked. "I've got an errand I want to run this morning."

"An errand?" She poured cream in her coffee cup but didn't look at me.

I hated lying to her. But where I intended to go today, she definitely could not go.

I was headed to a section of Savannah that wasn't a nice place to go even in 2023. I had no doubt it would be a hundred times worse in this year.

"How about this afternoon?" I asked. "Can you delay your visit until then?"

"I suppose so."

After that we talked about the weather. She knew I was going someplace I preferred to keep secret. And I knew she thought that meant I didn't trust her. The weather was a safe topic for both of us at the moment.

I knew from my online research that Savannah in the 1920s was a combination of squalor and wealth. The further one ventured from the ornate buildings of the city center, the more destitute the landscape became. On the outskirts of town, there were shacks made of scrap wood, leaning precariously in all directions, as if barely holding their shape together.

The neighborhood I'd taken the taxi to after breakfast was a rough one. As I paid the driver—with money I'd borrowed from Mary—and stepped out onto the sidewalk, I saw homes with splintered, sinking porches and dwellings leaning against each other as if for support. The street itself was lined with garbage, some of it blowing in the breeze.

I didn't have the help of a property owner's database in my search to find Mercy O'Gillis's family. But a quick trip to the Savannah Historical Society on West Gaston—an easy walk from Mary's townhouse—had proven immensely fruitful this morning. But my research allowed me to look up the name under marriages and births and then I found addresses. All of them were in the Tremont Park area. I didn't know whether the family still lived at any of these addresses, but it was a start.

It beat sitting home in Mary's parlor and praying things worked out for poor Henry Pickett.

I walked away from the historical society with three addresses—all on the same street. If none of them proved viable, I could start knocking on doors. It was a predominantly Irish neighborhood. Somebody would know where the O'Gillis's lived now.

Especially with the recent notoriety of Mercy's murder, I expected everyone knew the family.

The first address was on Hobson Avenue, and it was worse than I'd anticipated. The whole street was lined with unpainted shacks, some little more than wooden shells and others cobbled together from empty crates and scrap wood. One shed and a smaller shack shared the same corner. The former had no windows, and the latter was guarded by two feral dogs

Taking a deep breath, I went to the door of the smaller shack, and knocked. As I waited for someone to answer, I thought I could hear sounds of weeping coming from inside.

The door eventually creaked open, and an elderly man stood there. He had grey hair and sad eyes that told me everything I needed to know about what he was experiencing over his daughter's death.

"Hello, my name is Georgia Belle," I said. "I heard about what happened and I wanted to come and see if there was anything I could do to help."

He hesitated for a moment, then opened the door wider and stepped aside so I could enter.

"Come in," he said, his voice quivering slightly.

Inside the shack was filled with a mournful silence. Two young girls, wearing rags, clung to each other in the corner while an older woman—Mercy's mother I guessed—sat at a wooden table in the center of the room, her head in her hands. I sat down at the only other chair at the table.

"I didn't know Mercy," I said. "But I'd like to know more about her."

My words had the effect of watching a dying flower spring back into bloom. The old woman lifted her head and tears flowed freely down her face.

"Our Mercy weren't no tramp," one of the little girls said from the corner. "She was gonna be in the movies!"

"There, there," the old man said. "The lady don't want to hear about that."

"Yes, I do," I said. "I want to hear about anything you want to tell me."

"She loved music, our Mercy," the woman said, her eyes glowing as if remembering. "She played the viola, didn't she, John?"

"Like an angel," the man said. "She had such dreams. Dreams that would take her far from this place."

"Can you tell me," I asked hesitantly, "where Mercy was when she was attacked?"

I knew the answer to this but was hoping to get them talking and to expand on what they might know.

"She were killed in the garden at Savannah Hospital," the woman said. "She loved it there. She loved the peace."

She waved a hand to indicate the street outside.

"No flowers here. But there, she said she always felt like she were in heaven."

"And now she really is," one of the little sisters said softly.

As soon as they mentioned the hospital garden, my senses went on full alert. Yes, the garden was Henry's domain. It suddenly occurred to me it was also Gus Jones's.

I looked around the gloomy room and was surprised to see the walls covered with family photographs. This was a place of woe and mourning. But it had been a happy home not too long ago.

I listened attentively, offering words of encouragement here and there whenever appropriate - but mostly I just let them talk about their beloved lost daughter in whatever ways felt natural for them.

"Did she go to the garden often?" I asked.

"I know what you're thinking," Mr. O'Gillis said, his face creased with anger. "And for a long time, I couldn't believe it, could I, Edna?"

The woman shook her head.

"Believe what?" I asked.

"You know what they're saying about why she was in the garden? Girls! The other room!"

Both of the girls jumped up and ran from the room. I looked at Mr. and Mrs. O'Gillis. I was pretty sure I knew what they were going to tell me.

"Mercy brought in money that we needed," Mrs. O'Gillis said angrily. "You understand? Her sisters needed it! We needed it!"

I nodded. Mercy had been working as a prostitute. Old Mr. O'Gillis was staring down at his hands, still obviously ashamed of what Mercy had been driven to do to support the family.

"It were that dago bastard Spinelli," he muttered.

"Mercy worked for the Spinelli family?" I asked.

"Aye. They were to protect her, weren't they?"

I licked my lips. My research back in 2023 had told me that the Spinelli family was into prostitution and bootleg liquor. Drugs had yet to trump all other money-making vices in the South. I wanted to ask Mercy's parents if they thought one of her customers had killed her. But even I didn't have the words—or the nerve—for that.

"Like he killed her hisself," O'Gillis said bitterly. "Like he held the knife to her throat."

"Is...is that how she died?"

I hated asking the bereaved family these terrible questions. I felt a flinch of anger at Sam. I should be getting these answers from him.

"She...she had her throat cut," Mrs. O'Gillis said, her trembling hand going to her own throat as if imagining her darling girl's last moments.

"I'm so sorry," I said, feeling sick to my stomach at what these poor people were going through.

They offered me tea after that, but I couldn't imagine they had much to spare, so I declined. I wasn't sure I gave them much in the way of comfort, but I hope I did in some small measure, just letting them know that someone cared. As I stood up to make my departure, I went over to the wall of photographs.

I didn't need them to point her out to me. Mercy had to be the brunette teenager standing with her arms around her two little sisters, a smile on her face. The senselessness of such a vibrant life being cut down was overwhelming.

"She was killed because she were a dark-eyed beauty," O'Gillis murmured, harsh emotion in his shaking voice.

I did wonder what Alice Marshall and Julie Brown looked like when he said that. The fact is, most serial killers targeted their victims according to type and personal preference—regardless of what Ted Bundy did, who broke the serial killer mold in several unsavory ways.

Generally, serial killers were appallingly predictable when it came to choosing their next victim. And unless they were after brunettes of a certain size, being a beauty, dark-eyed or not, mattered not one whit to them.

47

I walked away from the O'Gillis home feeling sad and frustrated. I wasn't sure what to do with the information I'd gotten from Mercy's family. I wasn't surprised to see they were ashamed of her, but neither did they believe she deserved what she got.

I was surprised to see by the sun beginning its way downward in the sky, casting a warm orange light over the patch of green that was the Savannah River, that I'd spent more time that I'd realized with the O'Gillis family. I'd wanted to hear their stories of Mercy and to get a sense of who she was in order to see if there was any key there to how she died. Time had gotten away from me and now I could see the cobblestone street was bathed in the changing hues and shadows of the day.

I expected I'd have trouble finding a cab in this section of town, so I walked quickly, keeping my situational awareness at a high pitch, until I began to see more tended plots of flowers along the walkway and fewer potholes in the street.

The scent of magnolias and honeysuckle hung heavily

in the air. As I walked, I heard laughter and music from the nearby pubs carried to me on the breeze, while the occasional horse and carriage clattered by. An old man sitting on a bench beneath an old oak tree tipped his hat as I passed.

I felt relief to be in a less dangerous neighborhood when I suddenly realized that I was very close to the Spinelli compound. My 2023 research had revealed that Lydia Bartram lived in an apartment within the compound. I felt a flutter of nerves as I realized what I was thinking about doing. My brief interview with Lydia Bartram had been frustrating and had borne little fruit but perhaps a visit to her house—*without her in it*—would prove more helpful?

It was a terrifying notion. If I was caught by one of her family, I'd probably end up wearing cement pantaloons at the bottom of the Savannah River. On the other hand, if Lydia were to call the police on me, I'd just die a lot slower death in the bowels of some horrible women's prison somewhere in the county.

I walked quickly because somewhere in the back of my mind I'd made up my mind. I had no leads and only clues that confused me without clarifying anything. If I could just have five minutes inside the Spinelli lair, I might find something that could generate a lead.

The section of the compound where I'd found Mario the day before was a half block from where I was. I didn't necessarily need to break into Lydia's apartment—I just needed to make sure I didn't break into Mario's. Once inside, I could find my way to where I needed to go.

The house was two stories high with a front porch that faced the street. A black lawn hose lay coiled on the white concrete porch. There was a bay window on one side and two French doors on the other. Big leafy trees anchored the front yard.

Two small iron balconies with elaborate scrollwork were set into the second floor, facing the street.

I wasn't stupid enough to try to break in with my back to the street. Glancing in all directions, I slipped into the bushes that hugged the side of the house and headed for the back garden, assuming that most security efforts would be concentrated on the front.

I crept silently through the garden. It was hot and unless one of the family was out sunbathing—not likely—I didn't expect to meet anyone. Most people in Savannah in 1923—unless they were laborers—retired to the cooler recesses of their homes in midday. I knew there was a chance of running into servants, but most people of that class could be bullied or convinced that you belonged there if you acted like you did.

Somehow Lydia didn't strike me as a person who'd welcome having too many prying eyes and ears of servants around her.

I made it through the garden to the back of the house, my heart pounding and my palms sweating. A stroke of luck for me—the French doors off the garden were unlocked. I eased them open and slipped inside. The floors in the back foyer were made of glossy cherry wood and were accented by the soft glow cast by the overhead crystal chandelier.

I moved quickly down the hall to where I imagined the bedrooms might be. My heart pounded so hard the sound seemed to echo in my ears.

The first bedroom I came to was drenched in light. Motes of dust swam lazily in the air and a light breeze fluttered through the curtains at the open window.

It was definitely a woman's bedroom. On the dressing-table, there were trinkets and containers of varying sizes filled with perfumes and cosmetics. I spotted some earrings I'd seen Lydia wear the last time we met. I could almost see her reflected in the many mirrors before me, a hint of a smile playing across her lips as she inspected herself for any flaws.

My gaze shifted to the wardrobe where an array of dresses hung from hooks like ghosts silently watching me as I searched for any clues that might give me a lead. I opened every drawer but all I found were stockings and lingerie.

Then my eyes went to her nightstand where a jewelry box peeked out from under some papers. I pulled the box to me and opened it. Inside, was a tangle of gold and pearl necklaces and a few rings with semi-precious stones.

I picked up the tangle of gold chains gently between my trembling fingertips and stared at the object in the center of them.

It was the locket on the woman in the painting.

48

I stood in the bedroom staring at the locket in my hand as my mind tried to process what I was seeing. It felt as if the hairs on the back of my neck were standing at attention. Before I could decide what it meant—or even if it was the same locket—I heard footsteps in the hallway.

I jammed the locket into my dress pocket and whirled around to bolt out the door when a slight, dark-haired boy filled the doorway, his eyes wide at the sight of me.

I immediately recognized the resemblance to Mario and realized this must be Davey Spinelli, Mario's younger brother.

"I'm sorry?" he said as if it was his fault I was in his family's house—and his aunt's bedroom.

"Yes, hello," I said breathlessly, my mind racing to come up with a reason for why I was here. "Davey, isn't it?"

He looked around the room, taking in the open jewelry box on the bed, and then back at me. The expression on his face didn't register any emotion that I could discern beyond faint confusion.

"Your aunt and I were having tea when she had to leave abruptly."

"Oh," he said, nodding as if that were perfectly plausible.

"And I was just...powdering my nose before I left."

I didn't know if *nose powdering* was a euphemism for using the bathroom, but it seemed to suffice. Davey nodded again and even half smiled at me. I moved past him in the doorway and noticed he was holding a textbook.

"What are you studying?" I asked nonchalantly as I moved down the hall toward the front door, already realizing that going the way I came was not going to work.

"Medicine."

"You want to be a doctor?"

I don't know why that surprised me. It seemed so nonself-serving for a member of the Spinelli family. He seemed to read my mind.

"I'm not like my family," he said. "Or at least, I don't want to be like them."

This is why you can't just spray the whole hornets' nest, I thought. *There's always one good one in there who doesn't deserve to go down with the rest.*

"What does your family feel about that?"

"Well, they're paying my tuition," he admitted. "But I'm determined to dedicate my life to erasing what they did."

At least they weren't pressing him to go into the family business. Still, belonging to a renowned crime factory was a pretty big Albatross around your neck. As he walked me to the front door, I was tempted to ask him about the locket, but then I would have to admit I'd taken it from his aunt's bedroom and in the end, I figured he had enough on his plate without having to defend or betray his family on top of it.

I said goodbye to him on the porch and hurried down the steps and onto Cornwall Street, relieved to have gotten out without the aforementioned cement pantaloons. As I walked away, my mind was divided. On the one hand I was in no hurry to go back to Mary's house—especially since I still did not have anything that remotely looked like a clue or lead that could help prove Henry Pickett innocent.

Looking around, I recognized that I was near the speakeasy where the old man had told me about Lydia through the note a few days earlier, I thought it was worth the effort to see if he was around to be tapped for more information. I reminded myself that even back in my own time, true detection didn't tend to be done in the laboratory but out in the field. Shoe leather trumped forensics every time.

After scouring the block around the bar and the alley where my so-called assault had taken place, I found him sitting on a bench on Bull Street drinking out of a paper bag.

"Excuse me, sir," I said. "May I have a word?"

He looked up at me through rheumy eyes and blinked as if trying to place me. He had a week's beard stubbing his chin, his clothes were dirty and wrinkled. I could see that he wasn't quite as old as I'd thought at first. Just seriously down on his luck and heading toward drunkenness. His hands were grubby where he clutched the bag, his face scrunched in a frown. He opened the bag slowly, his eyes watching me the whole time, and took a long swig.

"You were there, weren't you?" I asked, sitting down beside him. "The day I was attacked."

He tapped his nose. "I seen it happen, didn't I?"

"Did you see me fall?"

He huffed. "You think I'm crazy."

"No, I don't. Tell me."

He leaned over conspiratorially, the blast of his breath nearly making me recoil.

"You just appeared. Poof! Out of nowhere."

I licked my lips as I realized what he was saying.

He saw me transport here from the future.

"And Mario? Did he see me, too?" I asked.

"He didn't see you go poof! He just saw you were suddenly there. He went to you."

"To see if I was all right?"

He snorted loudly.

"Is that what you think? He picked up the things you dropped. I saw that, too."

"So there was no assailant?"

"Huh?" He screwed up his face at my word.

"Nobody attacked me?"

"Nobody in this world, anyway."

I would allow that last bit to be the product of a man well on his way to a fully drunken state. But the rest of it made complete sense to me. Spinelli and Lydia saw me on the ground, they came over to see what they could find of value to steal from me. But I came to, so they sounded the alarm and said that I'd been attacked. It explained why my drivers license and phone had gone missing.

Spinelli and Lydia weren't witnesses to my assault.

They'd been trying to mug me.

"You don't want to hear about the other one?" the old fellow asked, frowning at me.

"What other one?"

"With the girl what got killed."

I stared at him. "What girl?"

He frowned as if trying to concentrate.

"Julie something?" he said.

I inched closer to him on the bench. Mercy had been killed in the hospital garden, and Alice walking home from the movies a block from the hospital. To make my burgeoning theory about Gus Jones work—that the killer liked to keep his kills within a certain radius of his lair—Julie's murder would have to be roughly in the same area.

"I knew her," he said. "Sweet lass. Working girl, but still."

That meant she was a prostitute, too.

I began to feel a throb of excitement. The third victim fit the pattern.

"Where?" I asked.

He frowned again and seemed to look out in the distance as if he could visualize the place.

"Calhoun Square?" he said. "In the alley there?"

I felt my heart rate speed up at his words.

Calhoun Square was close to the hospital!

"You saw him?" I asked.

"I seen him run out of the alley." He shook his head. "I went in straight after to see what made him run. I seen her lying there. Poor lass."

"Can you describe him?"

"Oh aye. I got a good look at him, didn't I?"

Later, after I left the old man, I made it as far as a block closer to Mary's townhouse before I had to find a bench to sit down again. What he had told me had seriously shocked me. It was not something I'd ever have guessed on my own. I definitely needed to calm down and try to make sense of what he'd told me.

Could it be? How possible was it? Did it mean he killed the others too?

I ran a hand over my face as if to assuage the effects of

the bombshell of the old man's revelation, of the terrible picture he'd described of the man he'd seen running from the alley where Julie Brown was slain.

Could he be wrong? Was he drunk at the time? But then how was he able to describe him so perfectly? No, there was no mistake. The person he'd described was not someone easily mistaken for anyone else.

It must be true.

I was so rattled by what he'd told me that I literally felt my knees go weak. I found my hand in my pocket touching the little locket like it was a sort of worry stone. I pulled it out to look at it, hoping to distract myself from the old man's indicting testimony when all of a sudden, the locket sprang open. I don't know why I didn't think to try to open it up before now.

Inside was a tiny black and white photograph. I tilted the locket in the light to see better.

My gasp caught in my throat as my mouth fell open.

The picture was of a young girl.

More precisely, me as a young girl.

49

ow can this be?
How can a locket which is well over a hundred years old have a picture of me in it?

I looked at the photo again. I realized that it wasn't a photograph but a very detailed likeness. But that was irrelevant. There was absolutely no doubt. It was me as a teenager.

Why did Lydia have a locket with a picture of me in it? Should I give it to Mary? Won't she ask me how I got it? She knows I have no money. The time when the painting was done was at least ten years from now. Maybe she won't recognize it because it hasn't been given to her yet?

I was frustrated and not sure of what to do with it.

Why is my picture in it?

I felt a strange mixture of apprehension, confusion and excitement. What was the significance of this locket? How did it come to have my picture in it?

Was I responsible for something that was yet to happen? Something that would bring this locket into my life?? Nothing made sense.

The background in the portrait looked vaguely familiar, but nothing jumped to mind as my having seen it before. This sketch had not been taken any time recently.

I held the locket in my hand. Why would Lydia Bartram have a locket with a likeness of me in it? Since when do pictures exist before the people they depict do?

More and more questions raced through my mind in a whirlwind. My future suddenly felt like a book with all of its pages written and bound together, but with no table of contents... except for whatever message this mysterious picture might tell me. And that I could not decipher. How could things be so connected across space and time without any explanation or logic?

Or at least none that I could figure out.

Was there any way that a picture of me as a teen could be connected to anything in this time? I ran my hands through my hair in frustration as I struggled to come up with an answer.

What if I gave the locket to Mary? Would she even know it was supposed to be hers? Would she recognize it even though the painting of her that I'd seen in 2023 was today at least ten years away from being completed?

I closed my eyes and forced myself to stop the barrage of questions for just a moment. I willed myself to experience nothingness for at least a full minute. When I opened my eyes I glanced back at my picture, my own eyes staring back up at me, and I quickly clicked the locket closed and shoved it into my pocket.

Enough! I can't solve every mystery that lands in my lap, and right now finding out the answer to a mysterious picture in a locket wasn't helping Henry Pickett to survive to next year.

I got up and began walking resolutely in the direction of

Mary's townhouse. I'd missed lunch again and nothing good ever came out of my brain when I was hungry. I would be in time for tea and Cook always had some kind of cake on hand to make sure that nobody fainted from lack of sugar. I could use a big slice of cake right about now, I thought.

I headed down East Harris toward Lafayette Square and Mary's townhouse, my mind still in a swirl of conflicting thoughts and ideas.

Why is it that the more I talk to people, the more I searched, the more clues and fragments I uncovered, the further from understanding what was happening I seemed to be?

The fact that Spinelli and Lydia appeared to be partners in crime fit a sort of picture but not the one I was trying to see. Their partnership didn't get me any closer to finding who killed Mercy O'Gillis and the others.

Something pinged in the back of my brain when I realized that. Something made me wonder to *whose* benefit it might be to distract the police from the real murders? Because describing my collapse in the alley as an *attack* only served Lydia and Spinelli, by shielding their true actions that day and by creating a smoke screen to divert and confuse the authorities.

Something about that thought intensified the pinging in my brain that told me I was onto something, but nothing would form beyond the annoying hum that told me there was *something* there if only I could identify it.

All three women were killed near the hospital. All three were prostitutes. It explained why they were out at night alone. But because I didn't know the details of their postmortems, I couldn't say how similar their manners of death were. Sam could tell me those details.

I felt a pulse of determination. I would ask him directly, and this time I would insist he tell me the truth.

I turned down the street that Mary's townhouse was on and did a quick check of my clothing and hair before going forward. I tended to forget I had a hat on and walking into the townhouse looking like I'd fought a wind tunnel and lost would only bring more unpleasant questions my way. And I could see that Mary was trying so hard to accept me as she found me.

I hurried down the street to her townhouse and climbed up the steps to the front door when suddenly a feeling of premonition grabbed me by the throat.

An uncomfortable tingling sensation rippled across my skin.

Something is happening inside.

I slowly pushed open the front door and found myself face to face with a man. His head and face were covered by a black mask.

He held a bloody knife in one hand.

50

My heart began to race as terror overcame me. I froze, unable to think or to act.

The man stared at me, his blue eyes searching mine behind the fabric covering his face. His gaze felt like he was trying to read my soul.

It sent shivers down my spine. I tried to think of a plan, but nothing came to me.

The man stepped forward and raised the bloody knife in the air.

My fear turned into a dull, immobilizing terror as I watched him slowly advance towards me, his weapon poised for striking. All fight drained from my body. All I could register was the sound of his footsteps.

He stopped a few feet away before finally lowering his arm again.

"You're late," he said, his voice high-pitched and shrill.

My fear seemed to crowd out all other emotions and conscious thought except one:

He's disguising his voice.

That thought was immediately followed by another:

He's someone I know.

With desperation quickly overtaking my brain, I frantically searched the foyer for anything I could use to defend myself with. A small glass ashtray on the hall table. A candlestick. A lightweight wooden box filled with mail.

"This is on your head, girlie," he said, his voice obscene and piercing. "Mark my words."

Gibberish words. Nonsense words. None of them made sense.

And that horrible unnatural intonation...

I licked my lips. The front door behind me was still open. But I couldn't turn. In the time I took to do it, he'd be on me, stabbing me in the back. No, I couldn't run.

If I lived to tell the tale, I'd say he was medium height. His hair and face were covered but his hands were large and gloved. Regardless of how he attempted to disguise his voice, he was definitely male.

"Afraid of a little mercy-killing?" he said, taking another step toward me. "Ring a bell? It Alice happens to me."

I swallowed hard. He was making puns about his victims.

"Been waiting for this," he said in that grating, unnatural voice. "Papers will need to print a public correction, won't they? Ring a bell?"

I saw his gloved hand twitch. It was the only warning I had before he made his move. I was already twisting away, reaching for the candlestick, praying it was heavy enough.

I grabbed it in one motion and brought it down on his outstretched forearm as he lunged for me. The knife flew out of his hand as his scream reverberated off the walls. He clutched his arm and turned toward me, eyes blazing with rage, his chest heaving as he searched the floor for his weapon.

I tightened my grip on the candlestick. It wasn't heavy enough to withstand another attack, but it was all I had.

Just then a door slammed somewhere in the lower level of the house. He hesitated only a moment before making up his mind and, cursing, he turned and bolted out the open door.

I raced to the door and slammed it shut, sliding the dead bolt against his return, my chest heaving with effort and emotion. I leaned against the door, feeling a cold sweat break out on my forehead as I gulped in deep breaths, my intense relief mingling with my still lingering terror. My eye fell on the glittering blade on the floor of the foyer.

Just looking at it I could almost feel it slicing into me. I had come within a hair's breadth of death. The realization weakened my knees, and I began to slump against the door to the floor.

That was the moment when I consciously saw the blood on it. I saw it just seconds before I heard the sound I should've heard before now.

A moan.

Terror stabbed into my gut.

Mary!

I pushed off the door and stumbled into the salon, looking everywhere at once, trying to hear the noise again over the pounding of my heartbeat thundering in my ears.

I found her behind the couch.

51

If Sam hadn't happened to hear the call come in from dispatch and recognized Mary Johnson's address, he wouldn't be here now. He'd been only seconds behind the responding officers and full minutes ahead of Detective Hawkins.

He found Georgia giving first aid to Mary whom he was sure at first was dead. When the ambulance arrived and took over, he led Georgia to a chair in the dining room. Mary's cook appeared, and he told her to make tea—milky and sweet—and bring any cake she had in the house.

"Enough for the coppers, sir?"

"No, just Miss Belle."

"Georgia," he said gently. "I'll be back in a moment. I need to call Miss Johnson's sister."

Georgia looked at him stricken.

"Yes, of course," she said. "I should've done that."

"Wait for me here, alright?"

She nodded, her eyes going to the salon where the medics were putting Mary on a gurney for the ride to the hospital which Sam took as a good sign. It meant she was still alive.

Hawkins showed up then, his eyes going all around the crime scene—which had now been well and truly trampled by no fewer than a half dozen people. It couldn't be helped, Sam knew, but that wouldn't placate Hawkins. He'd be furious.

Hawkins and his men had begun to process the scene, taking photographs, collecting samples and picking through the detritus for clues. A few men crouched by the sofa putting pillow cushions and ashtrays in plastic bags. As they worked, the detectives spoke in conversational tones to each other, their brows furrowed as they tried to find a picture that made sense of what had happened.

Sam went to the hallway and picked up the phone, quickly calling the Savannah Hospital and leaving a message for Sister Beatrice that her sister had had an accident and was coming in by ambulance. He came back into the salon and saw Hawkins standing over Georgia, his notebook out, his jaw set, stubborn, resolute. Sam wanted to support her, but he knew the sight of him might set Hawkins off. And that wouldn't help anyone.

"He thought I knew him," Georgia was saying. "He altered his voice."

"What did he look like?" Hawkins asked.

"I told you! He was medium height and masked."

"So you didn't see his face."

Georgia ran her hand through her hair in obvious frustration.

"No," she said tightly. "But I hit him on the forearm with the candlestick. Look for someone with a bruise."

"I thought you said he was wearing gloves."

"I didn't hit him on the hand. So, are you saying it's not worth checking?"

"I think you've read too many penny dreadfuls," Hawkins said. "Am I supposed to go around Savannah asking to see every medium-sized man's hand for a bruise?"

He snapped his notebook closed and glancing at Sam, rolled his eyes. It was clear he did not believe that Georgia had disarmed the man. Even Sam had to admit it was farfetched to think she had successfully defended herself against a maniacal killer.

"You can leave," Hawkins said to her. "You got someone to stay with?"

Georgia looked around, bewildered.

"She has a place," Sam said, as he walked into the room. "I'll escort her there."

Hawkins gave him a brief look and then turned away. Sam sat down next to Georgia, and she turned to him, the dazed expression in her eyes now replaced by an urgent vibrancy.

"Sam," she said, "the man disguised his voice. He knew I'd recognize him. It's someone I've met."

Sam had seen hysteria before. He knew the stages. He'd keep her calm. If she wanted to go to the hospital, he'd bring her. Otherwise, he'd need to find a place for her to stay.

"Are you hearing me?" she asked. "He admitted to killing Mercy O'Gillis. And Alice Marshall!"

That got his attention.

"Did you tell Detective Hawkins that?" he asked.

She snorted and glanced in the direction of the man who was now directing his men around the living room.

"What good would that do? I'm telling *you*, Sam."

He patted her hand and realized that the race to the house from the police station had gone a long way to calming his fears—that and seeing that she was unhurt—but he was still wrestling with how close today's tragedy could have been Georgia herself.

"Are you listening? I'm telling you he made a pun about their names! And mine! He was bragging about the killings."

"Maybe he read about them in the papers. All the names of the victims were listed there."

Georgia closed her eyes and pinched the bridge of her nose.

"Mine wasn't," she said in exasperation.

The air between them seemed to crackle with tension, as he watched her face heat up. She looked like a woman who was moments away from losing her temper.

"I'm telling you, he was *baiting* me, Sam. He knew all his victims. He *targeted* them. And today, he specifically came to Mary's house. Because he knew I was here."

"That makes no sense."

"Okay, let me ask you this," she said in frustration. "Julie Brown. Was she a prostitute?"

Sam felt actual goosebumps slicing the back of his neck at her words, her extraordinary confidence. If he had to describe her manner, he'd say she acted like a man.

"The Spinelli family makes their money from prostitution," she said. "Surely, you know this. Mercy was one of their girls. I talked to her family and even they know it. You have access to Julie Brown's file. You can find out if she was turning tricks too. Had she ever been arrested? Who posted her bail? Who paid for her lawyer? If it was someone connected to the Spinelli family, you'll know I was right."

Sam was overwhelmed with nearly every word out of her mouth, some vulgar and others just preposterous. And yet she was so passionate, so determined in her beliefs!

Suddenly Hawkins walked into the room, his face red

and contorted. Sam recognized it as the affect of a man frustrated by the lack of evidence and any useable witness testimonies. He'd already made up his mind that the case was unsolvable.

"Do I have to remind you, Bohannon, that you're not on this case anymore? For obvious reasons?"

Sam bristled at the insult. The whole department knew he'd been taken off the Savannah Killer's case for failing to make an arrest.

"I'm here in a personal capacity," Sam said. "The victim was an acquaintance of mine."

The big man snorted derisively.

"There's no way you knew Mary Thompson," he sneered.

"That's not true!" Georgia said to the detective indignantly. "Sam is a friend to both me and Mary!"

Sam quickly pulled her to her feet and prodded her toward the door before she had a chance to say any more to the detective. Just then the cook came back with a tray of tea. He watched two of the detectives come into the room and filch pieces of cake from the tray. Sam steered Georgia out the front door.

The only thing he could imagine was that it was Georgia's romantic nature that prompted her to talk about these ridiculous things—all due to her fascination with the novels that could very well get her killed!

He led her to the front steps of the house, his hand still on her arm. She tried to pull away once, but he was determined to be firmer with her—for her own good—and he held on tight. The last thing she needed to do was make an enemy of Hawkins. At the rate she was going, she'd end up in a jail cell before the day was out.

"You're not helping anyone," he said sternly to her. "Right now, you need to focus on Mary."

Georgia looked out the door where the ambulance had just pulled away from the curb on its way to the hospital.

"It's my fault," she said, despondently, her eyes filling with tears. "He was here for me."

At first Sam thought she was referring to Hawkins but the look on her face made it clear she was talking about the madman running around Savannah killing women.

For some crazy reason, she believed *she* was his intended victim. A nagging fear suddenly erupted in Sam's chest that told him she might be right.

52

The heat seemed to press on my face like a wool blanket. It seeped into everything, into the wooden walls and floor, into the chairs and benches of the hospital waiting room, and into the very marrow of the people sitting in it, absorbing it.

Three other people sat around me in the room, arms crossed, and heads bowed. It was a place of suffering and resilience, a place of hope and despair, and yet, somehow, a place of solace, too.

My stomach buckled as I remembered his voice. Why had I assumed he wouldn't sound like a monster? Like something out of a nightmare. It was unnatural. Like him.

I tried to imagine what might have happened if Cook hadn't slammed the door in the downstairs kitchen, making him decide to flee and fight another day.

I paced nervously in the waiting room, my worry and anxiety almost palpable in the air. I kept trying to calm my racing thoughts. Why hadn't I realized I'd put her in danger? How could I be so stupid?

My stomach growled angrily, but I couldn't bear the

thought of food. I turned to glance at Sam where he sat stoically in a chair by the wall, watching me in concern. I was sick about it all.

Not least of which was the fact that Sam didn't believe me when I told him what I knew about the man. So stubborn was his belief that women in his world were silly creatures incapable of logic that he couldn't stop for five seconds to really hear what I was telling him.

I turned away and stared out the window into the hot Savannah sky. But all I could see was that demon in Mary's living room. There was no doubt that he was trying to mask his voice, making it higher than it must naturally have been. He was worried I'd recognize his normal voice.

Who was he?

Of all the people I knew here in 1923 who I thought might fit the bill for attacking Mary—and be the serial murderer that all of Savannah sought—there were three possible candidates. All three fit the body type of the man I'd faced down in Mary's living room. All three had no alibi for the times in question. All three—from what little I knew of them—could easily fit the checklist of serial killer characteristics I'd brought back with me from 2023.

Lack of remorse.
Impulsivity.
The need to control.
Predatory behavior, manipulation.

Check, check, check and check.

I turned back to watch Sam as he returned from getting me a coffee. Now if I could just get this very stubborn man to work with me instead of continuing to believe I was crazy or a nuisance!

Sam handed me the coffee.

"The nurse said she'll be in surgery at least another hour," he said.

I nodded and then reached out for Sam's hand. I couldn't give up on him. He was all I had—heck, he was all Henry Pickett had, too. And truthfully, he was all the future female victims of Savannah had. I had to somehow convince him of what I knew.

"Can we get a breath of air?" I asked, setting the coffee down and standing up.

He stood up too, his face clearing and obviously pleased I wasn't pacing and glowering anymore. We made our way out of the waiting room down the hall, past the long stretch of patient wards.

Standing in the hall was Dr. Clay Ryan. He was laughing with a pretty nurse. He glanced at me as I passed and then turned away dismissively.

I saw the paperback book in his pocket again. Only this time, I was able to read the title.

Jack the Ripper.

53

We walked outside to the gardens that bordered East Huntington Street just past the entrance to the hospital. I felt an instant twist in my gut. These roses and tidy hedges were the result of the many hours Henry Pickett put into his job.

I went to a bench and sat down.

"Just let me say a few things," I said. "Then if you want to ignore my theories after that, I'll at least know I tried."

He sat down next to me. I could tell he was girding his loins for another screed from me on modern detective practices. One thing *that* told me was that he'd definitely forgiven me for running off before. It also told me he cared about me. I think I knew that before, but it was obvious now. I appreciated his giving me a chance to talk to him like this. I recognized it for the magnanimous, conciliatory gesture it was. Especially during this decade.

I picked my words carefully. One thing I knew from the little bit of research I'd done was that in many ways detective work in 2023 hadn't really changed all that much. Basic techniques such as interviewing witnesses and suspects, examining physical evidence, and reconstructing the crime scene were still the foundation for all crime investigations.

But with no surveillance, or DNA analysis—which in my day solves more than seventy percent of all crimes—most murders back in the twenties were simply never solved.

Or they were solved by laying the guilt at the feet of an innocent man.

"I need to tell you some things," I said. "And I need you to tell me some things, too."

He cocked his head. "Like what?"

"Well, I need you to tell me the details of Mercy and Alice and Julie's murders. What were the common points among them?"

He sighed heavily.

"You're not on the case anymore, Sam. I swear I won't tell anyone what you tell me."

He surveyed the garden intensely for a moment.

"All three were women of the night," he said, glancing at me to see how I reacted to that.

I nodded because of course I already knew that.

"All had been...interfered with." He didn't look at me when he said that. "And all had their throats slashed."

That I did not know.

"Serrated or scalpel?" I asked.

He blinked at me in surprise. "Scalpel."

"Same as Mary's assault."

"Except Miss Thompson is not...that is to say, she doesn't work as a...as a..."

"Yes, Sam, I know, of course. But don't you see? That's *not* a step away from this guy's MO. It's merely an inside joke on his part. An insulting joke, but a joke nonetheless."

He frowned as I prepared to explain to him in a simplified language that I thought he might understand.

"Look," I said. "The killer is aware that the police know he is raping and murdering prostitutes. To stab Mary—without raping her—is a message, don't you see? He's saying he groups Mary in with prostitutes. It's an insult. And because he didn't sexually assault her, he's delivering the further insult—in his mind—that he found her wanting."

Now, I know that rape has nothing to do with attractiveness or desire. It's a power thing. But I also believe this monster was delivering messages. Unfortunately, the Savannah police were struggling to decipher them.

"Bottom line. Mary was attacked because of me," I said.

"That's not true," he said.

"Okay, Sam, here's where you're going to have to be open-minded and really listen to what I have to say."

He nodded, still frowning. I'm not sure if he had a newfound respect for me or if he thought I was insane. Either way, he was watching me closely.

Here goes.

"I wasn't attacked in the alley last week."

His frown deepened. "You mean you weren't interfered with," he said, blushing.

"No, I mean, I wasn't attacked. At all. By anyone. I fainted. That's all."

"The doctor said you had amnesia. That you'd been hit on the head."

"Well, he's wrong," I said. *Or possibly lying.* "I might have hit my head when I fell, but I wasn't hit."

"You're not remembering correctly."

I knew he was going to have trouble with this next part, so I decided to just push on.

"In any case," I said, "when the two witnesses came forward—Havington and Lydia—and said that I'd been attacked, it was for two reasons. One, because they'd intended on robbing me when they saw me incapacitated but when I began yelling, they needed to pretend to have witnessed a man assault me."

Sam's eyebrows shot up and I realized he was seeing the possibility of what I was describing.

"And the second thing?" he asked.

"When the papers got a hold of the story of yet another victim—me, except I wasn't killed—the killer became enraged that it appeared to all and sundry like he had failed."

Sam's mouth fell open and his eyes looked out again at the garden. This time, I knew he was visualizing what I was saying. And it was making sense to him.

"He came after me today," I said, "to fix the problem. It was his reputation at stake. He even said to me: *the papers will have to publish a reprint* or something like that."

"You think he followed you to Mary Thompson's house?"

"No, because today, I wasn't there. But he has obviously followed me in the past. He knew where I was staying."

Sam was quiet and I dearly hoped he was taking it all in and giving at least some of it credence.

"We should get back," I said finally. "I want to be there when Mary gets out of surgery. If it weren't for me, she wouldn't be where she is now—fighting for her life."

"Don't be silly," he said, standing up. "Miss Thompson was injured because of a psychopathic murderer. It's actually *because* of you she's not dead."

"He was looking for *me*, Sam. Mary was hurt because she wasn't me."

"That makes no sense. The man broke in, saw Mary and attacked."

So, he wasn't buying my theory that the guy followed me. That it was the very fact that I'd *survived*—even though he never attacked me in the first place—that had galled him into coming to Mary's house.

"If you really believe that," I said, "then will Henry Pickett be released now?"

"No. Why?"

"Because he was in custody at the time of Mary's assault! *And* Julie Brown's for that matter. And since I was never attacked at all, he certainly can't be charged with attacking *me*. Not to mention, your first eyewitness—Havington—said my assailant was tall and blond, neither of which Henry Pickett is."

"Pickett is in custody for the murders of Mercy O'Gillis and Alice Marshall," Sam said, conveniently ignoring every specific point I'd just made.

I knew it wouldn't help to act as offended as I felt. I wanted to say that that was some pretty fast footwork. Pickett had been arrested *as my attacker*. How did he get retrofitted for Mercy and Alice's murders?

I decided to take a breath and try logic on him again.

"Sam, if the MO for all three killings is the same—Mercy, Julie and Alice—then the killer cannot be Henry Pickett *because he's been in custody for one of them*. You see that, right?"

Sam flushed with annoyance. I have to believe he saw the logic in it. But for some reason he was refusing to admit it.

I threw my hands up in frustration.

"Are you saying you think there's a *second* person running around Savannah killing women?" I asked in exasperation, raising my voice. "How likely is that? And since the manner of their deaths was not revealed in the paper how would this second killer even know about using scalpels?"

I couldn't believe how hard Sam was fighting to believe that they had the right man in custody!

There was no evidence to hold Henry Pickett. But if they let him go, they had nothing.

Clearly, as far as Sam and the 1923 Savannah Police department was concerned, even an innocent candidate was better than none. I tried to grapple with the reality of that revelation.

The result would be a dynasty of anguish and anger that would go on for decades, sowing resentment and despair to every member of the Pickett family for generations to come.

54

Sam turned away from me in frustration.

I didn't know whether he was just so committed to believing that the suspect they had in custody was guilty, or if he just didn't like me talking to him like this. Probably a little bit of both.

I focused my thoughts on the center fountain. Flowering bushes flanked it. The sound of it was soothing—as intended for those people with loved ones in the hospital.

Henry Pickett had designed this garden oasis. He'd tended it, groomed it, and probably loved it. He had worked to provide solace and comfort to those people needing it at the worst moments of their lives.

A breeze carried the scent of sweet pea and freshly mown grass around the fountain. Then, a woman was found raped and murdered here, and he became their person of interest.

"If Pickett didn't attack you," Sam said suddenly, "then what was he doing in the alley? An eyewitness saw him run away."

"No. She didn't," I said. "Lydia Bartram lied. I spoke with

her today and she said Henry annoyed her by not stepping out of her way and so she got back at him."

"She lied?" He looked incredulous at the idea.

"Think about it. She and her friend Havington were trying to rob an unconscious woman—me. By pointing the finger at Henry Pickett, she was able to distract attention from herself and her partner in crime."

"You believe Mr. Havington to be involved in this attempt to rob you?" He frowned in obvious doubt.

I sighed. I wish I didn't have to tell Sam all the major pieces to this puzzle. It required a whole lot of swallowing and acceptance before he was in a position to help me.

"Sam, Mr. Havington is Mario Spinelli," I said wearily. "He and Mrs. Bartram were together that day because they are having an affair."

He stared at me. I wondered how much time I should give him to digest that little tidbit. He got up and walked away from me. I knew it must really burn him that he hadn't known that Havington was Mario Spinelli. But hurt feelings had no place in a murder investigation. If I gave them credence now, I'd never get Sam to accept the facts that I needed him to accept.

Sunlight filtered through the flourishing flowers and trees, casting an ethereal glow throughout the garden. The crepe myrtles were in full bloom and the fragrance of roses and lavender filled the air. I found myself praying that Mary would have a chance to smell them again. She loved her garden so. Sam came back to the bench and sat back down.

"Anything else?" he asked shortly.

"Yes, since you asked."

There was now no reason not to tell him everything.

"In my mind there are three suspects—each of whom should be questioned immediately by the police."

He snorted and looked away. I could see he was angry with me for telling him things he should have found out for himself. I'd give him time to adjust. After all, this was 1923 and women had about as much stature in society as wayward puppies. Being schooled by one was just about the worst thing that could happen to the poor man. And he'd fought at Verdun, so that's saying something.

"First is Gus Jones," I said. "He hates women, and he has easy access to scalpels. Plus, he works at the hospital, so he is near all three murder sites." I held up my hand and ticked off the points. "That's motive, opportunity and means."

Sam looked out over the garden. I could not decipher his expression.

"The hospital orderly," he said.

"That's right. And then there's Dr. Clay Ryan. I've seen him twice and both times he had a paperback copy of the book *Jack the Ripper* in his coat pocket. May I remind you that the real Ripper was a barber who was killing prostitutes in London? In those days, barbers often did the work of surgeons. Dr. Ryan is a surgeon and has access to scalpels—as well as to each of the murder sites."

"I thought the Ripper was never identified."

I immediately realized my mistake. It was true that the Ripper had never been caught. But he'd eventually been identified by his DNA.

In 2014.

"Anyone else?" Sam said with an indulgent grin.

I was sorry to see he'd stopped taking me seriously. I was disappointed, but I wouldn't allow it to derail me.

"Yes," I said, holding my chin up defiantly. "The other person I think you should talk to is Seamus O'Brien."

55

"Oh, so, the butler did it?" Sam said, his eyes crinkling in amusement.

"That's beneath you," I said, tersely.

After what the old drunk had told me about who he'd seen running from Julie Brown's crime scene, I'd given Seamus's inclusion on my list of suspects a lot of thought. The fact is, I liked Seamus and I hadn't jumped to this suspicion easily. But there could be no mistaking the description the man had given me. Tall, dark hair, Irish accent and dressed in livery.

"First, Seamus doesn't have an alibi for Mary's assault this afternoon," I said, determined to ignore Sam's condescension. "And second, I spoke to a *genuine* eyewitness at the time of Julie Brown's assault who identified him as running from the alley where her body was then found."

It was true that if I trotted out the old man with the drinking problem as my eyewitness, Sam would likely not give him credence. But for the moment anyway, he'd stopped laughing.

"Okay," he said, still mildly smiling. "Well, I think your

friend Agatha Christie would be very proud of the work you've done today."

I was starting to wonder why I liked this man.

"What about Mario Spinelli?" he asked. "I thought you said he had this world empire of ladies of the night—just waiting to be picked off. Although, honestly, I don't think that sounds like a very sound business practice—to kill off your employees."

"Very funny," I said.

I'd already decided not to tell Sam about the purse-snatching incident with Mario because I knew it would upset him and because there was no clear end game to be achieved. But also, because I couldn't work out for myself why the head guy of a crime family would be snatching purses. But now, after seeing his patronizing attitude, I decided Sam should hear it.

"I ran into Mario Spinelli last week," I said, "at which point he tried to accost me on the street."

Sam stiffened at my words. "What? When?"

"It doesn't matter," I said, shrugging. "The point is, he snatched my purse and I fainted. And as I lay there helpless, he did *not* attempt to slit my throat, so I am hesitant to add him to my list of suspects."

Although, again, just because he didn't get the chance to kill me didn't mean he wasn't the Savannah Killer. My body had physically vanished back to 2023 leaving Mario holding my purse and wondering where I'd gone.

Sam frowned in confusion. His eyes blinked rapidly, and he clenched his jaw. He was the picture of someone feeling intensely protective but also angry.

"He tried to steal your purse?" he asked, incredulously.

It didn't even make sense to *him*.

"In broad daylight?" he pressed.

"Well, he was wearing a mask," I said.

"So how did you know it was Mario Spinelli?"

"When I interviewed him later, I recognized his aftershave."

"His aftershave."

"It was very distinctive."

"What do you mean *when you interviewed him*?"

This was starting to get tiresome.

"I went to his home to speak to him. He told me that it was him that picked up my card the day I was found in the alley—while he and Lydia Bartram were attempting to rob me, although he didn't admit to that. He said he gave the card to his younger brother, who handed it in to the police."

I could see Sam was gearing up to give me a scolding for successfully bearding a notorious family crime lord in his den —or maybe he was just cross because I was doing his job and he knew it—but I wasn't in the mood for it. I have a new but nonetheless dear friend who might not make it through the day and now that I'd told Sam all I knew, I was very disappointed that it appeared I was on my own for finding who had hurt her.

I stood up and walked back to the hospital without another word, making him scramble to catch up with me. The sidewalk leading back to the hospital from the garden was shaded by a line of cherry trees and the cement was covered with a confetti of pale pink blossoms. My footsteps were virtually muffled as I walked on the carpet of fallen petals.

I keenly felt the disappointment at the lack of respect in my conversation with Sam. I'd expected too much from him. But now I was left with trying to find Mary's attacker all on my own.

The first person I saw was Sister Beatrice who stood in

the waiting room, her rosary beads dangling from one hand and a Bible in the other as she talked to someone clearly waiting for a loved one in the hospital. The nun's focus on the woman appeared unwavering. Her face was still, but I could see the wrinkle of worry between her brows, as she clasped the woman's hands tightly.

I came into the waiting room with Sam right behind me and took a seat. Now there were no more distractions—only the horror of knowing that Mary was in surgery fighting for her life. I jammed my hands into the pocket of my dress and my fingers found the locket. I pulled it out without looking at it and began to hold it as one would a prayer bead or worry stone.

After a moment, Sister Beatrice came over to me.

"How is she?" Sam asked before I could.

"She is still in surgery," Sister Beatrice said, her eyes on me. "I would like to know how this happened."

"It was an intruder," Sam said.

"Did he break in?" she asked me.

"I don't know. I wasn't there at the time."

"But you were there when she was attacked?"

"No, I came afterward."

She looked frustrated. I could see how upset she was. She wanted to blame me and that meant blaming herself since she was the one who'd put me in Mary's house.

"Where was Seamus?" she asked.

I looked at Sam because I hadn't heard the answer to this, myself.

"He said he went out to get an afternoon paper for Mary," Sam said.

"Is that something he usually does?" I asked.

"Do not try to deflect upon poor Seamus your own failings, Miss Belle," Sister Beatrice said sternly. "The man is only guilty of trying to serve his mistress."

"I didn't mean anything by it," I said but we all knew that wasn't true. Especially Sam since I'd made it clear that Seamus didn't get a free pass as far as I was concerned.

"So she opened the door to this monster herself?" Sister Beatrice asked Sam.

"That is our understanding," he said.

"Was anything stolen?" she asked.

"We don't know yet," he said.

"Unless he could fit it in his pocket," I said, "he ran out with nothing in his hands."

Sister Beatrice turned her focus back on me. She was about to say something when suddenly she noticed the locket in my hands and her face went white as paint.

56

"Where did you get that?" she asked, pointing a shaky finger at the locket.

I stopped fidgeting with the locket and realized that if Mary had the locket in the painting—assuming it would ever be painted now—it made sense that Sister Beatrice might be familiar with it too.

"I found it," I said. "Do you...know it?"

The nun sat down hard as if she were suddenly having trouble supporting herself. Sam jumped up to find her a glass of water.

"How do you know this locket, Sister?" I asked. "You do recognize it, don't you?"

She fanned herself with her hand and looked around the now deserted waiting room. She looked everywhere but at me, her face reddening and a tear glistening in the corner of her eye.

"I know it," she said bitterly. "I know it killed my parents."

Sam came back then with a glass of water which Sister Beatrice drank thirstily.

"Sam?" I said, turning to him. "Can you give us a moment, please?"

He hesitated.

"Sure," he said. "I'll be just down the hall."

We both waited for him to leave before turning back to each other.

"That's an extraordinary statement," I said.

She glanced at the locket in my hands again.

"I can't believe I'm seeing it again after all these years," she said.

I knew prodding her wouldn't get her to tell me her story any faster. So I waited. A wave of defeat seemed to crash down over her when she realized she was going to have to revisit the story of the locket.

"My father gave my mother that locket on their wedding day," she said, folding her hands in her lap as she stared at the locket in my hands.

That surprised me but the more I thought about it, the more sense it made.

"My mother was not a religious woman, but she was a believer in the power of prayer and friendship. She put a lot of faith into the power of that locket."

"What kind of power?"

She bit her lip and looked away.

"Has Mary told you how our parents died?" she asked in a small voice.

"She said it was a car accident."

"That's right. Both of them." She looked at the locket again, this time as if it were a hand grenade that might go off. "The week before they were killed our house was broken into. My mother's locket—which was supposed to have gone to my sister Mary on her twenty-first birthday—was taken among other pieces of jewelry."

Killing Time in Georgia

I could see that Sister Beatrice believed there was a connection, but I was having trouble seeing it—even after going back and forth in time. I was tempted to ask her about the picture in the locket but decided that piece could wait.

"Well," I said. "Then it belongs to your family."

I held out the locket to her and she recoiled, nearly jumping out of her chair.

"Throw it in the river!" she said. "It's cursed!"

I was surprised that a woman of God could be so superstitious. The locket had been around Mary's neck in the portrait that someone would be painting in another ten years—if she survived. I would give it to her when she recovered.

We sat a little longer while Sister Beatrice got her composure back. Out of the corner of my eye, I saw Sam in the hall. He had that kind of look on his face that said he had news. My stomach fell when I saw it. It didn't look like good news.

Sister Beatrice must have deduced the same thing because she jumped up and hurried off to talk with him. I kept my seat, believing this a private family matter, when Sister Beatrice cried out and after shooting me a terrified look, ran off down the hall.

I felt a sudden sour taste in my mouth and my legs went weak. I wasn't sure why the doctors would tell *Sam* about Mary's demise before her own sister, but it seemed pretty clear that they had.

Was the misogyny back in this time so dominant that they would tell an unrelated male authority figure before they would a female relative?

I watched Sam walk over to me and waited for him to take his seat beside me.

"It's Mary, isn't it?" I said quietly.

He frowned. "I think she is still in surgery."

"Then what was it you just told Sister Beatrice?" I asked, not terribly concerned with my tone of voice now that I knew Mary was still among the living.

"A tragic accident," he said, shaking his head.

Before he told me, I flashed to the look on Sister Beatrice's face and her terrorized glance back at me before she ran down the hall and I swear I knew what he was going to say before he did it.

"It seems the taxi driver attempted to swerve. Witnesses said she stepped out in front of him."

I put my hand to my mouth, somehow knowing what he was going to say before he said it.

"It was Lydia Bartram," he said.

57

Chills raced up and down my arms, until I thought I was going to go into convulsions.

Lydia Bartram?

"She died before anyone could come to her aid," Sam said. "Run over by a cab."

"How can this be?" I asked in a whisper.

"Witnesses say she stepped into the street trying to avoid a puddle on the sidewalk."

"It wasn't an accident," I said.

"Georgia, it *was* an accident," Sam said, his brow knit in concern as he studied my reaction. "The driver had never had any prior arrests. He was completely distraught."

"But...how can she be dead? This can't be a coincidence."

"Surely you're not suggesting it's the Savannah Killer? Because the method of—"

"No, no, I'm not saying that," I said, bewildered. "I don't know what I'm saying. I just know this isn't a coincidence."

"You need water," he said. "I'll be right back."

When he left, I sat there, my legs vibrating—in fear? Shock? Disbelief? How could Lydia die just hours after speaking with me? Was she killed because she spoke to me? That made no sense! She was a part of the crime family. It made more sense for *me* to be killed for knowing something I shouldn't than for her to be.

I shook my head in confusion and disbelief, and my eyes dropped to my hands which were still holding the locket. A shudder of realization shot through me like an electric current.

Lydia died after I took the locket from her.

I thought I was going to throw up. I stood up and then sat down again immediately.

No! Lydia cannot have died *because I took the locket from her*.

Can she?

I stared at the locket in my now trembling hand, terrified even to put it down. My mind raced with the implications:

Having the locket was benign. Losing it was bad.

It had been bad for Mary—and her poor parents.

And it had been very bad for Lydia.

I tried to think but my mind was a whirling storm of disjointed thoughts and emotions. If I gave the locket back to Mary, would that make things better? Or would they stay the same? But then what if Mary lost it?

I watched Sam on his way back to me from down the hall, a glass of water in his hand.

? *I* had the locket now. If I gave it away, would tragedy befall me? But no, both times that bad things had happened it was after the locket had been stolen from the owner. Perhaps returning it to its rightful owner wouldn't trigger the curse?

Listen to me! I groaned. *I must be losing my mind to even be thinking such a thing.*

I straightened my shoulders with determination and tucked the locket into my pocket before reaching for the glass of water from Sam who was looking at me with a seriously worried look on his face.

I would return the locket to Mary as soon as possible.

∼

It was past dinner time when they finally wheeled Mary into a hospital room from her surgery. By then, Sam had left to check on some things at his office with assurances that he would return tonight. I was astonished that Mary wasn't being separated from the other patients. Beside her was a woman coughing and on the other side, a woman smoking a cigarette. I gave the smoking woman a dirty look but since cigarette shaming wasn't a thing in 1923, I'm sure she had no idea what my problem was.

Mary had dark circles under her eyes, which the bare overhead lighting made even harsher against her colorless cheeks. Her body looked frail beneath the white sheet. Her lips were parted slightly. Sister Beatrice stood next to her arranging Mary's pillow and taking her pulse.

I wanted to hold Mary's hand or do something other than just stare helplessly at her.

"What did the surgeon say?" I asked.

Sister Beatrice put a hand to Mary's brow before answering.

"They say it all depends on whether or not the wound site becomes infected," she said.

I stared at her for a moment when I realized what she

was saying. In all the drama of Mary's assault, I'd forgotten that the true danger was infection.

How could I have forgotten? Especially after Anna Wilkins died because she didn't have an antibiotic!

Where is my brain?

My heart raced with panic and urgency as I realized what I needed to do—as quickly as humanly possible. I snatched up my purse and my jacket.

"I need to go," I said.

Sister Beatrice turned to me with a look of horror on her face.

"I have to get back to my rounds," she said. "I assumed you would sit with her."

I could kick myself for hanging around an empty waiting room for four hours where I could do nothing to help Mary. Now that I could do her some actual good, I needed to race back to her house to get the antibiotics I brought back from the future. I couldn't believe I didn't think of it before now.

"I will not be gone long," I said.

I could see by the way Sister Beatrice's nostrils flared and her eyes met mine that my assurances did not cut it with her. Her hands were shaking like she wanted to wring my neck.

I searched for the words that might help her understand why I had to leave. But nothing I said or did was going to make a difference. I had been stupid, and I was about to pay the price for it.

I just prayed that Mary didn't.

"Look," I said, trying to keep my voice steady. "I care deeply about Mary..."

She shook her head and looked away, her eyes glistening with angry, incredulous tears. I wanted to reach out to her, but I knew it wouldn't do any good. She needed more than empty platitudes and promises; she needed me to stay here with Mary.

"Go," she said abruptly. "Do whatever you want. I'll ring for a nurse."

I left without another word, cursing myself under my breath the whole way, literally running down the hall to the hospital exit. I stood on the sidewalk for a moment heaving and breathless as I watched the street traffic.

I didn't have the money for a taxi, nor did I see one to flag down in any case. But I had two good legs. I stopped only long enough to pull off my shoes and tuck them under my arm and then ran down the block. I didn't care what I looked like, and I knew I looked like something out of a science fiction novel, running barefoot down a city block with the hem of my 1920's dress flapping behind me. I wouldn't be surprised if someone called the police.

Because I'm in fairly decent shape from my regular runs around Savannah in my own time, I made it back to Mary's house in under fifteen minutes. I knew that every minute counted when it came to the infection.

I groaned when I came to the front door and saw that the police were still there. At least I was fairly sure that that horrible Detective Hawkins wouldn't be, which was some help. I put my shoes back on and ran up the front steps, where I breathlessly told the policeman standing guard who I was and then pushed past him and ran up the stairs to my bedroom.

I went straight to my satchel and pulled out the small packet of syringes with a vial of the amoxicillin and jammed them both in my pocket, trying not to stab myself in the process. I turned to leave but only got as far as the bedroom door where I was confronted by Cook and Seamus both staring at me with suspicion.

"I can't stop," I said, attempting to push past them.

"How is the Missus?" Cook asked.

"She's out of surgery," I said. "She's going to be okay."

"Why did you come back?" Seamus said, frowning at my feet which even in shoes were obviously filthy.

"None of your business, Seamus," I said. "Which reminds me, where were you when your mistress was being stabbed?"

Cook sucked in a horrified gasp at my question and even Seamus looked as if he'd been punched in the stomach.

"I...how dare you!" he said with not nearly as much indignation as I would've thought a truly innocent person would've managed.

"Never mind," I said, pushing past them both. "I'm sure the police will take your statement if they haven't already."

With that, I flew down the stairs, my feet barely touching the steps. I landed with a thud on the bottom floor and hurried out the door, hardly aware of the two policemen still in the living room.

This time a taxi was driving past the house, and I stepped into the street and flagged him down. I still didn't have any money, but I was past caring.

"Savannah Hospital," I said breathlessly. "And hurry, please."

I sank back into the seat and closed my eyes, trying to regroup and corral my thoughts. I had to pray that my stupidity wouldn't cost Mary her life. I don't know why I didn't think of the antibiotics before. I just had to pray I'd get them to her in time.

As I sat there, I revisited the look on Seamus's face in my mind when I asked him where he was during Mary's attack. He didn't look guilty so much as surprised that I would dare to even suggest he might be involved. There was something wrong about his reaction, but I didn't have time to drill down into what that was just then.

"Here," I said to the driver as the hospital loomed into view. "Pull over."

He did and I climbed out.

"I'm sorry I don't have your fare," I said. "But I live in that house you picked me up at. Come back there and there'll be a nice tip in it for you."

He was not happy about it, but I was shutting the door so short of chasing me through the hospital, there was little he could do about it. I ran to the hospital, wondering how long I'd been gone and guessed it was thirty minutes.

Thirty long minutes.

It occurred to me that a short cut through the garden to the back entrance of the hospital would cut off a good three minutes, so I rerouted and ran into the garden from the side, past the bench where Sam and I had sat just a few hours before and down the path leading to the side entrance of the hospital.

Suddenly someone stepped out of the bushes, forcing me to slam on the brakes. I grabbed for a nearby bush to stay upright.

"Why such a hurry?" a familiar voice said.

It was, Gus Jones, the orderly. He stood before me, his blond hair sticking greasily to his forehead, his lips parted in a lascivious stare at me.

"Excuse me. I have somewhere to be," I said sharply to him, targeting a spot to his left to pass him.

He put out a hand and grabbed my arm, roughly twisting me around to face him.

"That's not very nice," he said, his teeth gaping in a grinning maw. "Why not be nice?"

"Get your hands off me."

"Don't be like that," he said as I twisted out of his grip. "I have something for you. Something I think you'll like."

I was a full step away from him when I caught a glimpse of what he held out in his hand. I stopped.

And turned back to him.

58

It was my cellphone.

He held it out in his hand as if he was luring a wild animal to him. His eyes crinkled into a grin at my reaction.

"Where did you get that?" I said.

"You can touch it if you want," he said with a leer, dangling it in front of me.

I knew not to announce that the item was mine. There was no point. But the fact that he had it—and I knew I'd lost it in the alley where I'd fainted—now put Gus Jones fully in my cross hairs. I didn't know what it meant, but it had to mean he wasn't innocent.

"Where did you get it?" I asked again.

He tucked it into his pants pocket.

"You can have it if you want it," he said. "Come get it."

I nearly laughed in his face.

"That's stolen property," I said. "The police will be eager to know how you got it."

That wiped the smile off his face pretty quickly, but things got better, faster.

"Georgia?"

Detective Sam Bohannon emerged from the garden path and strode over to where Gus and I were standing.

"Is everything all right?" he asked.

"No," I said, pointing a finger at Gus. "This man has just attacked me."

"What?!" Gus yelped, backing up into the rose bushes and then jumping away from their probing thorns. "She's lying! I never touched her!"

But Sam clamped a hard hand on Gus's shoulder.

"And he has stolen property!" I said as I began to make my way toward the side entrance of the hospital. "I'll give a full statement later. I need to check on Mary first!"

"You go on," Sam said, pulling out handcuffs as Gus squeaked in horror. "I'll find you as soon as I deliver this miscreant to the station."

"This is outrageous!" Gus shouted. "Unhand me!"

I disappeared into the hospital and took the stairs two at a time to Mary's floor. I ran to her room and stopped. Through the hall window overlooking her room I saw two physicians standing by her bedside along with Sister Beatrice.

I took in a gasp of breath as I moved to try to see better. Mary was still alive. I could see her face, still very pale beside the white bed sheet.

I tried the door, but a nurse was standing by it on the inside and stopped me.

"Sorry, Miss," she said. "No visitors until after doctors' rounds."

I was nearly vibrating with impatience but short of knocking her over and racing to Mary's bedside—which would probably earn me a cell next to Gus Jones—all I could do was wait. The doctors were nodding, and poor

Sister Beatrice looked as if she was going to burst into tears at any moment.

Come on! Hurry up! Leave!

But they were in no hurry.

While I waited, Sam strode down the hall to stand beside me. I panicked when I saw him.

"What did you do with Gus? Don't tell me you let him go!"

"I handed him off to a beat policeman who will take him to the station and process him."

I felt a wave of relief but noticed that Sam was looking at me critically as if parts of my story weren't adding up for him.

"The reason I knew about the stolen property is because he stole it from me," I said. "He took it the day of my...when I collapsed in the alley."

Sam withdrew my cellphone from his pocket.

"You mean this?"

I bit my lip trying to think of how I was going to explain what the strange gadget was.

"I had it with me when I fainted in the alley. Spinelli must have taken it from me like he took my drivers license."

"What is it?"

"It's a..." I tried to remember if I ever knew the word for flashlight in the old days. I couldn't remember if there was such a thing so I just called it what I knew it to be and hoped he'd chalk it up to whatever weird part of the country I must be from.

"It's a flashlight," I finally said. "It has a battery in it which I'm sure is dead by now."

I reached for it and pushed the button that normally would've turned it on. It was clear from my ease in handling it that Sam believed I was familiar with it.

"And you believe Mr. Havi—I mean, Mario Spinelli took this from the place of your collapse, and then gave it to Gus Jones?" Sam asked, frowning.

"Gave it or sold it to him directly or through one of his fences."

I could see by Sam's expression that he was taken aback by my knowing the word *fence* let alone the concept.

"I asked him where he was during the time that Mercy O'Gillis and Julie Brown were attacked," Sam said as he took the phone back from me and studied it.

That surprised me. In a good way. "What did he say?"

"He claims he has an alibi for both crimes."

I wanted to ask him what the alibis were, but even I know when I've hit my limit for aggravating men with healthy egos. For now, it was enough that Sam considered Gus Jones enough of a suspect that he at least asked the question. And it was also enough that that creature was at least temporarily in a jail cell and away from vulnerable patients who couldn't protect themselves.

Just then the door opened, and the two doctors with Sister Beatrice emerged. I'd already noticed that neither were Clay Ryan. I instantly moved to enter the room, but the nurse stopped me.

"Only one visitor at a time," she said.

I nodded and turned to Sam.

"You go," he said. "I'll be here when you come out."

I hurried to Mary's bedside and looked around in order to administer the antibiotic.

I'd learned to give injections in training for my job. It wasn't my favorite part of the drill, but it's not rocket science. carefully drew the clear liquid from the vial with a syringe taking caution to avoid air bubbles.

I'd brought alcohol swabs and, while I wished I had

latex gloves, I'd have to do without. I'd already washed my hands and was trying not to touch anything before I could swab Mary's hip. Suddenly the room door swung open, and Sister Beatrice entered.

Her eyes went from my hands to the sheet pulled back exposing Mary's bare hip—to the hypodermic needle I held in my hand.

"What do you think you're doing?" she screeched, as she ran to me and grabbed my arm.

59

I snatched my hand away from her and took a step back, the needle now gripped in my hand as if I intended to stab her with it. I saw her eyes go to the syringe and realized she was thinking the same thing.

An overpowering odor of antiseptic and blood seemed to fill the room.

"I don't know what you think you're doing," the nun said in a threatening voice.

"I'm saving your sister's life," I said. "The serum in this syringe contains amoxicillin, a powerful antibiotic that is used all over Europe to save post-surgical patients from infection."

She looked at the needle with suspicion.

"Where in Europe?"

"Switzerland," I said. "A friend of mine had an accident last summer and this drug—this miracle elixir—saved her."

"I am not about to allow you to inject some unknown foreign substance into my critically ill sister!"

I felt a wave of frustration. If necessary, I would attack the nun and administer the antibiotic to Mary—but that would likely involve my spending the rest of my tenure in 1923 in a primitive women's prison.

"Look at her," I said. "You know what you're seeing. Her skin is ashen and cold. She's shivering. Have you checked the incision site? I'll bet it's red."

I reached again for Mary's sheet as if to pull it back, but Sister Beatrice stopped me.

"No," she said, her eyes on her sister now and the fear in them apparent. "It's true." She hesitated. "There's pus too."

"Then, let me help her," I said. "This drug will prevent the infection from spreading. There is nothing to lose! If it's not as I say, she'll die anyway. This way at least she has a chance."

"This can stop the infection?" she asked, her eyes on her very ill sister. The war going on within her was all too visible to see.

I wasn't about to go into good bugs and bad bugs, even if Sister Beatrice did have a scientific bent to her which, being a nurse, I dearly hoped she did.

"It can," I said. "Mary needs every chance."

Her lips trembling, she slipped a hand under the sheet and took Mary's hand.

"Go ahead," she said. "I pray you are telling the truth."

I wiped a spot on Mary's hip and quickly inserted the needle, depressing the plunger. After withdrawing the needle, I looked around for a place to toss the syringe.

"Give it to me," Sister Beatrice said, holding out her hand.

I hesitated.

"I'm not sure this antibiotic is legal in this country," I said. "But I swear to you it is saving lives all over Europe."

I let her take the needle. In my mind, I think she figured that if I'd killed Mary—or hadn't saved her from infection—

she could use the needle as evidence to have me arrested. Otherwise, I assume she would dispose of it. I didn't blame her. She didn't know me. She had no reason to trust me.

I turned back to Mary as she lay in the bed. She looked so small and frail, her face so pallid that if I hadn't seen her chest rise with her breathing, I'd think she was dead.

I watched Sister Beatrice pull up a chair to Mary's bedside and take her hand again. I didn't see what she'd done with the needle. At this point, it didn't matter. I looked at Mary, so sick, so close to death and I felt myself suddenly close to tears. But I couldn't do that. Not yet.

I'd done everything I could for her, but Henry still had a noose hanging over his head. I couldn't stay here by her bedside when there was work to be done.

∽

It was early evening when Sam arrived at the Spinelli family home.

The home was large and well-maintained, a testament to the success of the family business. Sam felt a cold chill in the air as he stepped onto the porch. The lawn needed to be mowed, the branches trimmed on some trees, but it wasn't necessarily ragged from neglect. Upon closer inspection, he could see that the house needed painting, but wasn't run down. Clearly, Spinelli had made an effort to keep up appearances.

Sam was here to talk to Spinelli because too many things didn't make sense. Gus Jones kept insisting that "the dago sold it to me!" when questioned about the odd device that Georgia said was a flashlight. There was also the fact that Spinelli told Georgia he took the mysterious drivers card and gave it to his little brother as a token oddity.

And then there was the question of the purse snatching that Georgia insisted had happened—and that Spinelli had been the culprit.

All in all, especially with the accidental death of Lydia Bartram, it was time to bell the cat. Or at least ask him where he was during the critical times of the three murders.

Sam knocked on the door which was promptly answered by a young man with a scar on his face. The boy sneered when Sam showed his police identification.

"Who is it, Barney?" a voice called from the interior.

"A copper," Barney yelled back.

"Show him in."

Sam followed the young thug down a long hallway to a sitting room where Mario Spinelli sat in a high-backed armchair in front of cold fireplace. The room was filled with the smell of tobacco and sweat.

"I'm here to give official notice of a family member's death," Sam said stiffly.

"We've already been informed," Spinelli said, puffing hard on his cigar. "Is that all?"

Sam didn't speak or move. Finally, Spinelli looked up and motioned for him to sit.

The couches were draped with lace doilies and shabby throws—a hint to a woman's touch at one point. The carpet was a dark blue and very worn Berber. The furniture looked to Sam as if it had seen better days.

Sam sat in one of the big chairs facing Spinelli. When he did, he got a strong whiff of what smelled like rotten lemons that seemed to come from the man. He was reminded that Georgia thought she could identify Spinelli by his aftershave.

"I'm sorry for your loss," Sam said.

Spinelli turned to him, his eyes narrowing as he sized him up.

"Who was the bastard who killed her?"

"It was an accident. If any harm comes to the driver, you have given an officer of the law enough reason to arrest you for suspicion in his assault—or murder."

"I'll find him."

"And then I'll find you."

"Well, we'll see, won't we?"

Silence followed after that when Sam was able to hear the ticking of the hall clock and the sounds of the thug in the kitchen accompanied by the smells of cooking.

"You told the officer responding to the assault in the alley on April 17 that your name was Alvin Havington."

"Did I?"

"It is against the law to give a false name in a police statement."

"I think the officer misheard me."

"Havington and Spinelli sound nothing alike."

"I agree."

"As Alvin Havington it is believed you gave a false statement about the incident," Sam pressed.

"Oh? Remind me. My memory isn't what it was."

"You said you saw a man attack a woman in the alley. You said he was tall with blond hair."

"I do remember that."

"Your statement however conflicts with the statement given by your companion, Miss Bartram."

"Conflicts how?"

"You said the assailant had blond hair. Miss Bartram said he was a Negro."

Spinelli shrugged. "People see things differently."

"So you still stand by your statement that the assailant was blond?"

"I do. Is that all?"

"Not quite. The woman in the alley has revealed that she was not attacked after all. She merely fainted. There was no assailant. Not blond, not Negro."

"It's my understanding that the victim is addle headed," Spinelli said with a shrug. "But I guess you will have to decide who is telling the truth."

It was like attempting a conversation with a slippery eel, Sam thought in frustration. He decided to take a different tact.

"A man was arrested today with stolen goods he says he got from you."

"Did he, now? Do you have proof of that?"

Sam pulled the flashlight out of his pocket.

"Do you deny selling this to Gus Jones?"

"I've never seen that object before in my life."

"Where were you on April 1 of this year?"

Spinelli frowned.

"That's not when the young woman was attacked in the alley," he said.

"No, Mr. Spinelli, it's when Alice Marshall was killed on East Huntington Street."

"I see we've moved past allegations of lying on to accusations of murder."

"Right now, it's just a question. No accusations yet."

"*Yet* being the key word. As for where I was, I don't remember, Detective. I'll ask my secretary to have a look at my daybook, shall I?"

Sam knew that Spinelli was an accomplished liar. He hadn't expected a confession. But he had been hoping for something that might open up the possibility of a lead.

The young bodyguard came to the doorway.

"Dinner's ready," he said with a surly show of teeth as his upper lip pulled back in a snarl.

"Ah, the dinner gong," Spinelli said with a smile. "I'm afraid I must terminate our visit, Detective."

Sam stood and watched Spinelli as he hobbled to the kitchen. Was he faking it? Was this display for his benefit?

"Oh, by the way Detective," Spinelli said before entering the dining room. "I did want to remind you that there would be consequences if I were to be falsely arrested."

"Are you threatening me?"

"Oh, not you, Detective. I would never lift a finger to harm one of our city's finest."

He means someone near me. Someone I care about.

As the young thug escorted him out the door, Sam glanced at the thick dust that had gathered on top of the entryway umbrella stand in the foyer and it occurred to him that Mario Spinelli's criminal enterprise might not be doing all that well. He stepped onto the sidewalk in front of the house and looked up at it. The outside of the house was all about presentation but a thin scratch at the veneer showed the shambles underneath.

Was a rival gang raking in the lion's share of the illegal takes now?

Sam reflected back to Georgia's claim that it had been Spinelli himself who'd snatched her purse. At the time, the notion had seemed absurd. The head of a crime family doesn't shine his own shoes. Or do his own purse snatching.

Sam had seen only the young hooligan as Spinelli's security. The same guy who answered the door was also the cook? He hadn't been wearing a holster that Sam saw, but it was likely he served as security too. Although Sam knew there was a younger brother, with Lydia Bartram dead and his wife Mable in an insane asylum, there didn't appear to be any other family members to make up the Spinelli crime family.

Was the whole criminal enterprise just smoke and mirrors?

The more Sam thought about it, the more he felt like he was missing something important. It was as if some vital piece of information was just beyond his reach. He shook his head trying to clear his mind as he made his way down the sidewalk. That was when the image of Spinelli limping into the dining room came back to him.

Was the man really crippled? They had very little information on Mario Spinelli but something like that would have been useful to know.

Especially since crippled men might have trouble running from alleys after they'd just killed someone.

60

I went back to the townhouse to await word on Mary. Sister Beatrice had put a cot up in Mary's room and would be with her all night. I was exhausted and hadn't slept or eaten in hours. My head was swimming with the facts surrounding the three suspects I'd laid out for Sam. I knew one thing if I knew anything: unless I got him on board, even facts wouldn't make the difference for Henry Pickett.

I toyed with the idea of going down to the police station to see if I could get that ass Hawkins to listen to me. But if even Sam thought my theories were mad, what chance did I have of Hawkins listening to me?

It felt like two-ton weights were attached to my legs by the time I reached the front door of the townhouse. Seamus had let me in and was acting extremely jumpy—as well he should. Even if he wasn't the Savannah Killer, the fact of his absence this afternoon—still too coincidental for my comfort—had allowed the attack on Mary to take place.

"Will you be eating in the dining room, Miss?" Seamus said in his most obsequious tones.

"No," I said. "I'm too tired to be lady of the manor today. Tell Cook I'm happy with a tray in the library. Is there a fire?"

"There will be in short order, Miss," Seamus said, bowing deferentially.

I kicked off my shoes and padded into the library as Seamus lit the fire and then left to tell Cook about dinner.

I sat in front of the fire and let the flames warm me and soothe my jangled nerves. Staring into the hypnotic flames I thought about Mario Spinelli. I was still of two minds about whether or not he could be the Savannah Killer. From what I could see, he definitely fit the bill for having a lack of remorse. And he also exhibited a need to control as well as predatory behavior. All of those hit the mark. But was he impulsive? It's true he snatched my purse, but even then, he'd thought ahead enough to procure a mask.

I eased back into the chair and felt the day's stress begin to shift and throb through my shoulders.

And speaking of grabbing my purse—how much sense did it make for the head of big crime family to do that? I worried that around for a few minutes trying to make sense of it until I decided to put it away on a shelf in my mind. In my experience, trying to attribute normal behavior or rationality to psycho criminals usually didn't reveal much in the way of usable Intel.

Seamus came into the room and set down a tray of food on a small table near where I sat. The scent nearly made me weak in the knees. I saw fried chicken with mashed potatoes and gravy, the fluffiest biscuits dripping with butter, and green beans sprinkled with slivered almonds.

My mouth watered as Seamus handed me a cloth napkin.

"Would Miss like a glass of sherry?" he asked.

I tucked the napkin under my chin. I'd never think of doing it in my own time, but this dress was handmade and had to last me.

"Sure. That sounds good," I said, although I was pretty sure sherry was just as illegal these days as wine or spirits.

After he left to get the sherry, I dug into my meal as if I hadn't eaten for days. Every bite was so good, it nearly brought tears to my eyes. I'm ashamed to say I'd cleaned my plate before Seamus came back with the wine.

If he was surprised to see how quickly I'd gobbled down my dinner, he was too polite a butler to let it show.

I was relieved to see he brought an unopened bottle of the sherry and opened it in my sight. Not that I don't trust him. But of course, I really don't.

After he poured my drink, he bowed and left the room. I turned once more to the fire, this time with the glass of sherry in my hand and my thoughts went back to my altercation with Gus Jones.

Honestly, as much as I liked him for the role of killer—or at least the punishment that would await him if he were—I didn't really think he was smart enough to fit the profile. Serial killers tended to have greater than average IQs. And I didn't think Gus was faking his stupidity since one of the hallmarks of a serial killer is their arrogance.

As much as I hated to admit it, Gus just didn't fit the profile for the Savannah Killer. He was just a garden-variety sleaze who'd been getting away with bad behavior for way too long.

Seamus came back into the library. "Telephone, Miss."

I looked up and saw he'd brought the phone to me. It appeared he was really worried about what I thought he might have gotten up to while Mary was attacked. Or maybe I'm just becoming cynical in my old age.

"Thank you, Seamus," I said, wondering if I was really going to be able to sleep tonight in a house that I was not completely sure I wasn't sharing with a cold-blooded killer.

I took the phone receiver. "This is Georgia Belle."

"Good evening, Miss Belle," Sister Beatrice said.

I sat up straight. All the stress-relieving work the good food, fire and wine had done for me was gone in a flash. My stomach churned with dread.

"Yes, Sister," I said. "Is it Mary?"

"I wanted to let you know," Sister Beatrice said, "that Mary is beginning to improve. The doctors are calling it a miracle." She paused and I heard the break of emotion in her voice. "I wanted to thank you for what you did. For whatever it was you did."

"I'm glad to hear she's better," I said with a wave of relief vibrating through me. "God bless the Swiss."

We talked for a minute longer and I told her I'd come to the hospital in the morning. Just as I hung up, I heard a knock at the front door. I stood up, my back to the fire and drank down the rest of my sherry to fortify myself for whatever was coming next.

I heard Seamus speaking in the foyer and then Sam appeared in the doorway to the library.

"I wanted to tell you," he said in a rush, "that I think you're wrong." He paused. "But I think we're wrong too."

"Well, that's a start," I said, gesturing for him to come into the room—and feeling inexplicably happier than I can ever remembered feeling in my entire life.

61

The fire crackled in the hearth, its radiant warmth cradling the room in soft oranges and reds. The light outside had faded, leaving only the lamps and fire to illuminate the room. The logs crackled and popped as the fire sent sparks into the air.

I sent for sandwiches and coffee since Sam hadn't eaten and the meal arrived with the apple pie that Cook had made for my dessert. I was glad my outfits in 1923 were on the loose side since the food here was definitely going to ensure I put on a few pounds.

It was hard to wait for Sam to finish eating but he'd never get a bite if I started with all my questions. I considered it a very good sign that he'd shown up open to hearing evidence against someone other than Henry Pickett.

Finally, he wiped his mouth and settled back in the chair opposite the fire and lifted his wine glass.

"Dr. Clay Ryan has alibis for two of the three attacks," he said.

I felt a breathless excitement at the news.

"You questioned him?"

"He wasn't pleased to be, as he saw it, accused."

"I'll bet not. But as for his alibis, doctors are very persuasive and manipulative within the hospital. Who alibied him?"

"No nurses or interns if that's what you're thinking. He was at a gala the night of Mercy O'Gillis's murder—where no fewer than three hundred people saw him."

"He could've slipped out?"

"His date was with the chief of police's daughter. She was very attentive to him."

I winced. I had to admit that would be pretty hard to get around.

"What about Julie Brown's murder?"

"He was in surgery."

I sighed.

"Okay," I said. I hated to give up the doctor, mostly because he was someone I personally didn't like. But I suppose he might just be an ass with odd reading tastes.

"At least we've got two other viable suspects," I said.

He frowned at my language, but I didn't have time to choose my words to be more era appropriate.

I dropped my voice.

"I'm pretty sure nobody's questioned Seamus yet," I said. "So nobody knows if he has alibis for any of the attacks. And remember, he was also conveniently missing yesterday when Mary was attacked."

"Why would Seamus attack her?" Sam asked with a frown, clearly unconvinced.

"Serial killers don't need a reason for what they do. Or a motive," I said.

I was tempted to give Sam the list of characteristics of a serial killer that I'd brought back with me from the future, but I didn't want him thinking they were science fiction. I needed him to continue to take me seriously.

"And then there's Mario Spinelli," I said. "Clearly, he gathered up all the evidence in the alley where I was found incapacitated. Do you have any idea where he was for the other attacks?"

"I thought you said that the fact that he didn't try to kill you when he snatched your purse, took him off your list," Sam said as he poured himself a glass of the sherry.

Of course, I couldn't tell Sam that one reason Spinelli didn't kill me that time might be because when he jumped out at me, I vanished into thin air on my way back to the year 2023.

"Maybe he didn't kill me because he didn't have his scalpel with him."

He looked at me pensively for a moment.

"As a matter of fact, I've just come from Mario Spinelli's," he said.

"Seriously? You interviewed him?"

"I couldn't have you be the only one brave enough to enter the lion's den," he said with a smile.

"What did you find out?"

"Not much. He wouldn't admit to selling the flashlight to Jones or giving a false statement at the time you collapsed in the alley."

I was relieved Sam was no longer referring to that incident as my assault. But it was annoying that Spinelli hadn't admitted to any wrongdoing.

"However, he seemed to squirm noticeably when I asked him where he was when Alice Marshall was killed."

"That's saying something about an accomplished liar like Spinelli," I pointed out. "What did you make of it?"

"That I'd hit a nerve."

Killing Time in Georgia

"Do you think he was there?"

"Either that or he knows more than he's saying."

"He could be lying."

"Why would he lie?"

"You're a cop, he's a crook. It's what crooks do."

Sam smiled.

"Something else I thought was interesting," he said. "For a crime family there didn't seem to have much in the way of wealth. Or family for that matter."

I frowned.

"That might explain why he was doing his own dirty work," I said.

"Plus, he seems to have a physical impairment."

"Like what?"

"He limps. Did you not notice that in your encounters with him?"

Now that he mentioned it, the only time I'd seen Spinelli was when he was seated—or when he was standing in front of me. I'd never actually seen him walk.

I'd already matched Mario Spinelli up with the characteristics of a serial killer and except for the question about impulse control he matched pretty well.

Thinking of Mario made me think of Lydia Bartram.

"How did he take Lydia's death?" I asked.

"I think he was attempting to appear unaffected," Sam said. "But there was something about the way he received the news—which he'd already been made aware of—that made me think it was a hard blow."

"If what you say is true, her death seriously reduces the family population," I pointed out. "Kind of hard to have a crime family with only one brother who wants nothing to do with the family business and a wife locked up in a mental hospital."

"He threatened the driver of the car who hit her."

"I would expect nothing less of him," I said. "I didn't like Lydia Bartram myself, but I suppose *someone* found her lovable."

I got up to shove a piece of wood into the fire and then turned to face Sam.

"So that just leaves Gus Jones," I said. "He's a pervert with a penchant for assaulting women. But you'd know better than me."

"Pardon?"

"Does he have a record? Surely *someone* must have made a complaint about him over the years?"

"He has a prior for assault."

"Well, there you are! Why the hell is he working at a hospital? Whose bright idea was that? Never mind. So we've got Gus in custody."

"He has an alibi."

"I don't believe it."

"He claims he was sick himself."

"Easy enough to check," I said.

"A job for tomorrow," he said with a smile.

"Sister Beatrice called to say that Mary is improving," I said.

"I know. I stopped by the hospital first. She seems to think you had something to do with it."

"Not really. I'd brought back some homeopathic medicine the last time I was in Europe. It's pretty common over there."

Sam's eyebrows shot up at my mention of European travel. I should have remembered that that kind of overseas trip wasn't typically something the average person did in 1923.

Seamus came to refill our wine glasses and silently slip

away. I wasn't sure he wasn't standing right outside the door listening to every word.

"By the way," Sam said when Seamus left the room, "I really don't think the butler did it."

"That's because you like him," I said. "You don't actually have evidence that clears him."

"And you don't have evidence that indicts him."

I smiled over my glass of sherry. There was a warm moment developing between us, thanks to the wine and the sudden absence of stress in our relationship. Sam met my gaze, and I could tell he felt the same way. It would've been magical if not for the fact that the later it got the more times Cook came into the library to do totally unnecessary things.

I knew she was interrupting us in order to provide the semblance of a chaperone, which I suppose she felt the situation required. Even in 1923, I was certainly old enough to be in the same room alone with a man—especially a police officer—but it didn't matter to some people. Later, after Sam and I had debriefed and rehashed for hours—and kept poor Cook up way past her bedtime in the process—I walked him to the door, my skin tingling with anticipation. I had no idea how men in 1923 thought—I wasn't even too sure how they did it in my own time. But after the intimate evening we'd had, I hoped there was going to be a continuation of that connection between us.

Sam opened the door, and I felt the thick humidity of the Savannah night creep over my skin, startling me since we'd had the fire on, and it had given me the semblance of a cozy hideaway.

He turned to me, and I saw his face was flushed. There was no hesitation or doubt in his eyes as he pulled me close without a single word. Our lips met. The gentle pressure of his mouth against mine charged through me like an electric shock, igniting a fire within me.

I don't know how long the moment lasted because as far as I'm concerned time really did stand still when there was only Sam, the scent of him, the simple essence of him as we shared that first bittersweet kiss.

A kiss that somehow tasted like our last.

62

That night, hours after Sam left, I was still thinking about that kiss.

Long after I'd gotten ready for bed and climbed into the four-poster bed, I remembered the feel of his lips against mine. All the while, my heart had raced a million miles an hour. There was no doubt that the anticipation of that moment had been lingering in the air between us for weeks. Every part of me wanted to experience it with him again. And soon.

Somehow, even with all the drama of the day, I was able to fall asleep. I was bone tired, and my body needed to shut down. My mind even more so. It was sometime in the middle of the night when I heard a light tapping on my bedroom door. I'd locked the door and shoved a chair under the handle until I knew for sure that the Savannah Killer wasn't Seamus.

I fumbled for my cellphone on the bedside table. I'd found an adaptor in 2023 that worked with the electricity here and my phone was fully charged. I quickly checked the time. It was three in the morning.

"Miss Belle?"

It was Cook's voice.

I was up and removing the chair from the door in seconds, breathless with fear that she'd gotten bad news from the hospital.

"Yes?" I said, pulling open the door to see Cook standing there in her dressing gown and slippers. "Is it Mary?"

"No, Miss. Someone to see you and says it's urgent. She would not take no for an answer."

She?

My mind whirled trying to imagine who it could possibly be.

"Where's Seamus?" I asked.

"I don't know, Miss. Sometimes he goes out at night."

I'll bet he does.

"Give me five seconds," I told Cook. "I'll get my clothes on."

I closed the door and took in a breath. If it was another prostitute, perhaps a friend of Mercy's, she was likely here after my visit with Mercy's family because she had evidence to give about Mario and couldn't take the risk of anyone seeing her reach out to me in daytime.

And possibly because she was in fear for her life.

I pulled on the least amount of clothes I could—a wool serge dress with a matching jacket, with a pocket where I jammed my cellphone. I looked at the drawer where I'd put the Taser and tried to decide if I needed to bring it to a meeting with a terrified woman who thought she was next on the Savannah Killer's hit list.

"Please, hurry, Miss!" Cook said, her voice frantic with fear.

I slipped my shoes on and joined Cook in the hallway.

Cook was breathing heavily, her eyes wide with fear and her hands wringing together as she urged me down the hallway.

"Hurry, Miss," she said.

I wondered if possibly Cook recognized my mysterious visitor and if that was the reason she was so nervous. If Sam was wrong and Spinelli had more family than he thought, perhaps my late-night visitor was a female member of the crime family—perhaps a sister or even Mario's insane wife?

I hurried down the stairs and peered into the parlor, surprised that Cook hadn't parked my unexpected guest there.

Bewildered, I went to the door and pulled it open. But there was no woman there. Instead, a large brutish-looking man stood there, his hands holding a dark hood, his eyes malevolent and evil.

I turned to bolt back inside the townhouse, but harsh hands grabbed me and dragged me from the light.

63

My heart pounded as I fought the man. But he quickly pinned me in his arms before jamming the hood over me and slinging me over his shoulder.

I screamed but it was muffled by the hood. I thrashed desperately over his shoulder and pound his back. If I could get the hood off, I could try to bite a piece of his ear off! But he was running and jostling me until he slammed to a stop.

He said something to someone and then I felt him swing me down—the lurch in my stomach when he did nearly brought up my dinner. He tossed me into the car trunk and slammed the lid shut.

I was vibrating in pain and fear by then, bruised and shaken. I had no idea who he was or who had sent him, but I did at least have one glimmer of hope. He hadn't bothered to search me before grabbing me, so the Taser I'd snatched up at the last minute was still in my jacket pocket.

I felt the car when it began to move, slowly at first, and then faster. I lay there in the trunk, the car speeding along, and felt my heart racing in my chest, my mind spinning with every imaginable thought.

This couldn't be the Savannah Killer because I definitely heard him say a few words to someone. The Savannah Killer wouldn't have an accomplice. *Would he?*

I took in a breath, inhaling the musk and dust of the bag over my head and then the stale stink inside the trunk. I needed to calm myself to get ready for whatever was coming. I fumbled with the hood but when I got it off, I still couldn't see anything.

As the car raced and swerved in the late-night streets of Savannah, I found myself betting that my kidnapper was Mario—well, not the man who'd manhandled me because Mario hadn't struck me as being that strong. But if it was Mario, what sense did that make? Kidnapping me was not at all the MO of the serial killer. If he truly was one and the same, he wouldn't be able to help himself. His ego wouldn't allow him to bring a hired gun along to dispose of me.

It would be too much fun to do it himself.

~

The longer we drove, the harder it was to stay calm. I felt a cold sweat form on my forehead and the tight knot in my stomach tightened even further. My heart pounded against my ribcage like a drum. I worked to regulate my breaths—something I'd learned to do in yoga class for stressful moments—but it did nothing to calm the fear that was slowly overpowering me.

With each passing moment, I grew more and more terrified of what lay ahead. I could feel the fear bubbling inside me, threatening to spill over. I tried to keep my wits about me by focusing on the sensory details of my surroundings. I could see nothing, but the trunk of the car was cold. It felt as if I was suspended in a void where time no longer had any meaning.

The car had been speeding along at what felt like breakneck speed for what seemed like hours, but now it slowed. Finally, it stopped, but the driver didn't shut off the engine. I thought I could tell that my abductors were either switching drivers or adding another person to the car.

I heard them talking but I couldn't make out their words, nor how many of them there were now.

We drove on after that. At one point, I pulled out my phone and saw that only thirty minutes had passed since I'd been dragged off the townhouse steps. I touched the Taser in my pocket to give myself confidence, but I only had one charge. There were at least two of them, maybe three.

The cold that I'd been feeling just minutes before had been replaced by a thick humidity as the car came to a full stop, abruptly and without warning. I had my eyes closed tightly during most of the journey. I felt disoriented and scared listening to the engine ping as we sat there, unmoving.

It occurred to me I could shoot the first person who opened the trunk with my Taser but with only one shot there was the danger of them either slamming the lid shut before I could escape or the second person out there catching me. Either way, I thought I needed to wait and just prayed I'd get another chance.

Or maybe I was just too petrified to take proper action.

My mind was racing at a million miles an hour as I waited for the driver to come and open the trunk. Finally, I heard a door opening and footsteps—one set—walking back to the trunk. I hurriedly put the hood back on. Suddenly, I felt the cold metal of the trunk's handle being pulled up, followed by a flood of night air pouring over me.

Harsh hands dragged me out of the trunk until my feet found the gravel ground beneath them. He jerked off my hood and I stood blinking in the half light. It was dark but there was a light coming from the porch of an old shack that I could just make out the bare outlines of. I could smell the river.

The better to dispose of my body.

The shack was a decrepit wooden structure with a lopsided roof. The whole area was surrounded by a thick, dark forest of tall, gnarled trees. Even the air felt heavy, as though something sinister lurked inside.

"You couldn't just let it go?" my abductor growled in a voice I recognized. "I tried to warn you off."

I turned to look at Mario Spinelli. I don't know where his henchman was, but there was no doubt who had ordered my kidnapping. My mind was moving slowly as I tried to comprehend his words. So, accosting me in the alley and snatching my purse was his attempt to "warn me off?"

"You won't get away with this," I said.

"I'm pretty sure I will. Turn around."

He had a length of rope in his hands, clearly intending to bind my hands.

"Is that necessary?" I said, jerking my hands away. "Surely you're not worried I will overpower you if I'm not tied up?"

Without the use of my hands, I was as good as dead.

He snorted and threw the piece of rope down.

"Honey, nothing about you worries me. Let's move it."

He gave me a push toward the shack where I could see someone standing on the porch. He was in silhouette, but I guessed it was the man who'd dragged me off Mary's threshold. He turned and entered the shack.

Was he the one who was going to do Mario's dirty work?

I took two steps toward the shack. Two slow steps. And then I bent over in a coughing fit.

Most people will allow you to finish coughing up a lung before they recommence whatever activity or conversation they had planned. It's human nature.

Even people who are basically inhuman in nature.

"Hurry up," Mario said in annoyance as I coughed and coughed.

You know how when you're planning to do something risky and so even if the timing isn't right, you're just so eager to get it over with that you end up jumping the gun and ruining everything?

That's what I felt was happening when, still coughing, I stepped away from Mario, whipped the Taser out of my jacket and shot him straight in the chest. Instantly he froze and then began convulsing before falling hard to the ground.

I was electrified myself with adrenalin, nearly whimpering with urgency and single-minded focus. I tossed down the now useless Taser and grabbed up the ropes he'd dropped to the ground. I turned him over and used the handcuff knot they'd taught me in the police academy to bind his hands behind him.

Bet you're a little worried now, I thought grimly.

Mario was still vibrating and making unintelligible noises as I worked on him. I ripped the tail from his shirt and stuffed it in his still gasping mouth. I didn't care if he choked him to death. I just needed him not to alert the person in the shack.

The person waiting for me so he could kill me.

I felt for the keys to the car in his trousers, but they weren't there. Praying they were in the car, I got to my feet and turned toward the vehicle at the same moment I heard the door to the shed creak open behind me.

64

The car was too far away.

I'd never make it. And I had no car keys even if I could.

I turned to see the killer stepping off the shed porch. He was looking around as if trying to find Mario.

I backed away toward the car knowing there was no way I could race for it and make it. Even if I ran as fast as I could, the man on the porch would catch me. Terror rattled my chest until I couldn't draw a full breath. I watched him come, the scalpel in his hand reflecting the light of the moon.

A part of me had known on some level that it had to be Davey. The thought of him had flitted across my brain a few times in the days before, but it hadn't made sense then, so I didn't stop to seriously consider it. But now it made perfect sense.

After all, why else would Mario go to such lengths to distract me from what Davey was doing? Or to distract the police with false descriptions of my assailant? Plus, Davey was studying to be a doctor. He had access to scalpels and because of his studies he was often at the hospital—the killing field. He displayed the arrogance needed to pretend to be someone innocent with me. Check. And as for a complete lack of remorse, well, I was looking at a man right this minute whose eyes were about as cold-blooded as I've ever seen.

"Now this is very interesting what you've done," Davey said, as he came closer. "If I weren't going to take care of you myself, I'd love to see how my big brother would deal with you."

"So, it was you all along," I said, trying to sound so much braver than I felt. I made a gesture toward the scalpel in his hand. "You killed them all."

"Clever girl," he said and from the expression on his face, his admiration looked genuine.

"May I ask why?" I asked. "Why did you kill them all?"

He shrugged. "Why not?"

Naturally a serial killer doesn't have a motive. It had been a stupid question on my part.

"But, why prostitutes?" I asked, stalling for time. "Did somebody give you the clap when you were a baby?"

He flushed with anger.

"I was doing the world a favor," he said.

"That's funny. I thought your family depended on prostitution as the backbone of their business."

"Don't you remember me telling you I didn't respect what they did?"

"But your brother protected you," I said, glancing at Mario on the ground twenty yards from us. He was struggling with the rope around his hands and feet and attempting to scream through the gag.

I dearly hoped Davey wouldn't feel the need to release him. It was hard enough imagining how I was going to get out of this staring down one psychopath without having to deal with two.

"You know you're not getting out of here alive," he said.

"Sounds like you've seen too many Tom Mix movies," I said. "That's pretty corny dialogue for a serial killer."

"I like that term, by the way," he said. "It's clinical sounding but also terrifying. I'm hoping the press will coin it after I kill you. Or maybe by the next one. Or I might have to write in a suggestion in Letters to the Editor."

I know the rule of thumb for these sorts of situations is to keep maniac killers talking for as long as possible, but I was almost positive no one was coming for me. Waiting wouldn't serve me. The problem was, I wasn't sure what would.

"I have to say, I've had my eye on you for a long time," Davey said, licking his lips. "But now that I've got you, why don't we have a little fun? What do you say? The others wouldn't run. They were too terrified. They just lay there. What's the fun in that?"

"I'll run," I said breathlessly, my eyes on his knife.

"Something told me you would," he said with a grin. "How about a fighting chance? What would that look like?"

"The keys to the car?"

"Oh, funny girl," he said with a laugh. "Not quite *that* fighting. How about I give you a thirty-second head start? I'll even close my eyes. You might try hiding."

"Promise you won't peek?"

He laughed. "I don't need to cheat, duckie. You're mine no matter what you do. Ready? The countdown starts now!"

I turned and sprinted down the road toward the scrub pasture and the line of trees in the distance. The sun cresting over the horizon cast long, thin shadows over the vast expanse of desolate terrain. I leapt over a fallen log and raced over the uneven terrain, rocks and small shrubs tripping me up in my desperate attempt to put distance between us.

I pushed myself faster, ignoring the ache in my side and the fear that coursed through me as I literally ran for my life.

As soon as I crossed the pasture and hit the patch of woods on the perimeter I ran straight through a patch of thorny bushes, their branches lacerating my naked legs. The smell of decaying wood and new pine needles seeped into my nostrils as I ran. I was making my own path, leaving branches broken and leaves crushed behind me. My fear was like a living thing scrambling inside my chest as I ran.

I tried to listen for sounds of him behind me, but the noise of my panic was too loud. I stopped for a moment to get my bearings, my breathing loud and harsh in my ears. I glanced behind me and saw the clump of bushes I'd pushed through, now smashed and broken on the ground, leading a telltale path right to me.

Good enough, I thought, grimly.

"I'm coming for you, girlie!" Davey called out not nearly far enough away.

The sound of his voice spiked my fear and adrenalin. My eyes frantically searched for the spot I needed. When I found it—a flat stone under a bush—I pulled out my cellphone with shaking hands and set it on the stone. Then I pushed the Play button.

I didn't wait around to see if it worked. I dove into the nearby bushes, praying the leaves would have stopped shaking by the time he came into the clearing.

The clear, crisp tones of the female voice talent reading the last audio book I'd been listening to in 2023 pierced the quiet air.

"*...the glittering blue slice of Mediterranean sparkled in Amanda's rearview mirror. She smiled as she turned to look at Douglas in the passenger's seat of her Renault...*"

"Not much of a challenge," Davey said, his voice coming from just behind the ridge of bushes. "If you can't even stop talking for two minutes, I know exactly where you are. You make it too easy!"

It was light enough for me to see him when he entered the small clearing. He went straight to where I'd planted the cellphone.

"*...as he opened the door to the sound of Jenna's cries along with the three soldiers who went charging past him. She screamed at the shock of it...*"

"Come out, come out wherever you are!" Davie sang as he pulled back the branches of the bush where I'd set the cellphone.

So great was his arrogance that he even set his knife down so he could use both hands, probably assuming he was about to pull me out of my hiding place.

He never even heard me creep up behind him, the heavy boulder in my hands which I brought down on the back of his head with all my strength.

65

I left my cellphone and Davey where they were and rushed back to the car, expecting any minute that Davey would jump to his feet and race after me. I jerked open the car door.

The keys were in the ignition.

I nearly wept with relief when I saw them. I jumped into the driver's seat, my hands shaking. I started the car, thanking my Uncle Bill for teaching me to drive a stick shift.

I didn't know if I'd killed Davey or just stunned him. But I wasn't hanging around to find out. It was just light enough to see what I was doing and although this car was like nothing I'd ever driven in my own time, I knew the only way I was going to get back to Savannah before Davey woke up or Mario worked his way out of his rope bonds, was to figure out how to drive this car.

I don't know where the man who'd assaulted me at Mary's door had gone. Probably when the car had stopped and I thought they were switching drivers, he was sent off to do something else while Davey took his place behind the wheel. In any case, I was pretty sure I didn't have to worry about him jumping out from one of the bushes.

The last thing he would imagine was that a *woman* would be able to disable the head boss man and his brother, the psycho-killer.

I could barely believe it myself.

I drove for what seemed like hours, finally getting comfortable with the way the car handled, until I was eventually able to stop fearing that one of the Spinelli brothers would run up beside me. The car only went forty miles per hour at top speed.

Broader rays of sun light appeared over the horizon catching a dust cloud in the distance which glowed golden, like a child's painting. I have to say categorically, this is what the world looks like at dawn when you're just grateful to be alive.

I figured that since Pooler was due west of Savannah, the sunrise would happen in front of, as it was now. That meant we'd travelled west from Savannah, so I kept driving in the same direction. Worst case scenario I'd run out of gas near the coast. At least I was putting miles between me and the Spinelli brothers.

As I drove, I made my plans. I figured that unless Cook called the police—which for some reason I wasn't sure she would—and with Mary out for the count, there was nobody to come looking for me. It was too early for Sam to be missing me. For that reason, and because I no longer felt safe at Mary's house until the Spinelli brothers were picked up, I drove onto Highway US 80 which I seemed to recall had been replaced by I-16 which I was familiar with back in my time. It wasn't much of a highway—not by 2023 standards—but it was paved. I stayed on it until I saw the

Savannah River appear on my left side which I used as a guide the rest of the way into town.

I drove straight to the police station on Bull Street and parked the car on the curb, not bothering to even take it out of gear. I stumbled out of the seat, nearly sliding to the ground in the process, I was so unnerved.

The beat cop standing by the sidewalk strode over to me and then hesitated. He might have thought I was drunk, or he might have recognized me from two days ago when he tried to arrest me for prostitution because I certainly recognized him.

Before I could say anything, he clamped a hard hand on my arm and dragged me to my feet.

"I need to see Detective Bohannon," I said, gasping for breath.

"He ain't gonna help you, girlie."

I had been through so much in the past weeks, and all of it seemed to be leading up to this moment. How could it be snatched away from me now? I had been nearly on the verge of victory, but now I was being dragged by my arm and I literally did not have the strength to resist.

Just then, I heard a voice call out my name. I glanced around frantically to see Sam striding out of the police station, a look of concern on his face.

He took in the scene at a glance.

"What's going on here?" he asked, his voice firm and authoritative. "Get your hands off her."

The cop loosened his grip but still hung onto me.

"I'm making an arrest for solicitation," he said, his voice suddenly unsure.

"I know this woman," Sam said to the policeman. "Who is your supervisor?"

The policeman stuttered and looked at his feet, instantly cowed.

"He...I...he..."

Ignoring him, Sam turned to me.

"Are you okay?" he asked, his eyes filled with worry. "What's happened?"

Waves of relief wracked my body as the policeman released me. I stumbled to Sam and fell into his arms, momentarily unable to find the words to explain what had happened.

He pulled me toward a bench outside the front of the station and settled me on it.

"In your own time, Georgia," he said. "No rush."

"Sam," I said, taking in heaving breaths. "Davey Spinelli is the Savannah Killer. He and his brother Mario kidnapped me last night and tried to kill me."

The policeman overheard my statement and chortled with derisive laughter, but Sam glanced at the Model-T parked on the curb and reached out a hand to pull me to my feet, leading me gently toward the police station entrance.

Over his shoulder he barked at the policeman.

"Tell Detective Hawkins to meet me in the incident room immediately," he said.

∼

I didn't even get halfway through my story before Hawkins sent a squad of men racing out to the area where I'd been held and which they all seemed to know by my description. I could tell Sam wanted to go too, but it still wasn't his case.

Before Hawkins left to follow his men, I jumped up and grabbed his sleeve.

"Confirm to me that this means Henry Pickett will be released."

The man snorted scornfully and pulled his sleeve from my grasp.

"I ain't promising anything," he said.

"Then I am going to the press to tell them my story."

"Do what you want."

I blocked his way out the door. "I will refuse to testify against the Spinelli's."

"Georgia, no," Sam said, coming to my side.

"I mean it," I said to Hawkins. "Release Henry Pickett or rely solely on whatever physical evidence you can find to indict the biggest serial killer in Savannah history. Good luck with that."

Hawkins blinked at me for a moment.

"Fine," he said finally.

I indicated Sam. "Your agreement has been duly noted in front of a witness."

"Don't call me a liar, lady," Hawkins snarled. "You just make sure you say what's needed on the stand when the time comes."

On that note he grabbed up his jacket and stormed out of the room. I felt a flush of relief at his words.

I'd done it! Henry Pickett would not be lynched.

I came back to sag into the chair where I'd been sitting next to Sam. It was over. And now that it was, I didn't think I had the strength to put one foot in front of the other.

"I can't believe they dragged you out of your house," Sam said softly, breaking me out of my jubilant reverie. "How in the world did you escape?"

I took in a long breath.

"I used my...I have an audio recorder," I said. "It's like a gramophone only it's digital."

He frowned in confusion. I knew I was making things more complicated than they needed to be.

"They're all the rage in Switzerland," I said weakly. "Anyway, I set it under a bush like a trap and pushed the playback button and went and hid."

He was still frowning in bemusement, but he was at least trying hard to follow me.

"Then when Davey came upon it, at first, he thought it was me talking to myself, I guess. He walked over to it to try to figure out what he was hearing, and it gave me the opportunity to sneak up behind him."

"You could have been killed."

"Oh, I totally think that was the plan."

"I can't believe it was Davey Spinelli all along." He shook his head in wonder. "We never even considered the kid brother."

"I know. Mario knew what his brother was doing, which is why he tried to provide a smoke screen for him. That's the reason he gave a false eyewitness statement about my assault—by giving a description of someone who looked nothing like Davey."

"But why make up an assailant if he didn't see his brother do it?"

"I think he feared his brother had been there," I said. "He just used it as an opportunity to throw you off the track."

"And the purse snatching?" Sam asked.

"He said he was trying to warn me off because he knew his brother considered me unfinished business. He was trying to run me out of town."

"For your safety?" Sam frowned, unconvinced.

"Well, more for Davey's safety. I think Mario believed Davey was no longer thinking rationally. He was too focused on showing the world that he hadn't failed with my attack."

"And you say Davey confessed to killing all three of our victims?"

"He did. He bragged about killing them. And to attacking Mary, too. He didn't think I'd survive my kidnapping to tell what I knew. Detective Hawkins should be able to find the scalpel and any good medical examiner can then match it to the murdered bodies."

"You've been through hell, Georgia," Sam said, his eyes misting with pride and admiration as he regarded me.

"It was worth it knowing that no more young women will be murdered. And that Henry Pickett will be released."

He nodded.

"We have nothing to hold him on," he said. "Your testimony will be enough to indict Davey Spinelli."

"That and the murder weapon," I said. "And if I didn't kill him, you can bet Davey will want to brag about how he fooled you all. You'll get your confession straight from the monster's mouth."

I slumped back in the chair, exhausted and depleted from my night.

"I can't believe it's finally over," I said.

My thoughts raced back over the events of the evening. I remembered how scared I had been, how determined I had been to solve the case and bring justice to Mercy's family and the other poor girls who had suffered at the hands of this madman.

Suddenly, a wave of elation and pride washed over me. I had done it. I wanted to cry out in joy, to laugh in the face of fear—something that had hogtied me for as long as I can remember in my own timeline. I took a deep breath and smiled.

Suddenly, Sam clapped his hands together and giving me a satisfied smile stood up and held his hand out to me.

Let's go," he said. "The sun's up and I'm taking you to breakfast."

I stood, allowing myself to believe that this was really the end. Justice would finally be served. I was relieved and feeling so proud of myself as I followed him out of the office into the bright morning light.

66

The walls were peeling in places in the hospital ward where Mary and I sat on opposite sides of the bed, a small child tucked into it. She was blonde and her skin was very pale, almost translucent. She'd survived an emergency appendectomy—thanks in part to the round of antibiotics that Sister Beatrice was giving her from my quickly diminishing stash.

I held out the battery-operated fan to the child and she grasped it with delight.

"Oh, how do you make it work?" she squealed.

I could see her parents who sat at the foot of the bed watching the fan with marveling eyes wanted to ask the same question. The father's mouth fell open as the fan blew the child's curls around her face.

It was hot, naturally. And the hospital wasn't air-conditioned. We weren't even to September yet. In my own century September was even hotter than August.

I'd brought four fans with me from 2023. Two of them I kept in my bedroom—one to use and one to use when the battery ran out. I planned on being back in my own time before that happened.

I'd given the fourth fan to Mary, but I don't know if she uses it or not.

"It's magic!" I teased the child.

Mary shook her head as she watched the child's delight and after a few more minutes we got up to leave.

Mary had been out of the hospital for nearly two months by now. She had been recuperating slowly at home and between Seamus, Cook and myself, I think we were taking pretty good care of her. She and I had become even closer during this time, mostly because I told her stories based on the Harry Potter books.

I told her the stories were big overseas and would probably hit the States soon. I have to say I've gotten away with quite a lot using Europe as my excuse for having exotic or unbelievable items. I would've loved to have read to her from the Kindle app on my phone, but the police seemed to think they needed to keep my cellphone for evidence for the coming trial.

I had every intention of going back to my own time as soon as the trial against Davey Spinelli was over. That thought was not as easy as it sounded.

The day I'd conked Davey on the head with a boulder and Detective Hawkins had gone rushing out to arrest him and his brother had led to a very satisfying closure to the whole Savannah Killer saga. As I'd predicted to Sam, Davey couldn't resist bragging about his exploits—to the point I wasn't all that sure I was even needed to finish nailing up his coffin. But I said I'd stay and testify so here I am.

Of course, my testifying against the Spinelli Brothers meant I needed to be here an additional three months longer than I'd planned. And that was hard. Not just because I knew my mother would begin to wonder what kind of retreat I was on that kept me away for three months without calling, but also because the longer I stayed, the harder it was to leave.

To leave Mary. And Sam.

Mary and I walked down the cracked linoleum hallway toward the garden-side exit. We were planning on having lunch at a restaurant on Abercorn Street that we'd begun frequenting and I was finally intending to tell her about the locket.

I'd told Sister Beatrice I wanted to do it in my own time and she once more begged me to get rid of it. But I couldn't do that. The locket shows up around Mary's throat in the portrait. That was a fact. I didn't like the idea of messing with that.

As we opened the hospital door to the garden, I immediately scanned the grounds for signs of Henry Pickett. I knew he'd been given his old job back at the hospital and I've caught a glimpse of him now and then.

Today, as we walked through the garden to the gate that led to East Huntington Street, I saw him by a huge rose bush by the fountain—the very place where Merci O'Gillis's body had been found. He looked up as we passed and nodded. His gaze lingered on me a tad longer than with Mary I thought. I don't think he knew the role I'd played in his release. But something about the way he looked at me, made me wonder if he did. In any case, I was eager to get back to my own time to see how his freedom had translated into happier lives for his descendants.

Once out on the street, Mary hooked arms with me, and we strolled to *Grandma's Kitchen*. We stepped inside and the waitress seated us immediately.

An overhead ceiling fan created a weak breeze but no

real relief from the heat. The other diners around us were dressed simply. The men wore long-sleeved collared shirts and ties, the women mid-calf floral dresses. The only sound in the diner was the occasional clink of silverware on china and the murmur of conversations. The air smelled sweet and savory all at once. The menu ranged from meat loaf to fried chicken and fried fruit pies dusted with sugar that were to die for.

"Okay, Georgia," Mary said, putting down her menu. "Out with it. I know you've got something on your mind."

I couldn't believe how good she was at reading me. I've never had a friend who could do that so well.

"All in due time," I said. "Which reminds me. I heard you gave Seamus time off this morning."

"He has a niece getting married in Boston," Mary said, flapping a napkin out across her lap. "And he's been particularly attentive these last weeks. I didn't feel I could say no."

In the weeks after Davey's arrest, I'd learned that Seamus had in fact run from the alley in question—just as the old man by the speakeasy had told me. But it turned out that Seamus's alley visit was a result of a nasty little cocaine habit he had. In any case, this particular alley visit wasn't even on the same day that Julie was slain. Seamus had an ironclad alibi for that date. The old fellow had gotten that part wrong. I was relieved. I liked Seamus. I didn't like to think he was a psychotic killer.

We ordered our lunches and handed in our menus to the waitress.

"Come on, Georgia," Mary said. "What is it?"

I sighed and reached into my purse, drawing out the locket that I'd wrapped in a small square of paper. I slid the packet across the table to her.

"What's this?" she asked.

"This is a locket that was stolen from your mother seven years ago," I said. "Your sister tells me that your mother intended for you to have it on your twenty-first birthday."

"Really?"

Mary picked up the packet and unwrapped it. The gold locket dangled from her finger.

"It's beautiful. But how did you get it?"

"It was stolen from your mother in a burglary," I said, deliberately leaving out the part about her parents dying a week later. "I came upon it in Lydia Bartram's bedroom."

"She stole it from my mother?"

"I don't know how she got it, exactly. But since she was living in the middle of a criminal compound, I imagine she saw it in a pile of stolen loot and took it for her own."

"Thank you, my dear," Mary said, about to tuck it away in her purse.

"I was wondering if you could tell me who the picture is inside the locket."

Mary frowned and pulled it back open and popped the latch. I watched the tiny lid spring open.

"This makes no sense," she said.

"You know who it is?"

"I do, but it doesn't make sense that my father would give my mother a locket with this woman's picture in it."

"Who is she?"

"Well, I don't know the whole story," she said reaching for her glass of iced tea. "But as I understand it, she was someone my father had cared for."

"Why would your father...?"

"I told you it didn't make sense."

Just then our meat loaf and creamed corn arrived. I waited for the waitress to leave.

"Mary, the picture in that locket is the spitting image of me as a teenager."

Mary cocked her head to look at me as if trying to see the resemblance.

"Well, perhaps you're related to her in some way," she said finally. "I understand she's still alive. But she's very old."

There was no doubt this girl in the locket was a relation of mine. What other explanation could there be? Perhaps she was my great grandmother? I felt a strong urge to find her, having never known her in my lifetime. Both my great grandparents and my grandparents had died before I was born.

"In any case, thank you for the locket," Mary said picking up her knife and fork to tackle her fried chicken. "I promise to keep it safe."

67

Later that evening I had a date with Sam for a drive out into the country. I bathed and changed into another set of clothes since I guess what I wore at lunch for a perfectly nice restaurant wasn't fancy enough for a car ride.

Sam and I had been seeing quite a bit of each other in the last two months and, while I felt the end looming nearer with the coming trial, I could see that he was gearing up to pop a very important question to me.

And that made me irredeemably sad.

How could I stay here? First, I can't leave my mother, and second, how could I have any kind of meaningful relationship with someone I couldn't tell the truth to?

Just imagining telling Sam where I really came from made me wince. I felt like someone who'd been unfaithful and was being forced to keep the infidelity and the lies locked up inside.

It was not a good formula for a lasting relationship.

The sun was a blazing orange ball that hung low in the western sky by the time Sam and I drove north up the coast.

We'd left the bustling streets of Savannah behind and were now on an open highway, surrounded by an endless stretch of golden fields. The late summer air seemed to be tinged with the smell of pine and cedar, and the occasional farmhouse came into view with its white paintwork glowing in the dusk light.

I turned to look at Sam in profile in the driver's seat. He really was so handsome, and I had no doubt he loved me. Even in this century where just about everything I did and said was a shock to his system, he saw past that and loved me anyway.

That's a guy you want to hold onto.

Soon enough the road began to meander past the lush marshes of Hilton Head. The air was heavy with humidity and the scent of salt and seaweed. It was fully dark now, and the night sky was a deep navy canvas illuminated by a crowd of stars—stars invisible in my own time due to air and light pollution.

As we drove, a sense of peace came over me, as if I had finally reached the place where I belonged. As soon as I realized I was feeling this way, I pinched myself. This was not a dream. It was time to begin the ending.

"Sam," I said, "I got a letter from my mother today."

"Oh, that's nice," he said. "Why don't we drive down to Jacksonville next weekend? I would love to meet her."

"That would be great," I said. "Except I've promised her I'd go on a trip with her. To Paris."

"Paris?" He turned to look at me as if he must have heard wrong.

I was reminded that for most people during this time, European travel was only for the wealthy. He was quiet for a moment. I suppose he was reflecting on the fact that he really didn't know me all that well.

I hated to throw a wrench into his plans, but it was best for everyone if I did it before he proposed. Just the thought that he wanted to be with me—to marry me—but I was going to leave made me indescribably sad.

I knew all along that this was going to be painful but there are different degrees of pain. I was doing this for both of us. It was what had to be.

Suddenly, he slowed the car and pulled off on the side of the road. I was surprised and reminded myself that lack of traffic made this possible in 1923 whereas of course it wouldn't have been in my time.

From where we were parked on the highway I could hear the night chorus of frogs, and the occasional splash of a fish jumping in the water. Sam turned off the car and turned to face me.

"Georgia," he said. "I need to ask you something before you leave."

"Are you sure, Sam?" I said. "I'll be back before you know it."

He laughed. "It's an eight-day sail to Le Havre! And then eight days back? You won't be home for a month. This can't wait."

I knew when I was beat. The Spinelli trial had only just started, and I was needed here for that. There was no way around this. I was going to have to break up with him before the trial. The very thought of it was like a knife in my heart.

"Georgia Belle," he said solemnly taking my hand.

"Sam, you don't even know me," I said. "Not really."

"I know you as much as I need to," he said. "I know you're brave and funny and beautiful and kind-hearted and passionate. I don't need to know anything else."

Tears gathered in my eyes as I wondered if there was anyone like him in any time anywhere in the world.

"Georgia, darling," he said. "Will you marry me?"

He leaned in to kiss me and I felt an electrical pulse charge though me at the touch of our lips. I looked into his eyes when the kiss ended.

"Of course, I will," I said.

***

To follow more of Georgia Belle's sleuthing adventures across time, order *Scarlett Must Die, Book 2 of the Savannah Time Travel Mysteries.*

SCARLETT MUST DIE
Book 2 in the Savannah Time Travel Mysteries

Georgia Belle is engaged to marry the most amazing man she's ever known. The only problem is she had to give up everything—her work, her family and her friends, and her own time—to do it.

After freeing Henry Pickett from certain death in 1923 and agreeing to marry the handsome Savannah police detective Sam Bohannon, Georgia makes a planned trip back to the twenty first century to see her mother and decide for sure if she is going to remain in the past. While home, she becomes trapped in a perilous situation that threatens her existence in both timelines. If she can't solve the mystery before she goes back to 1923, the ramifications of her failure will ripple out much further than just one woman's personal happiness.

It will literally affect the next twenty years.

And the coming world war.

ABOUT THE AUTHOR

USA TODAY Bestselling Author Susan Kiernan-Lewis is the author of *The Maggie Newberry Mysteries,* the post-apocalyptic thriller series *The Irish End Games, The Mia Kazmaroff Mysteries, The Stranded in Provence Mysteries, The Claire Baskerville Mysteries,* and *The Savannah Time Travel Mysteries.* If you enjoyed *Killing Time in Georgia,* please leave a review on your purchase site.

Visit her website at www.susankiernanlewis.com or follow her at Author Susan Kiernan-Lewis on Facebook.